Columbus Day

First Published in the UK 2013 by Mirador Publishing

Copyright © 2013 by David Balaam

All rights reserved. No part of this publication may be reproduced or transmitted, in any form or by any means, without permission of the publishers or author. Excepting brief quotes used in reviews.

Second edition: 2013

Any reference to real names and places are purely fictional and are constructs of the author. Any offence the references produce is unintentional and in no way reflects the reality of any locations or people involved.

A copy of this work is available through the British Library.

ISBN: 978-1-909220-67-6

Mirador Publishing
Mirador
Wearne Lane
Langport
Somerset
TA10 9HB

COLUMBUS DAY

BY

DAVID BALAAM

FIC

Mirador Publishing
www.miradorpublishing.com

*To my first born, Nicole,
my first novel*

Prologue

It was the 1st June, the previous year – a date that George would never forget. He let the phone ring for a while before deciding to answer it. He was tired – physically and mentally. Eighteen months ago he had lost his lovely wife Aimee in a hit and run, then six months later he was accused of cyber theft. His whole life had been shattered. He was demoralized and confused, but above all he was angry, very angry at the hand he had been dealt. He was not a religious man, but like most of his contemporaries George believed in humanity, respect for others, love of his family, and many of the good solid virtues he had grown up with, including justice, and an eye for an eye. He had worked hard over the past ten years building up a good business, and he and Aimee had been blessed with three beautiful children - but then, all of a sudden, and without warning, it was taken away from him. His life had been turned upside down.

No wife
No job
No reputation
No reason to live

George put the whisky glass down and turned on the table lamp next to him, and picked up the phone. "Yes," he said, in a monotone voice.

"You bastard! – I know you did it and I want my money back, Morton!"

George remained calm. He knew exactly who the caller was. Oliver Barnes, the now chief executive of Barnes & Barnes International Bankers, but then, at the time of the call, he was Head of Investment. His father, Peter Barnes, was Chairman. The young pretender was working his way, albeit fast tracked, through the departments, until one day when his father, and the board, was convinced he would be a suitable successor.

George allowed himself a wry smile. "Oliver, how are you?"

"This is not a social call, Morton. The police may not be able to prove it was you but I know it was, don't I, Morton!" Oliver spat down the phone line.

"I have just heard that the police have dropped the investigation, so I can get back to putting my life together again." George stated, with an air of satisfaction.

"They are rubbish – I have other avenues, I can and will use, Morton. You can count on it!" Oliver continued to shout down the phone.

"I suggest you get on with your life, Oliver. Give my regards to your father." And he was prepared to hang up, when Oliver Barnes erupted again.

"*Where's my money, Morton!*" he bellowed once more.

"*Your* money, Oliver?" George's tone was casual. "I thought it was the bank's money," and went to hang up again, but added an afterthought.

"I don't owe *you* a penny, Oliver."

Chapter 1. March - nine months later

It wasn't completely dark, more dim than dark, and there was quietness all around. Only the sound of anticipation seemed to linger. The other faint sound was that of seagulls. The squawking was getting louder and louder – everyone knew it was nearly time – the swaying had stopped, and then they heard the sound of the heavy anchor descending. One by one they started their engines. Some revved the motor, as if on a starting block, which in a way it was. A shaft of sunlight burst through into the large iron room that was the vehicle hold in the belly of this floating car park. The giant door slowly retreated, like a drawbridge, and came to rest on the harbor floor, with a gentle thud. If there had not been a good queue control system it would have been a *free for all. Young Turks* revving, and then charging into the sunlight, as if into battle. And some not so young, in their Audi TT's's or Mercedes SL300's, keen to show they still had some spirit in them, but resisting the temptation to show-off, especially with the wife gently tapping their arm and saying, "Now dear, we are not in a race."

George, too, could almost feel the urge to press the throttle a little more than he should, but thought better of it. After all, he thought he should show some self-control with his son, Christopher, sitting next to him.

Slowly the cars in started their exit into the daylight, and onwards to wherever they had planned. Over five hundred cars. Five hundred different journeys. George wondered if any of them would be as exciting or adventurous as his might be. He would never know of course, but George liked to think of people taking paths, and where they would lead. His path was to a new beginning. A new country. A new life.

Only four cars ahead and they were out into sunlight. That glorious sun which he would be seeing a lot of from now on. They cleared customs and headed out of the harbor, looking for the signs to the E-804 out of Bilbao. It had been a long twenty nine hours since they had left Portsmouth, England, and George was starting to feel elated.

Of his three children, Christopher and Bonnie, the twenty six years old twins, were there to see him off, (especially Chris as he was driving down with his Dad), and some close friends. They had had a meal and said their goodbyes. Bonnie tried not to show too much emotion, but could not hold out on the last hug.

"It's not Australia, its Spain. Any of you, including your sister, can be with me in a few hours by air."

"We know, Dad," Bonnie said thoughtfully, wiping away another tear. "It's just that we, err, some of us," she said, glancing at Christopher, "thought you would never actually get this far."

"I said nothing of the sort," snapped Christopher, "it was Alex who had doubts. We just want you to be happy again, Dad."

"Look after each other and yourselves." George tried to say with some fatherly authority, which only started Bonnie being tearful again.

George also said goodbye again to his friends, Roger and Carol, and Colin and Judy, who had given them some privacy as a family, but now all waved and cheered as Roger, the court jester, reappeared from somewhere carrying a bunch of 'Good Luck' helium balloons, which he tied to the rear bumper of the Transit. The mood was lighter now thanks to Roger, and George appreciated this. They all had a final hug and kiss, and said *au revoir*, as he and Christopher got into the hired Transit van and pulled into the ferry queue.

Christopher put on his iPod headphones, and in the quiet of the van George thought of his other off-spring, Alexandra.

Alex was their first child. She and George had said their goodbyes a week earlier when he stayed with her, and his son-in-law, Tom, at their house in Cheltenham.

As Alex, being the elder, George for some reason always thought of her as more sensible and level headed, which may have been unfair on his other two children, even if a little true.

They had talked for hours, just as they had done over the

past seven months when he first broke the news, but she knew that with only six days left before he sailed, she was just going over old territory – satisfying herself she had done everything plausible to dissuade him from '*going over there*', as she put it.

It was hard saying goodbye that day, but he left with the knowledge that he is not *that* far-away, and with the internet they can talk every day, if they really want to. In reality, families apart do not talk to each other that often, so George was confident he would not be on Skype every day revealing what he had been up to, and asking *how is the weather in England*?

George had bought a good size converted farmhouse in a small town called Calabaza, situated in the north east of Spain, two hundred miles due south of Bilbao. He could have taken the Plymouth ferry to Santander and had a more straight-forward drive to Calabaza, but it would not have been fair on family and friends to expect them to go all the way down to Plymouth from London. So he did the Portsmouth – Bilbao route instead, and now they have a three hour journey ahead of them.

George had been to Calabaza twice before. The first time with Carlos, the estate agent from Aranda de Duero, the nearest large town. They had looked at five properties that day, covering over one hundred miles. Carlos was very keen to get a sale, but George was not in a hurry, and wanted to get it right. The last property, as always, was love at first sight. *El Pino,* as it was then, is a converted farmhouse, and had been done so with much love and care by the previous owners. It had five bedrooms, a large living room/dining room leading to a good size modern kitchen on one side, and a spacious terrace balcony overlooking the village, and it came with a mature olive grove. It was however the view from the terrace that actually clinched it for George. The view was stunning. The farmhouse was unusual in so far as it was on a high point overlooking the village on one side, with the wide snaking Rio Arandilla on the other. They had arrived at around five in the afternoon and spent a good hour looking it over. A stone stairway from the end of the hall led to the first floor with two large bedrooms, both en-suite. At the end of the corridor more stone stairs led to the top floor, and a corridor which had the master bedroom, en-suite again, with a wonderful walk-in shower. Next to this bedroom was a smaller spare room which some may have used as a nursery, but could make a good extra study/play/junk room. From the master bedroom, as in all the bedrooms, the view was intoxicating. All the rooms had windows facing westwards over this spectacular landscape. The one exception was the last bedroom. This was to be found in the basement. Stone stairs from the end of the entrance hall lead down to a small corridor with rooms leading off on either side. To the right was a small room ideal for storage or a wine cellar. The room to the left was a good size bedroom with a basin and wardrobe. However, there was no window or air conditioning, and George was not sure anyone would want to sleep there in the summer.

The house was decorated simply and cleanly with modern lines, but keeping much of the Spanish feel in the colors, especially terracotta, blue hues and sandstone. The outside walls were made of local stone and not cemented smooth, or painted white like the more familiar *pueblos blancos* of Andalusia in the south.

George stood in the large airy living room facing the balcony and considered the smaller room off to the right, which was currently the dining room. It was a good size room, and he knew it would be his study/office/chill out room. He could see it just as he wanted it to look.

George could have negotiated harder, but Carlos could see he wanted it, and like all good salesman he was protecting his commission. The price was not really an issue anyway, it was within budget, including all the work he planned to have carried out, so around six-thirty that evening he and Carlos drove into town to find a bar and seal the sale. They entered from the north of the town along narrow streets looking for signs of life. Carlos eventually asked directions and found an old quaint-looking bar called *El Tango*. They parked in a side street adjacent to the bar, and sat outside with a cool *cerveza* and discussed the house, and what George needed doing to it.

With Carlos speaking good English, and George not very good Spanish, they managed to agree Carlos would oversee the alterations he wanted doing before he moved in. Looking about him, George realised he had not actually checked out the town to see if he would like it, but decisions like this, he felt, are done with a mix of gut-feeling and fate. He promised himself he would make Calabaza his home, and he would make it work. He had hardly taken notice of the attractive dark-haired waitress who served them, and why should he - he was house hunting, not wife hunting, but she noticed him, and saw the house sale papers on the table as she put down the drinks and a bowl of green olives.

By the time they returned to the farmhouse the sun was nearly setting, and the view to the west over the mountains was even more breath-taking. On that evening, on the last day of June, George knew he had started his new life, although, ironically, it would be nine months before he would be reborn.

As it turned out Carlos had been a great help and they became good friends over the following months, sometimes talking for hours by Skype video, and of course e-mailing each other. George had made one further visit in November to sign the papers and finalize the legal affairs, of which there are many when buying a property in Spain.

Now, after nine months, and a three hour drive, he had arrived at his new home. Carlos was waiting for him with his wife Alyce, to greet him, and help him unload his entire possessions from the back of a Ford Transit van.

To some people the house may have looked much the same as when they first saw it, but there had been some significant alterations. George had agreed to buy most of the furniture from the previous owners; beds, wardrobes, lounge sofa and chairs (although not to George's taste, but ideal for a while), and rugs and chattels, as they were described in the agreement. But the major alteration was the sealing off of what was once the dining room adjoining the lounge area. This sanctuary was now his office and music room. George had built solid louver style doors, which looked elegant when closed, but were far stronger than normal wooden doors, and had an electronic locking device and alarm fitted. The room was wired with the latest broadband connections so he could continue his highly sensitive work, and communicate with the outside World.

When his computers, music systems, monitors and other 'important' items, including; cooking utensils, a set of Sabatier chiefs knifes, his favorite saucepans and a set of La Creuset oven to tableware, had been unloaded, he left Chris to unpack them while Carlos showed him over the house again, pointing out all the work that had been done. As they walked through the hallway to the lower ground floor, George noticed on one of the walls was a set of *Toreador Picas* in a cross swords display.

"Ah," said Carlos, "the previous owners left these as a gift. They arc highly prized lances belonging to some famous Toreador from many years ago." He said with some pride.

"They look dangerous, but I suppose they add some flavor of Spain to the décor." George said, as they continued their tour. Very little, in fact, had needed to be done in the rest of the house. Some painting here and there, and some window shutters repaired. On the balcony Carlos pointed out a loose section of railing that still needed to be repaired, and promised George he would send someone round soon.

Later that evening they had a wonderful meal cooked by Alyce, to welcome George to his new home.

George had managed to unpack the iPod speakers and set it up. He played Gotan Project while they ate, much to Christopher's annoyance, but he was on his best behavior today, so allowed his dad some indulgence.

Alyce did not speak English, but she had some French, which both George and Christopher appreciated, so they managed to have a conversation of sorts. Carlos was also translating, and seemed to enjoy it, and was very proud of what he had done for George. They drank more wine and talked about George's new life, their lives, and everything else people do over a good meal, and several bottles of excellent *Pesquera Ribera del Duero Crianza 2005*, which Carlos had provided as a welcoming gift.

George slid out through the open patio doors and smelt the warm evening air tinted with scented pine from the nearby forest. The sun had set hours ago, but there was a full moon and a clear sky with many twinkling stars which lit the view he had first seen those nine months previous. If he had any doubts it was too late, but he did not have doubts about the decision to move here. Maybe about leaving his children and friends, but he had to leave England and start anew – to be reborn. Here on the 1st March his life begins again, and he raised a glass to the heavens, and whispered a toast. "*To you my love – I miss you.*"

Christopher walked over carrying a bottle of wine. "Top you up, Dad?"

George shook his head. "I think I've had enough for one night son."

"I thought I heard you talking to yourself just now. What were you doing - toasting the night sky?"

"Something like that." George left it at that, and Chris did not seek further explanation, mainly because he was not thinking clearly, and because it would not have occurred to him his dad still talked to his deceased mother.

In the lounge Carlos was asleep on the sofa, and Alyce was clearing the plates.

"No, no, please, por favor, Alyce. Mañana si." She smiled, and reluctantly stopped, and sat next to Carlos, who stirred. "*Sleep well my love,*" she whispered to him in a strange mix of Spanish and French. He was not drunk – just happy and content. They carried him up to the guest room on the first floor and placed him on the bed. "Gracias George." She turned and gave George a kiss on one cheek. "Gracias, buenas noches," she said with a sweet smile.

"Thank you Alyce, thank you both, for everything." George whispered, and gently closed the door as he left the room.

Chris took himself off to the lower ground bedroom, but not before giving George a hug. He looked at him with that slightly satisfied, blurred expression you get after a good few drinks. He hugged him again and staggered tentatively towards his bedroom. Nothing needs to be said on occasions like this between father and son, except, "That's the front door son, your bedroom is downstairs to the left."

"I knew that." Chris replied, raising his left hand as if to steady himself, then turned left and disappeared downstairs.

Back in the lounge George sat alone. It was 11.45pm. He was exhausted. He had meant to call the girls but sent them a quick text instead. *"We made it. Had a good journey. Will call or email tomorrow. Love Dad xxx."*

He started to clear away some more of the dinner plates but thought better of it. He was tired, and fatigue was overtaking rapidly. Alyce and Carlos had made up two of the beds - the guest room on the first floor for themselves, and the master room on the second floor. It was just as well, as George had no energy to make a bed. He got into bed and lay there staring at the ceiling picturing Aimee's face for all of sixty seconds before he fell asleep.

The next morning, George was woken with a shake of the shoulder. "Hola, George, are you sleeping all day?" Carlos was standing over him with a cup of coffee and a smile.

"What time is it?" George managed to utter.

"Late, 7.45, and we must leave for work."

George suddenly cleared his head and remembered where he was. "So sorry, Carlos. I meant to put the alarm on, but I don't think I have unpacked it yet."

"No problem my friend. But we must go. Alyce says good-bye. I will call you later in the day to see how you are. Also, I have left a note in the kitchen about Senora Torres, the house cleaner you asked me to find. She is coming for an interview around twelve o'clock."

"Carlos," George said, half sitting up in bed, "thank you my friend. I could not have done all this without you."

"I have enjoyed it, George, and anyway, you will soon get my bill, si," he smiled and winked, and left George to his coffee and thoughts.

George heard the car start and drive slowly down the gravel lane, fifty yards to the main road.

All was now quiet. It's the one thing he noticed right from the start. The quietness and stillness of this place. Not just the house, but the surrounding area. Life was lived at a slower pace out here, and George was going to have to get use to it very quickly.

He stood in the bedroom, looking out of the window at that beautiful view. "I'm never going to tire of this," he promised himself. He stretched and sighed, *'today is the first day of the rest of your life, George.'* Not very original he admitted – but true at least.

Yes, a new life. No more England, no more bad weather (hopefully), no more rush hours, no more over priced everything. He was excited at the prospect of this new life, and what adventures lay ahead.

The most important decision this morning however, was if he should shave. "What would it matter if I had a day's growth?" But, thirty-eight years of shaving every day is hard to stop just like that. It's like trying to stop smoking after many years, although he had gradually cut back over the last five years, to the point were he could have one every now and then and not feel guilty. "Perhaps I could shave every other day," he convinced himself. Looking at his reflection in the bathroom mirror he thought he had worn OK for his age. He still had a good crop of black hair even if it did have some slight graying on the sides, but that was distinctive – wasn't it? No need to worry just yet. His boyish pear shaped face needed some sun, but apart from that all looked good.

Then what to wear? That was easily solved. He shaved, after all, and showered, and put on kaki shorts and a white cotton kurta shirt he had bought in India. He looked once more in the mirror, looking for self approval. Aimee had been his best critic when it came to dress sense, and he missed the off-hand remarks from her about colour coordinating and shoe suitability. He smiled at the thought, and saw her nodding her approval to his chosen attire.

What next!? Time to explore and to get know his new house, finish the unpacking, and wake one lazy son.

As most of the furniture had been included with the property there was not a lot to bring over, apart from the computers, his music collection and the aforementioned prized kitchen paraphernalia. He also had the usual linen, towels, books, personal things, favorite mirror, mugs, several 'good luck' gifts from friends and neighbors, plus several boxes containing things he could not decide whether to leave or discard - so he had brought them with him.

Six months after Aimee died he finally started to sift through her belongings. Bonnie and Alex had come over for the weekend to help – he could not have done it alone, and besides, girls know what's what when it comes to clothes. Aimee had been a slim size ten, so many of her clothes would fit the girls. Bonnie, as usual, was more selective than her sister, and only took two recently new tops, and a summer skirt. Alex on the other hand seemed to take almost everything. She was organised. She had boxes for what she wanted for herself, boxes for the charity shop, and boxes for the dump, although that box was harder to fill. She found it difficult to throw anything away that could have a use, if not for herself, but for someone less fortunate. Consequently the '*dump*' box ended up being renamed '*charity two*'.

After that George found it easier to clear out odds and ends he may have otherwise kept, so by the time, nearly two years later, he came to move, much of what was left were a mix of essentials and memorabilia. A lot of the larger fixtures and fitting and furniture were sold with his house, so everything he ended up with fitted into the Transit van.

George found a pen and note pad and started to write a list. He had always been methodical. This came from his discipline working as a computer programmer. The mind has to work logically in his line of work, and this translated in to his private life – something that infuriated Aimee he remembered. He stopped writing and smiled. "*Sorry love, got to get organised,*" he whispered.

By ten thirty he had done most of the washing up and decided it was time to wake Chris. He made a strong coffee and took it to the downstairs bedroom. He knocked and went in. Chris had found the room hot, and with no window to open he had kicked off the bed sheets and was lying naked in the fetus position. He was not sucking his thumb, but George thought it an amusing story if he added the sucking of the thumb at a later stage. "Your wake up call young man." George put the mug on the floor next to the bed and rescued the sheet, and threw it over his son. "Not a pretty sight, Christopher. Long time since I've seen you naked."

Christopher was suddenly awake, pulling the sheet tight around his neck. "Hi Dad, sorry about that," dismissing the event as quickly as possible and changing the subject.

"What time is it?"

"Ten thirty... in the morning."

"Very funny – hard to tell down here in the bunker."

"Have your coffee, and a shower, and come on up for some breakfast."

George left his son with an echo of complaining mumblings and smiled to himself. He was glad Chris had come out with him, even if it was only for one day. Waking up alone in a new home, let alone a new country, was something he knew he would have to do tomorrow, but for today, a friendly face was comforting.

Christopher eventually made it to the lounge. He was wearing the same faded Jeans and T shirt he had worn for the journey down. "Didn't you bring a change of clothes?" George asked, although it was more a statement than a criticism. "I've just showered and everything, so I do not smell," he said, lifting his right arm and sniffing his armpit. "May have to pinch some deodorant before I leave."

"Ok, but borrow some shorts. Jeans will be too hot in this weather, especially if you are working."

"Working! You said nothing about working, Dad. Driving yes. Working, no!" he said defiantly, with hands on hips.

"OK, how about you help me finish unpacking the van and we may have time for a game on the Wii before you leave."

Christopher suddenly became alert. "Excellent. I'll take you for a few rounds in the ring."

"Or maybe a gentle game of golf," George suggested.

"You wimp. Just because you have never beaten me at boxing."

George smiled. "True, but you have never beaten me at golf."

The next couple of hours were spent tidying up and unpacking most of the remaining boxes.

They were working outside in what was the old barn where the van had been parked overnight, but was now used as a general storage building. It was a good size; around one hundred feet deep by fifty feet wide, and the open beamed roof gave it some character. The previous owners had used it more recently for building materials, and for olive storage, but given time it could even be transformed into a self contained living apartment. For now, it still had the musty smell of a barn. Wafts of diesel fuel seeped from the walls, and nesting swifts had taken residence in the eaves.

George had been methodical as usual. Boxes had been marked according to their contents; '*Kitchen*' or '*Spare Bedroom*' or *'Garage.'*

"I didn't see a garage, Dad, where do you want this box?"

"For now son, that can stay here. This can serve as garage and workshop."

Christopher then found the box marked '*games, CD's and leads.'* "I'll take this one in and set up the Wii."

"OK, but how about some lunch. I think we should take a walk into town and see what we can find. I still need some provisions."

"Always time for a quick game, Dad, then we can eat. Anyway I think we deserve a rest, don't you?"

George had to agree. Work and routine were going to take on a new emphasis here. Getting use to the heat for one thing. The house was cool and had some air-conditioning in the main lounge but not in the bedrooms. *Acclimatization* – that was the word someone had said to him. *'It could take a year or more – if you survive that long George.'* George had promised himself he would survive. Day two and he was still here.

By the time George got back to the lounge, Christopher had set-up the Wii console and one of the PC screens. George hadn't bought a TV yet, but planned to put one on the wall opposite the computer room. Provisions for a wall TV had been made during the renovations, and the connector socket was the only thing visible on the white wall.

"I'll leave the laptop to you to set-up, Dad. Looks a great system. Did you get a good deal?"

"Yes it is, and yes I did as matter of fact," but not expanding on the details, or reason as to why he wanted a complete new computer system. There was, in fact, no real mystery. Technology changes rapidly these days, and for both business and pleasure George also wanted to keep up-to-date, and he did not feel like using the laptop or server the police had taken and pulled apart over the last twelve months. Anyway it had been three years since his last upgrade, so with a shopping list he visited his specialist PC supplier and ordered a complete new system, built to his own specifications.

"What's it to be old man..."

George took the bait and gave his son a clenched fist tap on the shoulder.

"If that's all you've got then I'm going to thrash you old man."

"Any more of the *old man* and you won't be fit to drive anywhere."

Christopher loaded the game and they took hold of the plastic Wii paddles, one in each hand.

"This is going to get warm old..." Christopher stopped in mid sentence, "sorry, dad, so I suggest we disrobe."

"I can take the heat even if you can't. Let's do it." But Christopher had removed his T shirt and jeans and stood ready for action in his boxer shorts. They took position in front of the screen.

"Round 1...go!" he shouted, and the men started to box.

The rules are much the same as in real boxing, and after three minutes the bell went.

"Nearly had you there old man."

"Don't get cocky son, its early days. George wiped some perspiration from his brow. "Perhaps I will take off the shirt."

Christopher winced at his dad's naked torso, but thought he looked all right for a guy of fifty seven.

"Ok, let's get serious."

'Round two' came the announcement.

Another three minutes and the bell went again.

"That can't be three minutes," Christopher complained. "I nearly had you on the ground."

"Save your energy son or I will take you in the next round." George said in all seriousness. "I know what's missing – music."

"OK. But only if I choose," Chris insisted.

"Sorry son, house rules. My house, my music."

George darted over to the sideboard where he had left the iPod from the previous evening and turned it on. It was still plugged into the small, but powerful speaker. The room was filled with music – one of his favourites, Giraffe Walk by Mr Scruff and the Quantic Soul Orchestra – great rhythm for boxing.

Back in position in front of the screen, George and Christopher started round three.

They had all the moves. Ducking a left hook, blocking a right hook, protecting the face from a barrage of blows. All carried out in good humor but with a will to win, which is inbred in all who partake of any form of games. From playground 'conkers' or 'marbles,' through to any competitive activity – the goal was to win, no matter if it was your son or your dad you were playing.

Now the music was kicking in. The rhythm of the tune made each of them more confident with every blow. Father and Son – playing together. George enjoying life, probably for the first time in over two years, without a care in the world.

To anyone watching them, to all intents and purposes, they were in fact, shadow boxing. And what made the scene even more curious, if the casual observer could not see the computer screen from a certain angle, was the sight of two half naked men punching the air and shouting unrecognizable words above loud music.

This was the scene that greeted Senora Rosa Torres. She stood dumb-stuck, jaw dropped, looking in disbelief at the scene before her. Senora Torres had made her way up the winding iron steps on the side of the house that leads to the terrace, instead of walking up the sloping driveway to the front door on the other side. She was a little out of breath as it was, having walked from the end of the lane where the bus had dropped her off, and climbing the steps to where she now was. All manner of thoughts were racing around her mind, from *"What in God's name is going on?"* to *"Have I come to the right house?"*

She finally came out of her shocked trance and started to tap on the patio glass doors, which were locked. Tapping was not working. She clenched her fist and wrapped her knuckles on the glass even harder. "Hola, hola," she called out, but no one could hear her. She shook her head and sighed, as people do who have given up on their quest. She picked up her shopping bag, turned, and descended the iron steps and back along the road to the bus stop, to take her back to sanity.

As round three finished George instinctively turned towards the patio doors. "Did you hear anything Chris?"

"Only you huffing and puffing," he offered with glee.

George walked over to the sliding doors and opened them, allowing the music to escape into the midday air, and into the lives of whoever was in ear shot.

"Probably nothing." George left the doors open and returned to the game.

"This has gone on too long. Want to call it a draw and go get a drink?"

"Dad, I don't believe what I'm hearing. You are actually capitulating?" Christopher was ecstatic.

"No, not capitulating at all. I said call it a *draw.*" George replied, trying to sound sincere.

"Whatever old man," Chris shrugged, secretly relieved, "as long as you're buying lunch."

George took a quick shower and changed his shirt. Christopher sprayed himself in a large quantity of his dad's deodorant, and dressed again in his own jeans and T Shirt.

Ten minutes later they were ready to go. "Hell!" George was at the front door. "I don't know where the house keys are."

"Hardly anything to take here." Chris said sarcastically, trying to hurry his dad along.

George looked hurt. "Apart from my cherished possessions, there's the PC and Wii,' he exclaimed, while looking thoughtful. 'I'll give Carlos a ring, he will know."

"Didn't Carlos leave a note in the kitchen or something?" Christopher remembered.

"Of course." George headed for the kitchen.

He saw the yellow sticky note, which was partly hidden behind a jar of coffee. *'The cleaning lady is coming at 12.00 o'clock. Her name is Senora Rosa Torres.'*

"Damn." George looked at his watch. 12.45. "I wonder if she's coming."

He opened the kitchen drawers. Various cutlery, and a bottle opener. "Handy," he thought to himself, "but not what I need right now."

"Hmm, dad, these look like door keys." Christopher was standing at the other end of the lounge jangling a bunch of keys.

"Where were they for heavens sake?"

"On that small table in the hall, under the shrine." Christopher was pointing in the direction of the Picador lances mounted on the wall.

"Well done son, let's go."

They drove out of the driveway into the narrow lane, then the fifty yards to the main road and turned left towards town. They drove in silence for while.

George realised there was a lot to do at the house. He needed to get to *know* it for a start. He had had one social evening on his arrival, only yesterday, and now he was playing games and going drinking with his son. Why was he not feeling guilty? George was usually a methodical man. Methodical at home and at work. Was he slipping? Had the last couple of years taken away that sense of achievement and pride? No one who knew him, or knew what he had been through, would think any the less of him if it had.

Aimee's death.

The suspicion of a crime.

Not working for a year.

Enough to break any man. No, he was not feeling guilty. Why should he not take time out with his son? Precious few fathers do. Even less when the son is twenty-six years old.

He glanced over to Christopher.

"Dad. You OK. Why are you smiling?"

They parked the van in the town centre and stood at the edge of the square.

"OK, which way?" Christopher asked, looking up and down the street for signs of life.

"Is it always this quiet?"

"No idea son. I seem to remember some life last time I came here with Carlos. We found a Bar. On a corner. We sat outside and had a beer."

Christopher took the initiative. "Come on. Let's take a chance and go right."

They walked down a road with a mix of typical Spanish terraced houses interspersed with a few shops. The walls of the houses were mainly white or pale cream, with dark wood or painted window 'louvre' shutters. They passed a baker which was closed. Then a row of assorted shops. A ladies hairdresser. "Handy dad." Christopher offered. George smiled but did not rise to the bait.

Next to that was what looked like an ironmonger. Then more houses. The road widened slightly and then there was a T Junction. Strung above them spanning the width of the street was a banner announcing a forthcoming event. "Must be life somewhere. They're having an event of some sort. Can you read it?"

George studied the banner but the sun was directly above them and was making it hard to see, even with sunglasses on. He made out *Festival of something, April 24th* but not much else.

"Can't read much of that. The sun's in my eyes."

"Lame excuse. Come on then, let's find this bar if it exists. I'm getting thirsty."

George looked left and smiled. "I think it's this way. I seem to remember we came along this road from that direction. "Yes, I'm pretty sure we go left."

More houses, and on the right an entrance to a play ground. It seems children all over the world play on the same apparatus. There was a slide. A round-a-bout. An up and down thing which the name had escaped George. There was a large wooden house for exploring, and of course a sand-pit. The notice on the entrance gave opening times plus what was a list of Do's and Don'ts which George could not read, and in the bottom right corner was the EEC logo. "I guess they had funding for this." George thought to himself.

Spain had done well out of the EEC and spent most on its roads and infrastructure. Many towns and villages had been expanded and benefited from the low cost housing projects, although George had not seen any sign of that yet in Calabaza. Now Spain had entered a recession, and unemployment was running higher than ever, George was not sure what the long term economic situation would be for Spain, his new home.

They walked on, past more houses, and then George spotted the bar. "There, on the corner." He was pointing to a building fifty feet away to the left. "We parked down that side road. We've come in the other end of town that's all."

George and Christopher stood on the opposite pavement facing *El Tango*. The pavements were wider on both sides of the road here, and the bar had two tables and chairs outside. There was an old awning pulled over the front window, giving much needed shade to the tables.

"Yes, we sat there and planned the purchase of the house." George looked pleased with himself.

"Excellent. Glad dementia has not set in yet. Can we go inside, out of the heat?"

Christopher crossed the road, but George stood staring at the bar. It had seen better days he thought, and needed a paint job. The once bright terracotta walls were now faded to a milky yellow. There was a red OPEN fluorescent sign in the window which George thought was out of character with this old building. The name painted across the frontage had faded, and the 'o' in Tango could hardly be seen. Above the bar was what looked like a two story apartment. The window on the first floor was closed and shuttered. Paint flaked off the old brown wooden louvers. The top two widows were open but had no shutters. Around the top of the building ran a bricked fascia, and George guessed there was some sort of roof terrace. A rusty drainpipe ran the length of the font wall, completing the sad image of this old establishment.

George sighed, not really knowing why. He crossed the road and they entered *El Tango.*

Chris pushed open the heavy glass door and stepped inside. It was dark, and it took a few moments for their eyes to adjust to the surroundings and geography of the room. When their eyes did adjust to the dim light, they were genuinely surprised by the interior.

It was as if time had passed it by. There were several wooden tables and chairs in the centre of the room and in front of the window, where sat four elderly men drinking iced coffee and playing chess. They had looked up with interest when the two strangers entered the bar, but said nothing, although nodded in reconnection.

Christopher was more forthcoming. "*Buenos días* gentlemen," he said, waving a hand in greeting.

The bar on the left wall stretched about thirty foot, and like any bar worth visiting, it had three shelves along the back of the bar wall, each around twenty foot long stacked with every conceivable spirit and liqueur you could imagine. Many, of course were Spanish or Portuguese, especially Northern favourites such as Rioja and Tempranillo, plus a mix of American, English and Scottish sprits.

But what caught George's eye was on the far wall. It was a floor-to-ceiling painting of dancers - traditionally dressed men and women in the Tango pose, and a guitarist sitting playing, with beads of sweat trickling down his temple.

Maria walked to the end of the bar were George was standing, looking at the painted wall in admiration.

"My husband painted it." George turned around quickly, and for a second forgot he was in another country. "You speak English," he said rather tongue-tied.

"Si, yes. You are English are you not?" She answered, without expression.

"Is it that obvious?"

"Well, yes, and I heard your friend speaking it," she gestured to Christopher.

"Ah, he is not a friend, he is my son, and I can disown him any time if he misbehaves," George said, feeling a little more confident.

Christopher was now standing next to George, and extended his hand to Maria.

"*Hola, buenos días Senorita*. My name is Christopher."

Maria smiled, or perhaps was laughing to herself, at the poor excuse for what she heard as her own language.

"Hola, Christopher." She replied, taking his hand.

George thought he had better follow his son's lead and extended his hand, but did not chance the mother tongue just yet. "Hello, I am George Morton."

"Welcome to Calabaza. I am Maria and this is my bar." George was still holding her hand and was surprised by the length of her fingers. *'Probably a pianist'*, he heard his mother say somewhere in the back of his mind. She always had a saying for something attributed to other people's looks or character. She would have liked these hands. Maria was not stunningly attractive - she was more like a mysterious dark haired gypsy. Tall, and with a good figure from what he could make out under the apron she was wearing. Her skin was tanned smooth for her age, which George was guessing was around fifty something, give or take a few years. And even in this light he could see her eyes were a beautiful clear emerald colour, and could not stop from staring into them longer than he should have.

"*Senor.*" Maria said, withdrawing her hand and disguising a smile. "Can I get you something?"

"A bucket of cold water probably." Christopher suggested, giving his father a look of disgust.

Maria looked puzzled. "Take no notice of him. He is leaving tonight. I would like a cappuccino please Maria."

"I only have instant coffee. The machine is broken." Maria replied, looking slightly embarrassed for the excuse.

"Come on old man, it's gone mid-day. Two beers *por favor*, Maria."

"Si." Maria opened the cool-cabinet at the end of the bar and took out two bottles of cerveza.

"Any tapas Maria, we missed breakfast this morning."

"Sorry, no. We do not get enough business to offer Tapas, but I can make you a toasted sandwich. *Jambon y queso*, err... ham and cheese?"

"Sounds good to me, Dad, want one?"
"No, I'm fine thanks, Chris."

George and Chris sat opposite each other at one of the tables in the middle of the room.

"What are you grinning about, Christopher? Act your age please. I am staying here after you've gone remember, so do not embarrass me."

"Would I?" Chris looked hurt at the thought, but smiled again. "No worry's dad, your secret is safe with me."

George was taken-a-back. "What secret?"

Christopher leaned forward and whispered. "I saw the way you looked at... what's her name over there," nodding in Maria's direction.

"Don't be..." then realizing he had raised his voice, lowered it to a whisper, "don't be daft Christopher. I have just met her, and I have no intention of starting a relationship... *with anyone.*" He gave his son a look to establish his seriousness on the subject.

"Ok, sorry. Just a joke dad. I won't say another word." Chris said, holding his hands up in surrender, and suppressing a sheepish grin.

"Good. I hope not." George replied, in a mater-of-fact way.

They sat in silence for a couple of minutes when Christopher noticed the Jukebox.

"Excellent!" he stood up and walked over to the wall mounted music box, a few feet behind George.

"Wonder what it takes. Got any Euros, Dad?"

George froze and closed his eyes. They had left in such a rush the key episode had taken his mind of other important considerations, such as money.

"It looks pretty old dad. It's still got a selection of original 45's."

George gestured to his son and called over in a low voice. "Chris, come here. We have a problem."

Chris wasn't sure what his dad had said, but was more interested in the Jukebox. Thinking George had a coin, he went back to the table in expectation.

"Chris," George was looking directly at his son, and again in a low voice, "son, listen to me. Have you got any money on you?"

"No, of course not. That's why I asked. . ," and stopped in mid-sentence. "You've come out without any money haven't you?" Christopher took a sharp intake of breath. "This is going to be interesting. She's probably got a giant of a husband out back. I feel sorry for you old man." Christopher said shaking his head.

"Oh really. I'm not the one having a sandwich, eh?" George had seen a young woman come from behind the bar, where he assumed the kitchen was, and came to their table.

"Es este bocadillo para usted?" The young waitress asked George.

"No, for my idiot son."

She looked at George, then at Christopher. Shrugged, and placed the plate in the middle of the table.

Christopher grinned. "Lucky for me she doesn't understand English."

Talking with his mouth full, Christopher posed the question. "Do we make a run for it pass the geriatric posse over there, or volunteer to wash up. It's only one plate after all."

"I don't think it works like that. I'm going to talk to Maria and explain. After all, I have to come back here," and George left his son to eat, and went back to the bar.

Although two large ceiling fans were rotating at full speed, George was till perspiring. Maybe from the heat, but certainly from the uncomfortable feeling of having to admit they had not one Euro between them.

Maria was back behind the bar talking to the waitress.

"Hola." George coughed. "Sorry, Maria can I talk."

"Si, of course. This is Angeles, but we all call her Angel, which she is some of the time." Maria introduced her to George, and Angel immediately said something to Maria, which they both found amusing.

"I must start learning more Spanish." George promised himself. He gave the two women a puzzled look, as he knew they were talking about him.

"I am sorry, we are not laughing really. It is just my son is called Jorge, and Angel said if I called out his name who would come to me."

"I see, I think...how old is your son Maria?"

"Nine years next month."

It was George's turn to look surprised. Was she younger than she looked? Does this climate make you look older? He really did not want to get into a personal conversation now. He just wanted to get over the embarrassing problem facing him.

"Maria, this is very embarrassing for me, but it seems we have come out without any money between us. I know this is not a good first impression, but it is an honest mistake."

Maria was whispering a translated version to Angel who looked aghast, and a little amused.

Maria stared at George for what seemed like ages.

Angel was staring at Christopher, and then spoke to Maria excitedly.

George turned to see his son waving back and smiling. He gave a 'thumbs-up' for the sandwich.

"Angel says you leave your son as hostage while you go and get some money, and take your time."

George sighed. "As much as I would like to I don't think he would be... erm.," he tried to find the right word... he pulled a face of clenched teeth..."of any help to your friend. He has a partner," he said, raising his eyebrows, hoping for a sign of understanding.

Maria translated. Angel looked at her, then at George, then at Christopher who was still smiling. Angel shrugged and muttered something to Maria, and went back into the kitchen.

"Angel said to make you wash up, for a week."

"Gladly, of course. I am sorry about this. I am not leaving the country. I have just moved in to the old farmhouse *El Pino*. You may know it." George said hopefully.

"Si, I do," and smiled a smile that melted Georges heart. "We had heard it had been brought by a foreigner. Ana and Julio were very nice people. They have retired to Andalucía by the sea. Lots of Spanish retire to the sea." She paused, as if thinking of a solution. "Forget the payment. It is a welcome drink. As long as you come back."

George was relieved. "That is very kind of you. Please say sorry to Angel and your husband for my stupidity, and of course I will return. Gracias Maria, muchas gracias."

"I will tell Angel, but not my husband. He is now dead."

George didn't see that coming. "I am very sorry. How long has it been?"

"Seven years ago."

George was about to say something, but hesitated.

"My son did not really know his father." Maria explained.

"I'm sorry. It must be hard for you here."

"We survive," she smiled, not elaborating any further.

"Of course." George was now feeling embarrassed and started to turn away when he thought of something.

"Maria, can I ask something else of you."

"Si"

"Can I put a coin in the Jukebox? My son wants to hear one of the old records."

"If it works yes, but it has been broken for a long time. I have not taken it down. We play the CD now," and she pointed to a modern JVC midi hi-fi system behind the bar, with speakers placed at each end of the bar on the top shelf.

George was genuinely disappointed. "Do you know what is wrong with it?" He asked, never one to see something not working when it should be.

"I do not know the technical words. It just stopped one day, and a local electric man said it could not be fixed. They do not make the parts any more. It is very old," she shrugged.

"As I seem to have a lot of spare time, and I owe you a debt, would you allow me to look at it to see if it is truly not working." She said nothing, so he continued. "I have some tools I brought with me. I need to get the house straight, and finish unpacking, but I will come back later in the month if that is OK. What time do you open?"

"I am downstairs around eight, after I have taken my son to school," she said, "but you will be wasting your time."

"Then it's a deal. I will see you again soon."

George went back to his table.

"Blimey dad, what was she talking about? I couldn't tell if she was going to get rough with you." Christopher smirked.

"Well, she was actually very good about it. It was the other woman, Angel, by the way, who wanted to get *you* roughed up." He let the thought settle.

"Bloody hell – really. What did you say?"

"I was very discreet. I said you had a partner, and she understood. That's why she left and went back outside. Seems you've broken another heart. Come on, let's get back and get you on your way."

They headed for the door and George nodded to Maria who was still at the bar recalling their recent conversation, and her thoughts on this new man in town. "See you soon," he called out, and left the coolness of the café for the heat of the street.

Maria was brought out of her thoughts a few moments later by the door opening, and Senora Torres bursting into the bar.

"It's them, it's them!" she blurted out, and pointing vigorously in the direction George and Christopher had turned. "The two dance crazy weirdoes living in the farmhouse. I went there for a job and they were dancing naked." And she proceeded to show her stunned audience, which included her husband, of how she remembered seeing the two men dance. At this everyone burst out laughing, and Senora Torres continued to dance around the bar waving her fists in the air.

"Ok, you know the way back to Madrid."

"Sure, Dad. Due north I believe."

"Not funny. You have plenty of time to get back and return the van and get the plane. Call me on my mobile when you are at the airport."

"Stop fussing, Dad. It's no big deal."

George *was* fussing. Part of him wanted Chris to stay for a while longer. He knew as soon as he left he would be alone to face his future.

"Here's two hundred Euros for petrol, etc. Have a good meal at the airport, not that fast food stuff."

"Thanks, Dad, I will."

They looked at each other for a while then hugged, and Chris kissed his Dad on the cheek.

"Good luck Dad. Enjoy the rest of your life." Chris said in a solemn but sincere tone. He climbed in to the van and started the engine. "By the way, dad, don't play hard to get with Maria," he called out, as the van slowly passed George, and down the gravel drive to the main road.

George wanted to give a quick and witty reply but was lost for words. He realized then his children not only expected him to find another partner, but it was OK to do so. George smiled to himself, and then walked back inside to start his new life.

He spent the next week opening boxes and putting the house in order. He wasn't rushing – no need to. Senora Torres came back two days later, this time with her husband for protection, or moral support, but the language was a problem. George could understand pleasantries and order food and drink etc. but asking someone to come in two days a week to wash, clean and iron was beyond his vocabulary. Then he had an idea just as Senora Torres was leaving in frustration. "*Un momento Senora, por favor.*" He went over to the laptop and opened up Word. He wrote:

"Please come two days each week. Need cleaning, washing and ironing clothes. Is that OK? Thirty Euro each week."

Then he clicked on the translator option in Word and the following appeared;

"*Por favor llegado dos días cada semana. Necesidad de limpieza, lavado y planchado de prendas. Es aceptar. Euro treinta cada semana.*"

He gestured for Senora Torres to come over to the computer. She looked at the screen where George was pointing, somewhat proudly. "Here, can you read this?"

Senora Torres put on her glasses and leaned closer to the screen as if she was approaching a dangerous animal. She read in silence. The grammar may not have been perfect but she understood the jest of it. Especially the Euro thirty part.

"Si Senor George" she said straightening herself up and removing her glasses. *"Muy bien, acepto la oferta. Vendre los martes y los viernes de las nueve hasta la una poe que tengo que preparer de comida para mi marido antes de la siesta. Esta usted de acuerdo?*

George didn't get all of that, but understood nine to one, although was not sure if she agreed on two days, and if so, which ones they were.

He eventually found out the following Tuesday morning at 9.0am. Senora Torres was knocking on the front door. George opened the door bleary eyed in nothing but a pair of boxer shorts.

Senora Torres looked him up and down and muttered something to herself which George was not able to understand, but on reflection, was oblivious.

She walked past George into the kitchen. She placed her large Jute shopping bag on the counter and unpacked a wide array of cleaning materials, cloths and brushes.

George was suddenly awake. "Ahh, sorry Senora. Forgot you were coming*. Perdone Si*, I will get dressed."

He turned and ran upstairs and threw on shorts and a T Shirt.

Back downstairs Senora Torres was making coffee for him and placing the receipts for the items she has brought on the counter. George looked at the receipts and understood. "Of course. I will give back the Euros, Si no problem." She looked at him without smiling and gave him the coffee.

"This is very good of you but not necessary." George gave a deep sigh. "There must be a better way to communicate." Then he remembered the laptop again. He got up quickly from the kitchen stool, which gave Senora Torres a fright. She watched him go over to his office and open the louver doors by entering a pass code in the digital padlock.

He returned to the kitchen with the laptop and opened up Word. "This is how we will communicate again, and leave messages for each other, Si." He said smiling at Senora Torres who was not too sure what was going on. He typed the following and pressed 'translate':

"We can talk to each other by typing a message here and translate it."

"Podemos hablar entre sí escribiendo un mensaje aquí y traducirlo."

Again, not perfect grammar, but Senora Torres understood what he was on about.

"You have a go", he said pointing to the keyboard. "Si, go on. Just type."

Senora Torres typed gingerly with one finger. "*Con que quiere que empiece?*"

George showed her how to highlight the sentence and press *translate.*

"*With what you want to start?*" appeared in the translation box.

"Excellent – we have contact." George was about the give Senora Torres a celebratory hug but thought better of it.

They spent the next half hour agreeing on what needed to be done and showing her around the house. The only exception was she was not to go into the office. He was happy to clean there. He explained the equipment was sensitive and he would look after it. Not that she could do any real damage, but just to be safe.

Later, George learnt Senora Torres proudly announced in El Tango she was now an expert on the computer. Her husband said she should ask for more money with these extra skills.

Over the next few weeks the house took shape nicely. All precious nick-knacks had been found and unpacked. He and Aimee would collect, where possible, a flyer or program from the many shows and concerts they loved to go to, and frame them. George stared at the line of familiar artist's faces and remembered each concert with affection. Rabih Abou-Khalil, Jan Garbarek, e,s,t, Richard Bona, Hiromi, Paolo Conte, Joe Zawinul, Trilok Gurtu, and for old time sake, Leonard Cohen from his World Concert in 2006, the last one he and Aimee went to see together. *This is one thing I will resume now* he promised himself – he had not been to a concert in over three years. It was time to start again.

Panic had struck George one day when he couldn't find some favorite CD's he knew he had packed. They were in fact Aimee's favourites as well. She particularly liked pianist Keith Jarrett, and the Irish group, The Cores. George was normally a focused sort of guy – he had to be in his line of work – but somehow, now, in this new environment he was distracted. New surroundings, new sounds, new colors, smells, light; everything was new to him, and he found he was enjoying the experience of going against the *norm*. The other problem, or advantage, of being alone to do what he wanted to do, and when he wanted to do it, with no particular agenda, was that he had time to think a lot.

He had done plenty of that during the twelve months he was under investigation, but that was a case of being more obsessed with the facts of the case, and being very angry at what had happened to him. Of course he thought of Aimee during that time, but in a different way – wishing she was there with him, giving him moral support and telling him everything would be OK in the end, as she always did. There was no one now to turn to each day to just *let it all out.*

Now, alone in his new house, he stopped to think of what Aimee would have made of it. Would she have agreed with the move? She loved England for all its faults but she liked to travel, and they had had many happy holidays in Spain with the children, but she was always pleased to be back home.

George was glad in a way she did not have to suffer the trauma of that long year he was under investigation. The anguish at not knowing if he was going to be prosecuted and hearing whispers behind her back about her husband *'the thief'*. And *'was she in on it'* as well?

He opened the patio doors and walked out onto the cool flag stones. The sun had not come-a-round to the patio side, but it would in about thirty minutes, and the stone would be much warmer then, and last all day.

George smiled, and allowed himself to think Aimee was watching over him, and she was enjoying seeing him happy – alone maybe - but happier than he had been for a long time. He looked up to the clear blue sky and blew it a kiss. "You'll be *my someone to watch over me*, wont you my love?"

31

He could hear the tune playing in his mind – her favorite version of course, by Keith Jarrett.

Chapter 2. April

With Senora Torres's help, George spent the rest of the month putting the house in order, and getting to know his new home, the town and the locals.

The most difficult part was settling into a different time-zone. He had been use to late mornings and late nights at home over the past year or so - there had been nothing to get up for, and no work, as he was banned from working. He read novels, watched films, and sometimes worked on a laptop Christopher had lent him. Only a few loyal friends kept in touch. Funny, how suddenly your friends and relatives pre-judge you when they have been close to you for many years. George could count on one hand the good friends that have stood by him, including his in-laws, Thomas and Eilidh.

They were sorry to hear his decision to move to Spain, but understood, and promised to keep in touch, either directly, or via their grand-children. George hoped they could visit one day, but although Thomas was a sprightly seventy-five, Eilidh was rather frail now and suffered from arthritis, but said they would look forward to reading all about Calabaza and the new house, and seeing lots of photographs. George had enjoyed the walks with Thomas that cold January weekend before he left England, and was happy to sit with him in the Old Thistle Hotel bar and talk about his *lost* daughter over a pint of ale. Thomas could never bring himself to say 'dead'. She was 'lost to them', and therefore one day will return. George would place his hand on Thomas's hand and nod silently, wishing to hell if only that were true.

His own parents had died ten years ago, two years apart. Aimee had been very close to them and really missed them. Christmas was never the same again – and never can be now Aimee has been taken from him as well.

George soon found that 'lying-in' was not an option in Spain. Although sunrise in early April is around eight a.m., the sun is very bright, and without blackout curtains, which he did not have, it was almost impossible to stay asleep. By the end of April sunrise would be even earlier, at around seven a.m., and gradually get earlier and earlier throughout the year.

George also found that despite Spain having a reputation of eating late, many folk in the provinces retire early. One tradition George was not sure about was the siesta, which is still observed all over Spain. Did he feel like taking a 'nap' at two in the afternoon? Not just now he decided - there was too much to do around the house. He did however find time to relax with a late lunch on the balcony, and read, or just watch the world go by - although no one was actually going by. Instead, he just appreciated the views from the balcony and the sounds of Mother Nature.

He did get into a routine of emailing the children once a week, plus a Skype call when he wanted to see them. It had only been four weeks since he had left England, and the self-denial of not expecting to miss his children was beginning to fray, but a quick chat on Skype helped to relieve his misgivings.

Although George had been into town several times to work out the geography, and find shops, he realised he had not seen Maria again to look at the jukebox as he had promised. Maria had been getting progress reports via Senora Torres, when she called in after the morning duties at the *'foreigner's house'*, as she called it. Not that there was a lot to gossip about. *"He is typical man – not very tidy in the bedroom. Does not eat properly."* Senora Torres would reel off a list of observations that everyone in *El Tango* was eager to hear. Maria however was not so interested, and thought it not right for his privacy to be discussed in such a way. She made a mental note to have a quiet word with Senora Torres.

Maria was also slightly put-out that despite his apparent eagerness to revisit the cafe, even if it was to look at the jukebox as promised, he had not been back in over three weeks.

George had not forgotten the jukebox, or Maria, or his promise. He simply had not had the time he thought he was going to have to get back there. Now four weeks later he realised he must go soon. However, one pressing problem had been transport. George had walked the half mile to the village a few times to buy groceries in the local Spar store, but carrying bags of shopping back was not going to be a pleasurable pastime for long. He needed transport. A small second hand car for now would suffice. He did remember however seeing a pushbike in the old barn, and with a good rubdown and some oil on the brakes it seemed adequate for now.

George gingerly pushed open the heavy glass door of *El Tango* and entered the dimly lit establishment. It was eleven a.m. on Tuesday morning, and all was quiet. No customers yet. No Maria or Angel. "Hola," he called out. "Hola, anyone here?" No answer. George ventured further into the bar and stood facing the entrance to the kitchen. He considered going behind the bar and into the kitchen, but thought better of it.

"Hola," he offered once more, but still no answer.

He walked over to the jukebox on the far right of the room, and studied it closer than he had done on his previous visit.

It looked a lot bigger than the remembered. *"How the hell am I going to get this home?"* he asked himself.

The make was a Rock-Ola 1485. It played fifty 45rpm vinyl records - a total of one hundred selections. First appearances looked promising. Nothing looked out of place - just dust and dirt. George located the plug socket near the floor and hesitantly plugged in the jukebox.

Nothing happened. No lights. No noise. Nothing.

He looked around just to make sure no one had come in and was watching him – so he gently shook the box. Then shook it again. Nothing. He sighed, and took up a thinking pose.

"It's going to have to come off the wall" was his conclusion. But how? The box was just over three feet high and around three feet wide. It also looked heavy. (George

found out later it was actually 700lbs, and was glad he did not know that at the time).

He could see no obvious signs of fixing brackets on either side. He pressed his face to wall and looked behind the shiny chrome box. "Ah, I see." The unit looked like it was mounted on one long facing plate which was fixed to the wall – not the box itself – making it easy to lift off for servicing. That's the theory anyway. George held the jukebox on either side and tried to lift it off the bracket. It did not move. Either it needed some lubricating, or it did not come off that way. As George did not have any oil to hand, he decided to try and lift it again. This time he took a stronger stance – he bent his knees and gripped the underside right corner with his right hand, and the left side of the box nearer the top with the other hand, and pushed upwards. The jukebox moved. George gave a faint smile. "Not beaten yet then George," he said out loud. He took the stance again, and with determination pushed with all his might. This time the box moved several inches, but as it had been untouched for many years, part of the fixing had seized tight on the left side of the bracket. George knew he was almost there. It just needed a final push, but he did not have the strength to budge it further, and if he let down the side that had moved, he would be back to square one.

George had not heard the glass door open a few minutes earlier. The tall man in the shadows had been looking at him with curious interest, *"¿Qué le está haciendo a mi jukebox?"*

George turned his head slowly towards the door squinting. He could make out someone there but they were in the shadows. "Hola." George called out, rather breathlessly. "Could you help me please?" Hoping the person in the shadows could understand him. The only reply was the same question, *"¿Qué le está haciendo a mi jukebox?"* The man's voice was calm but firm.

"¿Qué le está haciendo a mi jukebox?" He repeated the question, but now his tone was sharper.

"I am sorry, I do not speak Spanish that well." George offered. He tried to look behind him to see if Maria was there. "Maria!" he called out with a slight tone of despair. "Maria, if you are there I could do with some help."

"*You do not speak Spanish at all I think,*" *the* voice at the door said, in broken English.

George was taken by surprise. "Yes, err no, not much at all – who are you – never mind, this is getting heavy, can you help please?"

The stranger moved in to the room from behind the shadows, and George saw for the first time Vincente Cotrina. George froze for a second taking in the physic of the man. Vincente was over six feet tall. He had a craggy suntanned complexion under what looked like a week's stubble, and long thick wavy black hair, with a hint of grey. Probably in this late sixties, but looking very fit, George guessed, which was what he needed just now.

George blinked, and returned to the situation in hand. "I'm sorry, but this is heavy."

"*¿Papa, ayudale por dios?*" It was Marias voice.

George looked around and was relieved to see Maria come out from the kitchen.

She looked at Vincente then at George. "George what are you doing?"

"Maria, thank God. I did call out but no one heard me, and then I tried to remove the jukebox myself and got stuck. Then this gentleman came in and... err. . here we are."

"Papa, please help," she said in English.

"*¿Qué él está haciendo con mi jukebox?*" He asked Maria, demanding an answer.

George looked at Vincente, then Maria. "He's your father?"

Maria turned to George. "Si, he is, I'm sorry, I did not hear you come in."

"Do not apologize to him for me being your father." Vincente raised his voice to Maria.

"I did not say that! Please help him Papa and I will explain everything."

"*Jorge* is it. How long has *Jorge* been here? What is going on?" Vincente had still not moved from just inside the door. He stood there, defiant, with arms folded.

Now Maria was getting cross. She walked over and stood directly in front of her father and looked up into his sparkling blue eyes and spoke to him in Spanish, and from her tone, George guessed, she was not too pleased.

"Papa, if you had been here, and not gone away without telling anyone where you go, and for how long you are going to be away, you would know what is going on. Now help him with that thing, *please."* Pointing to George, without taking her eyes off of her father.

Vincente walked slowly over to the jukebox and leaned over to George and whispered in his ear. "Do you have children?"

"Si, err, yes I do." George replied.

"My condolences Senor." He said with sigh. "Excuse me Jorge. Let me take over." George tentatively released his grip. The jukebox did not move.

Vincente took the same pose as George and griped the sides and lifted. The back of the jukebox responded to the upward movement, and reluctantly released its grip from the rusty bracket.

Vincente placed the jukebox on the floor, as if it had been sack of feathers.

"Now, Maria, my darling daughter. Tell me what has been going on here."

"*George Morton*" George extended his hand to Vincente. Vincente looked at him with suspicion, and did not shake his hand.

"Papa!" Maria decided to take control. She continued in her own language. "Come and sit down and have a coffee. And you George. Come and have coffee."

"Maria, I must apologize for not coming back sooner with what I owe you."

"What! What does this man owe us? He has only been here five minutes and he is debt." Vincente turn to George for an answer.

"Excuse me, err . ." George looked at Maria for help.

"Papa, this is George Morton. He has moved into the farmhouse."

Vincente still did not offer his hand.

"Maria, please explain. I think he is going to hurt me."

"Both of you sit down!" Her voice was as firm and

commanding as any school teacher putting her class in order.

Maria continued to explain to her father who George was and why he was here this morning. George could not understand a word, but was more concerned with the way Vincente kept looking at him.

When Maria had finished talking, Vincente turned his gaze on George, saying in a calmer tone, "Why do you want to mend this music box?"

George was not sure if this was a trick question, but decided to tell the truth. "Because it is broken," and shrugged.

Vincente smiled for the first time since he had entered the bar. "Good luck to you Jorge." and then turning to his daughter. "Now, where is my coffee and my favorite waitress?"

He leaned back in the chair and smiled as if he did not have a care in the world.

Maria got up to fetch coffee. "*Papa... behave please.*" George understood by Maria's expression, if not the words. That awkward moment then came when two people who feel uncomfortable with each other, not knowing what to say. In George's case the later was literally true. Fortunately, Vincente broke the ice, or was about to. He smiled such a wide smile, George instinctively asked "Why are you smiling like that?"

"Did Maria tell you my grandsons name is Jorge?"

George smiled too. "Yes... she did," he offered hesitantly.

"Have you met him yet – he is a lovely boy."

"No. I have only been here once, with my son, who helped me move in at the beginning of March."

"Si." Which was more of a confirmation than an acknowledgment, as if Vincente already knew that.

Just as George was about to ask Vincente a more probing question like, where *have* you been, or what do you do around here, he was interrupted by a squeal of delight from Vincente, seeing Angel approaching with the coffee.

Vincente immediately rose and greeted Angel with two kisses, and from what George saw, accompanied by a firm pat on the bottom. Angel hugged him and kissed him again on the lips, and they entered into a long dialogue, in Spanish, which must have included *'where the hell have you been for four weeks'*, and *'why did you not call me'*, all of which no Spanish conversation would be complete without the gesturing of the hands, raised shoulders and finger wagging, which was abound.

Maria joined the group and George took the advantage to stand up and make his excuses to leave the 'family' reunion. Maria, however, interrupted the other two with a scornful look and with hands on hips. "Leave the staff alone Papa. Angel, get back to work." Angel obeyed, and blew Vincente a kiss as she turned and walked to the other end of the café to clean the tables.

"Papa, please stop encouraging her – she is younger than me – it's embarrassing."

"Maria my lovely, it's only some fun – she likes to flirt."

"Si, she is not the only one."

Father and daughter looked at each other momentarily, in a calculating way, without speaking.

George took his chance again to leave in the calm of the moment.

"Thank you for the coffee, but I think I should leave now."

"Jorge!" Vincente called out, seeing an escape route. "Do you want help to your car with the music box?"

George looked perplexed. "Ahh... I actually do not have a car yet."

But without time to explain further, Vincente saw a good excuse to leave his simmering daughter. "Si, good, I will take you in my pick-up, OK?"

"That's very kind of you. Are you sure you have nothing else to do." George asked, looking at Maria.

"No, nothing," also glancing in Maria's direction. "Maria, I will collect Jorge from school on my way back, OK?"

With a faint smile she raised her hands in defeat. "Ok, but no treats, and bring him straight home Papa." Then she seemed to remember something, and called out as the two men picked up the jukebox, "and Papa, he is not to ride in the back, Papa please say so."

"Si, Maria, not in the back – now may we go, this is heavy."

George and Vincente carried the jukebox out into the sunlight, which nearly caused George to drop his end. "Just over there." Vincente nodded in the direction of the car.

Car, however it was not. It was the biggest, shiniest pick-up George had ever seen.

A Dodge 3500 with brunt red metallic paint. They put the jukebox down behind the truck and Vincente opened the drop-down tail-gate. "OK Jorge, on three in to the truck. *Uno, dos, tres,"* and it was in. George was breathing heavier than usual which Vincente noticed. "You must drink more water out here. You are not use to the heat I think."

"It's not that – I'm probably not as fit as I should be either."

"Oh really – I thought you boxed," Vincente replied without any hint of sarcasm.

George looked at him suspiciously. "No," he replied slowly, "never boxed."

"Ok, never mind – let's go."

George, still looking puzzled by the question, got into the pickup.

Vincente started the engine and the monster purred. He was obviously proud of his Dodge.

"5.7 litre V8 engine. 383 horsepower. 3.42 Axle Ratio. 17" steel all weather tires." George realized he was reading a list of memorized specifications.

"It's a great car. . err truck. How long have you had it?"

"Nearly eight months." Vincente smiled back.

George was not surprised. It's still his new toy.

They drove in silence for most of the five minutes to the farmhouse. Vincente knew the way. He had been there before as a friend of the previous owners, and more recently when renovations were being carried out.

"Do you think you can mend the music box Jorge?"

"I'm not sure. I need to open it up and see what parts can be replaced."

They turned in to the drive and Vincente parked close to the front door.

George went in and through the lounge to open the patio sliding doors. "Ok, let's take it through to the patio. I will have more room to work on it there."

The two men maneuvered the heavy object carefully through the living room and on to the patio floor.

"Bueno." Vincente looked at the view. "I remember this - it is still a good view."

"Did you know Senor and Senora Caldas well?"

"Si, as well as anyone in Calabaza. They have lived here all their lives. They turned in a good olive crop each year as well. Are you going to continue with the olive grove?" Vincente asked with interest.

"I'm not sure. It would be a shame to see it die off if there is a market for them." George had not really considered the fate of the olives, but now Vincente had mentioned it, it was another thing to add to his list of *things to do*.

"Have you lived here long?" George asked, out of genuine interest.

"We moved here when my wife died, twenty years ago. But that's a long story."

George got the message – no more questions, but he did register the coincidence in their circumstances.

"Would you like a beer?"

"Ah Si. Cerveza will be good."

George took two cold bottles of Estrella from the fridge. "Do you prefer a glass or the bottle?"

"Glass, por favor Jorge. I am too old to drink from a bottle."

George smiled. His thoughts exactly. He poured the cold beers and they sat on the patio.

"Cheers." George raised his glass.

"Salud." Vincente touched glasses and sipped the beer.

"This is a good beer. Do you buy it here?"

"Yes. I have not ventured further than the town for shopping yet. I must look for a car soon."

"Ah, you must see Martin the Mechanic. He is good with cars."

"Thank you, but I need a car first before I have it serviced."

"Si, si, but he can also find you a good cheap car. Tell him I send you."

"Thank you. I will look him up. Do you have an address?"

"Just ask anyone in town. They all know him." Vincente said, looking around and into the lounge area.

Vincente smiled, looking at George. "Have you made many changes to the house?"

"Yes a few." George clicked. He wanted a guided tour. "Would you like to see the rest of the house?"

Vincente was on his feet. "Si, lead the way Jorge."

In the lounge George gestured to the kitchen area. "No real changes here, just painted the walls, and added a few rugs on the lounge floor." George was walking and talking and heading for the landing to go upstairs, but he turned to see Vincente studying the louver doors to the office.

"Some change here, Jorge?" he said, nodding to the doors.

"Ah, yes my office. I converted the dining room. Just my computer and work files."

"Si, but why the locks?"

George had been asked the same question by Christopher. *"What are you hiding in there Dad. Crown Jewels?"*

The answer would have to be the same.

"My work is sensitive. I am in software security, and I have an obligation to my clients." George replied, with as much composure as possible.

Vincente seemed unimpressed. "Of course," he said, but sounding unconvinced.

After that Vincente seemed uninterested in the rest of the house, and hardly glanced in each room, just giving a nodded approval and moving on.

Back downstairs, Vincente looked at his watch. "I must collect my grandson from school for lunch. I don't want to upset my daughter, *again*. How many children do you have Jorge?"

"Three. Alex, she's thirty, and then we had twins, Christopher and Bonnie who are twenty-six."

"They must miss you, Jorge."

"Not so much. They moved out some years ago and have their own lives to live now."

"Ah, families should keep together Jorge. It is different here. Our children look after us in our old age."

They shook hands outside. "Thank you Vincente for your help. I could not have done that alone."

"Si, it's OK. Hope to see you soon Jorge. Don't be a stranger in the bar. Come in for lunch and we can talk some more. Adios Jorge."

George waved as Vincente maneuvered the Dodge down the slope to the main road, and wondered why he had not asked him about his wife. George shrugged at the thought, and returned to the patio to inspect his new project. The Jukebox.

***

Around 10.30 that evening George had a Skype call from Alex. "Hi, love. Nice surprise. Everything OK?"

"Yes, Dad, nothing has to be wrong to call does it?"

"No, but it's a weekday. I thought you two were early birds."

"We can be when we want to. Anyway, moving on, how are you? Are you eating OK."

"Yes I am, and yes, and no. Again!"

"Yes and no to what?"

"The same two questions you asked me last week. Am I happy and am I missing home?"

"OK, sorry, Dad, but we are all concerned about you. There was something else however I wanted to ask." Alex said looking serious.

"Ok, what's that – you two want to come over soon?"

"No... yes... but I will come back to that. No, what it is I had a call from a guy asking about you."

George look alarmed. "What guy. Who was he?" he asked, sounding anxious.

"Dad, wait. I don't know, he didn't give his name. He was calling from a secure line so I couldn't get a call-back number. He asked if I knew what you had done. What did he mean Dad? I was scared and Tom wasn't home. Why did he call me?"

"Oh darling, I'm so sorry. He's probably a nutter. Did he say anything else?"

"No... I put the phone down. What did he mean? Was it anything to do with your work or the police enquiry?"

George drew breath. *Why now* he thought to himself. *And why go after my children*?

He tried to put Alex's mind at rest. "Don't worry Alex - it's a crank. Report it if he calls again, and just to be safe, tell Chris and Bonnie to be aware of any strange callers. On second thoughts I will call them myself tomorrow. Now, what was that about visiting your old man?" he said, wanting to change the subject as quickly as possible.

"Ah yes . .we... that is Chris, B and me wondered if you are ready for visitors."

"Of course, anytime. When?" George was excited at the thought of his kids visiting.

"How about for your birthday." Alex said "and to remember mum. It will be three years," she said with more than a hint of sadness in her voice.

George smiled reassuringly back at the screen and touched her face. "That is a lovely thought," he said quietly. Each year they had gathered to remember their mum, and George had encouraged them to continue the tradition, wherever they may be. Not so much in a solemn way, but to celebrate her and who she was. To cook her favorite food, play her music, and generally talk about her. Alex found it very hard the first year, and the others felt awkward talking about their mum. The second year seemed better, with Christopher bringing some of Aimee's favorite films, and Bonnie actually reading a poem. Alex however was overcome again with emotion and could not bring herself to say anything. They had all sat huddled together on the sofa and watched Moulin Rouge, one of Aimee's favorites. Everyone cried, and no one said a word.

"We had a conference call last night. Well Chris and I did. B was on the line for two minutes to say yes, and left us to make the arrangements. Nothing new there then."

"I wish you two would get on better. You're not kids anymore."

"I know Dad. It takes two to Tango and all that. I give her every opportunity to . "

"OK, OK." George raised his hands in surrender, "just be sure you leave your differences in England. I don't want my *Karma* spoilt."

"*Karma,* Dad – what's going on out there? Sounds interesting."

"Nothing – I mean it's so relaxing here. You'll love it. So will Bonnie."

"OK, I'll call when we have made the arrangements. We may need picking up from the airport. Have you got a car yet?"

"Not yet... but I know a man who has."

***

George reflected on Alex's mystery caller. Who was causing trouble out there? George pondered on this for some time and concluded there could only be one trouble maker – Oliver Barnes.

He didn't contact Chris or Bonnie as he had promised Alex, as he was sure there would be no need.

***

Peter Barnes had reluctantly accepted the inevitable that the money was gone, and at the January board meeting reported that the case had been closed, and the money was 'written off' - lost, conveniently, in the wake of the Icelandic bank fiasco.

Oliver Barnes was, however, not satisfied with the outcome. He was furious with the decision. "How can you sit there and calmly agree to write-off five million pounds. You should be out there hanging him upside down until he confesses."

His father sat behind his old polished mahogany desk, transfixed at his son's outburst.

"Oliver," he said as calmly as possible. He was aware of his high blood pressure, and the warning the doctor had given him on his last check-up. *'Take it easy Peter unless you want early retirement.'*

"....firstly do not talk to me like that. I am not just your father but also Chairman of the bank, and expect more respect from you."

Oliver went to respond but was cut short. Barnes senior

raised his hand. "I am not finished. Secondly, the board has made a decision to close the matter. We have assessed the damage, and we will take the loss. After the insurance settlement is taken in to account the figures will look better than many of our competitors who have taken similar losses through the World's *financial fiasco* of the past coupled of years." He paused to shake his head as if in memory of a lost friend. He looked up suddenly. "Thank God we were not truly compromised in that as well. That may have been a loss too far. Most banks will survive, albeit in a new structure, and with new mandates, but some will go to the wall and God help them, all because of the greed within our own financial institutions."

Oliver Barnes listened with a mix of bewilderment and incredulity, and realised then it was time for a change at the top.

***

George walked into town the next day to retrieve his push-bike and decided to see if he could find Martin the Mechanic, Vincente had recommended.

He thought of looking in at El Tango to see if Vincente could give him an address, but decided to cycle around and see if he could find it himself, and discover more of where he lived at the same time.

Calabaza is not a large town but George realised he had not ventured further than the Calle de Casteno, a long road leading west from the Calle de Algarrobo, where El Tango is situated. Along Calle de Casteno he had found several shops including a convenience store he used for provisions. He now cycled further along this road to see where it took him. Some locals nodded to him or waved as he passed, and George felt a tinge of pleasure that these people would greet a stranger so openly. At the end of Calle de Casteno he came to a T Junction. Cycling around is all very well but it could be counterproductive, and tiring, so George decided to approach one of the friendly faces that had acknowledged him as he passed by a couple of minutes earlier.

"Hola," he called over to an elderly lady crossing the road in front of him. "I am look for Martin the mechanic..."

The woman stared at him, smiled, and continued on her way.

George turned right into Calle de Cerezo, where to his delight he discovered several more shops. There was a butcher, an art shop selling local paintings, gifts and pottery, a wine shop, delicatessens and an electrical shop. He decided to ask directions in the gift shop hoping they would understand some English. Unfortunately they did not speak English, but George somehow made them understand with mimes and gestures he was looking for the local garage.

As it turned out he was only a few hundred yards away in the other direction. Martin's garage was in Calle de Aliso, a small road with just a handful of old terrace houses and what looked like a disused shop next door to the garage. Above the garage was a double-story flat where Martin lived.

A man in his late-thirties was working on an old Honda. "Hola." George said, and to his surprise the man replied in English. "Hello, can I help you. You must be the Englishman who brought El Pino."

"Does everyone know of my arrival?" George enquired.

"Well, most people will. The previous owners were well known here. There is even a street called Calle de Pino the other side of town," he said with some pride.

"Your English is good." George said, holding out his hand

"I lived in Oxford for a few years working at Ford," replied Martin.

"Ha," George replied, "a place I know well."

Martin stood up and shook hands with George. "George Morton."

"Martin Gardel. Do you have a car that needs looking at?"

"No, not yet, but I am thinking of buying one so I can see more of this wonderful country."

"Ha," said Martin with some enthusiasm, "you need an open top tourer. I know someone who has one for sale. It is a 1988 Roadster in good condition – I know, I service it. Do you like classic cars George?"

"I was thinking of something a little newer and something to suit my age more. A Seat Leon convertible maybe."

"Yes it is good, but the older cars are more fun, yes?"

George could not help but admire the man's enthusiasm. There was also something about him George could not put his finger on. Not the accent, but something in his manner. Yes, he reminded him slightly of his own son, Christopher, but probably a little older.

"If you see anything suitable let me know. Leave a message for me at El Tango, or please call in and see me at home."

Martin raised an eyebrow. "So, you have met the lovely Maria. What about our mayor, Vincente. His bite *is* worse than his bark." Martin emphasized.

"Mayor?" George asked. "I did not know that. When I came over last year to finalize the sale I saw a different man."

"Si, Senor Sanchez Snr. He died last January. Vincente was elected soon after."

Martin moved closer and lowered his voice. Not that anyone else was around to hear. "Be careful of our Mayor Vincente. He is a powerful man and not to be..." Martin searched for the right words. "... double crossed, especially when it come to the lovely Maria. Si, you know what I mean?"

George was not sure he did. "Thank you Martin. I will be careful, but I think Maria is old enough to look after herself."

Martin shrugged and picked up a spark-plug remover from his tool box. "Si she is, but all I say is when Vincente is around, be careful when it come to her."

George realised the young man meant well, and there maybe something in what he was saying, but George just smiled and nodded, not wanting to get into a long discussion just then, but made a mental note to learn more about the mysterious Mayor Vincente.

Having said goodbye, George cycled back via the delicatessens and brought some ham, bread and salad for lunch, and by the time he had reached home, decided a car was needed sooner rather than later.

***

The next morning George sat at the computer and searched Google for "Rock Ola".

12,800,000 entries appeared.

"Excellent, bound to be something here, but need to narrow the search a bit."

He keyed in Rock Ola 1485. This time 856 entries appeared. *That's better* and scrolled through the list.

He spent the next few days emailing and calling specialist Jukebox suppliers and was surprised to see so many still selling spare parts for these old models.

Eventually he found a very helpful man in England, Mr Wilson, not far from where he used to live in Windsor. He emailed a request for the 1485 manual and spare parts list, which he paid for with PayPal. It took over a week to arrive, but that gave him time to explore the heavy beast.

The Rock-ola 1485 was made in 1962 and could hold fifty 45rpm vinyl singles. It was a popular model in small bars and cafes all over world, especially in countries wanting to hear the emerging new 'pop' music from America. Spain however was an exception. Franco was still in power and the authoritarian state discouraged foreign culture. Because of this Spain had been largely isolated by the international community for many years until 1953 when she was reconciled, thanks mainly to the USA, who helped her to kick-start the economy. The rest of the 1950's brought rapid wealth and acceptance, and some say, unfortunately, the start of cheap package holidays. The rest is history.

George removed thirty-seven rather old 45's from their racks and put them to one side without really looking at them. He knew the jukebox could hold fifty in total and would like to see it complete one day. He tried to imagine the residents of Calabaza listening to the popular music of the day. He knew it was made in 1962 so it could have been installed anytime that year, or the following year perhaps. Just what did the population of Calabaza listen to way back then? America had Elvis, and the new Rock 'n' Roll sound dominated the charts. Some of the most popular artists in the USA then, were; Perry Como, Nat King Cole, Tony Bennett, Elvis Presley, Bill Haley and the Comets, Chuck Berry and Doris Day.

Europe however still preferred home-grown artists, even if they were copying the new sounds of the decade. France had Johnny Hallyday. Italy adopted the most popular America/Italian artists of the time; Frank Sinatra, Dean Martin, Bobby Darin and Perry Como for instance, (all of whom had an Italian heritage), but they also had their own stars like Domenico Modugno, Luigi Tenco and Milva (Ilva Biolcati).

George picked up a handful of the 45's taken from the jukebox and read the titles;

Las Muchachas De La Plaza De Espana - *Visconti, Mario*
Bambino - *Lasso, Gloria Y Su Orquesta*
Estudiantina Portuguesa - *Gamez, Celia*
Usted - *Garrido, Lolita Y Su Orquesta*
Flamenco - *Rosalia*
La Chicha Ye-Yé - *Concha Velasco*
El baúl de los recuerdos - *Karina*

These looked to George all very... err . Spanish. No USA or UK imports here, and until he repaired the jukebox there was no other way of listening to them.

He had checked over all the parts and was satisfied they were correct, but said a silent prayer that he could make this work, which was unusual for George, because he never prayed.

What was so special about this job? Did he want to make it work and impress Maria, and the locals, and now her father? Would it help him to be more accepted in the community? Or was it just something else waiting to be mended, and no one really cared if it ended up on the council tip, like many newer pieces of modern day technology do.

This did worry George. Was he doing it for the right reasons? Did Maria think of him as a new friend, or just a customer wanting to help out, and taking advantage of his generosity? *Did she think of him at all?*

Well, he had gone this far in buying all the parts; he may as well finish the job.

He imagined Aimee smiling at him with his head buried in something to repair. They weren't short of money but George would always try and repair something once broken, or had died of old age; toasters, kettles, CD players, video players and especially computers. Aimee had lost count of the computers in the loft. Some of their short lived arguments were generally over the repair, or sometimes non repair of an essential appliance, like a toaster or kettle. She would give George twenty-four hours and then if the said appliance was not returned fully functional she would go out and buy a new one.

This had resulted over the years with a good stock-pile of duplicated products. However, as each of their off-spring left the family home they were presented with a useful, second hand, fully working appliance.

He blinked a tear from his eye at his memories. He did miss her.

It was nearly three years ago Aimee had died in a car accident. That was the official line – an accident. Actually her car had been shunted by a drunk, under age driver, with no tax or insurance, and not old enough to prosecute for manslaughter. No one had been held accountable. No one had been punished.

Every day the papers report killings, fights, stabbings, riots, and thefts and it seemed the whole country was going to pot. Over one thousand people a month leave the UK for a new life abroad, mostly over fifty-five's, disillusioned at the way things had become - or rather the way things were not as they used to be.

Many go to Australia, especially the younger ones, and some to the USA and Canada, but most of the 'older' generation look for their '*place in the Sun*' in Europe.

George was totally convinced he was no different to all those other discontented souls looking for a place in the sun.

Earthquakes, war, oil spills, famine, corruption, murder, religious extremists. All of these were good enough reasons to find 'shelter' elsewhere, and turn ones back on the world. George also added a *broken heart* to his list.

But was that fair? Ordinary people in the adopted country still have to live *their* lives knowing what is going on in the world. As do the children he left behind. As do friends and colleagues. Is it denial, not wanting to know what happens in the world? Is it cowardice? Yes, some of each, but more than that, these modern day evacuees want to remember how things were when they were young, when *their* country was civilized, authority was respected and youngsters were polite. *'We all want to escape to the past'*, George said out aloud - then smiled at his own supposition.

Most of these 'ex pats' also accept that change needs to happen for the wealth and growth of any nation, but too many anomalies have been introduced onto the world stage which no one seems to have control over. In these modern times of twenty-four hour news, and the constant analysis and post mortem of global atrocities, some citizens just want to hide away and let the world get on with destroying itself, hoping they will be the last to hear about it. He remembered something Peter Mayne had written in his book, A Year in Marrakesh - *'I shall be content in the centre of my universe and leave the universe to do the spinning.'* "Yes," George thought, "that's exactly how I want to live my life now".

George was not prone to nightmares or bad dreams, but he did fear for his children, and for several nights he had woken in a cold sweat dreaming of the day the world would end. The question was, he asked himself, was it the real world, *or his world*.

He had found the whole idea of living in England unsavory after Aimee's death, but had not banked on leaving so soon – until the second disaster hit him. He was accused of a major cyber theft.

George had been working for six months after Aimee's death when one of his clients, the private firm Barnes & Barnes International Bankers of Jermyn Street London, had reported a cyber theft, or 'missing funds' as they called it. George wrote high level security software for banks and financial institutions, and someone had skimmed off five million pounds without any trace. George was the immediate suspect and the police worked hard to prove he was behind it. They took every piece of hardware he owned (including what was in the loft), all his software and files, and effectively closed him down for twelve months.

Word got out. No one gave him work. He was not allowed to work.

The reality was the police did not have enough evidence to prosecute. Secretly, they thought he did it, but even their best high tech forensic guys could not find any trace back to George. The finger was pointing to him and no one else, and he was disillusioned with the way he had been treated in the whole affair. Guilty until proven innocent. The way things are done in England now.

After awhile he started to get work back from some dedicated clients who knew his worth – which really touched George. During the twelve months lay-off however he had plenty of time to take stock and consider the future, and the only logical conclusion was to start it somewhere else.

He needed a new life in new surroundings with new people. He was not old, approaching fifty-eight, quite healthy, and able to work anywhere in the World in his line of business.

The children all lived miles apart and only ever got together at Christmas and special occasions. They had, however, been fully supportive of him during the investigation. Alex even wanted him to move in with them, but the thought of sharing a house with Tom, Alex's husband, persuaded George to decline. Having done that, he could hardly move in with either of his other two children. On reflection, Bonnie would not have entertained the idea – against her street-cred to have dad staying, and he was not sure how he felt about sharing with Chris, his son. His only gay son.

So he stayed in the house he had lived with Aimee for the past twelve years in Windsor, and planned his future.

He eventually felt he had been given a second chance in life. Time to see something of Spain, a country they both enjoyed and visited often. His 'interests' could be run from anywhere, thanks to modern technology. A few hours a day to ensure everything is ticking over, and it seemed an ideal way to 'wind-down gently', with the added bonus of living in Spain and indulging in his favorite hobbies; cooking, travelling and music - and now, repairing broken Jukeboxes.

***

Oliver left his father's office still not convinced that the right decision had been taken. Without consulting the board of directors he called a private security firm to investigate further. Oliver contacted Jackson Security who were on the banks list of approved 'contractors and suppliers'. This meant they had been checked out by HR and passed all the required ISO criteria to be given work by the bank. Work which Oliver Barnes wanted to be carried out as quickly and as quietly as possible. His father, he felt, had handled the whole affair badly. The board had been persuaded to launch a 'quiet' investigation headed up by Chief Inspector Cox, who his father knew well. *Probably from the same club or lodge,* Oliver thought. CI Cox however did not have the manpower to continue the investigation unless the bank made a public announcement of the theft, which it did not want to do. Although George Morton was the prime suspect, and Oliver felt this in his bones, nothing could be found to link him to the money. No computer traces, no bank accounts, no suspicious phone calls. In fact, since his wife died he had led a quiet, sober life. Oliver did have to admit he could not fathom out *why* Morton would want to carry out such an audacious crime, especially so soon after the death of his wife. He could have been planning it before she died, and therefore having done his homework decided to go through with it. After all, he had nothing to lose.

He knew Morton had had his computers confiscated, but the police did not have the manpower to track his every movement. Now he had fled the country Oliver Barnes needed someone to find him and get close to him, but more importantly to get him his money back so he could impress the board.

***

Since George had moved to Spain, the weather had been considerably warmer than springtime in England, and he had become accustomed to waking up to blue skies and sunshine. However, one morning in late April, a week before Easter, George woke up and knew something was different. He opened the wooden shutters and rubbed his eyes and actually shivered for a moment. There were no blue skies and definitely no sunshine, but there was plenty of rain, consequently the morning temperature was down by several degrees. George rubbed his shoulders and yawned, and thought of diving back in to bed to keep warm, but suddenly froze. "Shit," he said out loud and ran downstairs as fast as he could.

He grabbed the patio sliding doors and fumbled with the lock. "Come on, open." Then the door slid across to reveal the rain, which was now coming straight in to Georges face. He looked across the patio only to have his fears confirmed. The Jukebox was lying where he had left it, in pieces and uncovered. He pushed the doors fully opened and dragged the carcass of the Jukebox into the lounge, quickly gathering up the loose pieces of engineered parts he had left scattered around the patio, and on the coffee table. He closed the doors and looked at the battlefield lying in front of him. Then he noticed the kitchen clock. 8.15am. "Bugger . .." Senora Torres would be here in forty five minutes. He scratched his head and breathed deeply. He could push everything into his office but that would only be short term, and only make more mess. Then he remembered the basement room. "Of course. The basement." He picked up the most easily transportable pieces and ran downstairs with them. After two more trips he just had the cover and the base left. The cover was reasonably easy to maneuver, but the base, even without the motor unit and all the records, was an awkward piece of hardware to pickup by one person. He heard the distinctive sound of Mr Torres's old Honda climb the slip road to the front door. "Damn it. She's early." George had no choice but to lift and drag the remaining skeletal casing into his office. He closed the office doors and quickly pulled off his T Shirt to wipe the wooden floor, just as the key in the front door turned.

Scanning the floor to ensure all wet patches had been wiped clean, he almost dived into the kitchen and tossed the sodden garment into the washing machine, just as Senora Torres entered the lounge. George was standing there in just his boxer shorts and a smile. Senora Torres shook her head. '*Boxing mad*' she said, but George had no idea, and just stood there grinning.

Chapter 3. May

Easter had been a lonely time for George, as had all the major holidays since Aimee's death, but especially Easter and Christmas. Anniversaries and birthdays were other occasions to stop and reflect. He had hoped the children could have come over for Easter, but they had committed now to later in May, nearer to George's birthday.

The Skype sound rang out from the computer and the video camera instantly came alive. It was Alex.

"Hi, Dad, it's me, Alex, are you there?"

George walked over to the computer and sat in front of the large high definition flat screen, on which he could see his smiling daughter's face.

"I must reset the camera to only come on when I want it to. One day it will be very embarrassing."

"Who for Dad, you or me?"

"Me most likely, if you catch me in a state of undress."

"In that case please do reset it." She laughed and smiled at the screen. George could almost reach out and touch her. Having this communication – this state of the art communication - was the one thing that helped George to decide make the move to Spain. Without it the decision would have been very much harder. Speaking on a phone was one thing, but being able to see your loved-ones as well, was very reassuring and comforting.

George smiled back, and gently touched the screen where Alex's face was.

"Hey, don't touch the screen!" Alex raised her voice and gave her dad a scornful look. "You always shouted at us for doing that," she said more calmly, and with a mischievous smile.

"You're right of course, but sometimes rules can be broken," he replied softly, and looked away for a second.

"Why so thoughtful Dad. Anything wrong? Any regrets?"

"No, on both counts. I'm fine; it's just nice to see you."

"That's good – then how about for real." She said almost casually.

"Excellent – have you got tickets yet?"

"Yes, we fly out on the 27th on the Friday afternoon. We have all managed to wangle a day off work, although you know Bonnie, she never stops."

"The break will do her good. Do you want picking up?"

"No, Chris has hired a 'people carrier', so I assume we have a lot of luggage just for two nights. He is as bad as B when it comes to clothes," she said thoughtfully.

"And what about Tom? Doesn't he want to come over? George asked.

Alex looked down for a moment.

"Maybe next time dad but not now, it's just family this time." Alex was clenching her teeth. She did this every time she was anxious, and George noticed.

That was the downside of video calling – you can see the other's expressions – warts and all. On a phone line you may say the same, and make the same facial expression, but at least you can't be judged.

"What's going on Alex?" George looked concerned now.

"Don't look like that Dad. It's just that Chris and Bonnie and me thought it would be nice to come down together for a few days. Just us. Just family." She did it again – the teeth thing.

"That's a nice thought, but how will Tom cope?"

"He will be fine. He's a big boy. Don't worry," she said, now with more reassurance, but George was still not convinced.

"You seem to have this planned out well."

"You know me Dad. I'm a planner and a *lister*," she said, in a knowing and mocking tone.

"You do take after me in that respect – planning and making lists. Your Mum could never see the point in making a list when she knew she would never keep to it." George half smiled, reminiscing.

"I know, Dad." Alex's voice was quieter – respectful. She let the moment hang for a few seconds. She could see her Dad's face remembering, and a tear started to form in her left eye. She slowly raised her hand and wiped it away before George could see.

"So?" Alex came back to the subject of visiting, and George's face lit up, as if he had been startled out of a sleep. "What are the sleeping arrangements? I can share with B if you want."

"You can if you two are OK with that, but all three spare rooms are made-up and ready, so make your mind up when you get here." George said with a smile.

There was a silence for a while. Was Alex wanting to say something but not sure how to?

George broke the silence.

"I suppose you are still a 'veggie'?" George winced in jest as he said it.

"Yes, of course, but still love fish, so plenty of..." she couldn't remember the name, "that lovely fishy thing you did when you came here last."

"Oh yes, the fish Tagine. I'll see what I can do. But we still eat meat here, so don't be too alarmed at what I cook. Anyway, I like to cook something we can ALL eat, and not treat you as different." George smiled. "Special maybe, but not different."

Alex frowned back at the screen. "Don't let Bonnie and Chris hear you say that, it's not fair."

"I know, I know." George put his hands up in surrender. "It's just that you were special to us being the first born, after your Mum's miscarriage."

Alex knew this and had heard it before, but it made her feel uncomfortable, and somehow even more distant, and older, than the four years between herself and her brother and sister.

"Talking of which – how are my other off-spring?"

"They're fine, Dad. When did you last speak to them?"

"I have left messages on Skype for Chris but he has not returned them, and because Bonnie will not use the video camera I bought her, I have left text messages – all to no avail. I could be dying and no one cares," he said with a heartfelt actor's cough.

"Of course they care, we all care Dad, but you know

them, unless it is an emergency they do not always respond. I will have a sisterly word in their ear." Alex smiled .

"You take care love, and say 'Hi' to Tom for me." George said with genuine affection for his son-in-law, but also wanted to see if Alex would respond to his name. He was sure she was keeping something back.

After closing the connection he cursed himself for not asking if she had received any more strange calls, but she would have said, wouldn't she?

George sent an email to his old friend Colin Jackson.

"Hi Colin. Hope all is well back at the ranch. Any news from our old German friend? Keep in touch. George"

An hour later the email jingle sounded to announce new mail.

"Hi George. Good to hear from you. Our new German friend did contact me recently and asked for my help in finding some lost property. My retainer should keep me busy for a few months, but not much longer.

Kind regards. CJ"

So, George mused, Oliver Barnes is pulling the strings now, hence the 'new friend'. Their 'old friend' would have been Peter Barnes. 'German friends' referred to the bank's London office in Jermyn Street. I hope Colin can keep the wolves away for a while longer, George reflected.

***

George spent the next few days getting the house ready. He finished painting the downstairs bedroom, replaced a broken glass pane in his bedroom and asked Carlos to send someone over to check the railing on the patio as he had promised to do – with a section feeling loose, and with a twenty foot drop, he was not taking any chances with his children.

He continued working on the Jukebox but it was slow progress after the drowning it got. He spent hours drying out the parts and making sure they were serviceable. He could not get the pickup arm to work but everything else did; the lights, the turn-table, but the arm would not move to collect the record. He puzzled over it for days, and decided to put it to one side until he could talk to Mr Wilson in England.

Later that week he visited Maria and Vincente. Mainly with a progress report on the Jukebox, but to tell them his children were visiting at the end of the month, and to invite them to an evening meal.

"Are you sure you want us there?" Maria asked sincerely.

"Of course I do, I want them to meet you, and Vincente of course," he added quickly. "Where is he by the way? Not gone AWOL again has he?"

Maria gave George a puzzled look. "Not gone what . ."

"Ah . .sorry... it means gone missing without permission, which is what he does, so you told me."

Maria smiled. "Yes he does, and no he has not... well not yet. He is fishing."

Maria sat in silence for a moment, but George could see she wanted to say something. "What is it Maria? Are you worried about meeting my children? They don't bite." He said, trying to ease her concerns.

"It's just... will they think you are seeing me... I mean... how will they feel about . ."

"Hey, it's OK." George leaned over and took Maria's hand. "You are a good friend. I want to show you off. If they think differently then I will tell them...," George hesitated.

Maria cocked her head in anticipation of an answer. "Si George... tell them what?"

"Watch this space," he said smiling, and leaned closer and gave her a gentle kiss on the cheek. Maria may have responded with another kiss or touching his face, but any decision was interrupted by the arrival of Vincente entering the restaurant from the kitchen.

"Buenas días, George, how are you, and where is my Jukebox?"

"Buenas días, Vincente, I am well and so is your Jukebox." Telling a small white lie was easier than explaining the problems he was having. "I hope to have it finished by the weekend." But declined to say which weekend.

Maria spoke to her father in Spanish to explain why George was there.

"Ah, very good George. What are you cooking?"

George knew full well what he was cooking, but did not want to pre-empt this by telling Vincent and have him comment on every single ingredient. "Not 100% sure yet Vincente, but it will be on an international theme," he said, with a broad smile.

"We look forward to it. And to meeting your family," Vincente replied, giving his daughter a sideways glance.

"Very good, and do tell Jorge I have a surprise for him as well which he will appreciate, especially when he gets bored of listening to seven adults talking all the time."

Maria looked quizzically at George, but Vincente had not noticed anything. "Seven George?" Maria asked.

"Did I say seven? Sorry... I meant six of course." George said with a worried look, and sat absentmindedly for several moments.

Vincente was not sure what he had missed but thought he should say something. "George!" he said with gusto. "I have some trout I have just caught. Would you like one or two?"

This sounded good to George, and he came around from his personal thoughts with a smile. "That would be nice. Thank you."

"Ok, I will go and get them. Do you want me to fillet them for you?"

"No, its fine. I'll manage, but thank you for asking."

Vincente went through to the kitchen and Maria smiled and leaned forward and kissed George on the cheek. "Thank you," he said. "What was that for?"

"For being a friend," and squeezed his hand just as her father returned with the parcel of fish.

"Here you are George. Two fine trout."

"Many thanks. Perhaps Maria would like to come and have dinner with me." George said looking in hope at Maria, who had let go of his hand. "That would be nice, but not tonight George." She said with genuine regret.

"Ok, how about Friday. You may want to taste my cooking first." George said jokingly.

"I am sure you are a wonderful cook, and yes, OK, Friday will be fine. Can I bring Jorge?"

That was unexpected. Why can't Vincente baby sit? "Yes of course, please bring him. Shall we say around 7.30." He said, trying not to sound too disappointed, but was sure he could see Vincente smiling out the corner of his right eye.

George had two days to come up with an impressive dinner for two, or two and a half. He flicked through all his favorite books; Nigel Slater, Jamie, Delia, Floyd and Rick Stein, and jotted down a list of ideas. Nothing too elaborate, but something tasty.

Then panic struck. He had no idea of her likes or dislikes. He had seen her eat chorizo and tortilla in the bar, but apart from that he knew very little about her. He could speak to Vincente, but George was not so sure her own father would know all her preferences.

George had still not bought a car, so he took the twenty minute bus ride into Aranda de Duero, the nearest large town. He had done this several times when he wanted different shops or to use the market, or just to wander around the old town and take in the atmosphere.

The indoor market was good here with a wide range of fish, meat, vegetables and fruit. He was already on nodding terms with several of the stall holders, but his knowledge of Spanish food names needed to be addressed soon. Looking at the dictionary too often was becoming an embarrassment. Not only that, George wanted to be accepted – and not thought of as another *'touristo'*.

He often thought people stared at him. It was obvious he was not Spanish, but try as he may, he could never accomplish the art of *blending in*. He didn't mind being looked at as he knew in time the novelty would wear off. He did however keep catching a glimpse of what looked like someone watching him, which made him curious, and a little paranoid.

Did this person want to be seen, or are they just bad at stalking. George found a café, sat inside ordering Espresso and Tapas, and started to mentally compile a list of reasons for someone to spy on him. He could only think of one.

From where he sat he had a good view of the street and could see everyone who passed by. Perhaps it was his imagination – or was someone really following him. Did Oliver Barnes send Jackson Securities over to spy on him? "Stop being paranoid," he told himself. He surveyed the street once more and was satisfied he was only scaring himself.

Having finished his Tapas and coffee he stepped outside on to the busy pavement and casually glanced around. No, nothing, no one watching him as far as he could see. Just mind games.

***

Colin Jackson sat across from Oliver Barnes in silence. Oliver had called in Jackson Security to brief them on how he wanted George Morton found and the money returned. He was explicit enough to give the impression he was not concerned about George Morton's 'safety', but just wanted the money back.

Colin Jackson sat in silence listening to the brief.

"So, there you have it Mr Jackson. Can you deliver what I want?" Oliver Barnes asked sternly.

"You are different to your father." Jackson observed sourly.

Oliver frowned, and leaned forward over his desk. "I am NOT my father. Understand that Mr Jackson. I am doing what should have been done months ago. I just hope the trail has not gone cold."

Colin Jackson, although ex-SAS was not your pre-conceived idea of a six foot tall, heavily built muscular army officer. Having served in the Falklands and the Gulf War, he had made a promise to himself, and his wife, he would resign as soon as they started a family.

Plans however do not always go the way you want them to. Catherine, his wife, gave birth to their daughter, Evie, in 1991 towards the end of the Gulf War, but Bosnia followed so quickly on its heels that Colin's unit was re-commissioned, and he served three more years before he could resign.

With infrequent visits home, father and daughter did not

really know each other until she was nearly four years old. Colin by then was thirty eight, and decided to put into practice the only trade he knew – security. He set up Jackson Security, and in nearly twenty years had built up a good reputation at home and abroad. That reputation was not now going to be put into jeopardy by one hot-headed suit sitting opposite him.

Jackson spoke quietly in his soft East Lothian accent, which disguised his strident and demanding army voice.

"Mr Barnes, firstly we are not in the habit of 'taking people out'. Secondly, if we discover any new evidence relating to the *alleged* crime involving Mr Morton, we will make a full report to the police. Do I make myself clear?"

Oliver Barnes shifted in his chair. "Perfectly, but I want results, and *I want my money back,* Mr Jackson." Oliver said, without a flicker of emotion.

***

Vincente stood in the hall feeling impatient. "Maria, are you ready? It is nearly 7.30."

"Si, papa, I am just finishing my make-up." Maria called down from her bedroom.

"Make up? It is dinner, not a date, my child." Vincente called back in frustration. Maria stopped a second to consider this remark. She thought her father needed to get out more often. But on the other hand, she asked herself, was she dressing up for a meal with a friend or a date with a man? She did like George, but did she feel anything more for him after only knowing him for a couple of months?

"Maria!" her father's voice filled the house.

Vincente drew right up to the front door. "I pick you up at 11.00. Be ready OK?"

He turned to Jorge in the back seat. "You keep an eye on your mother, yes," and winked at the boy as if Jorge knew what he was saying.

"Papa, stop it. Don't talk to him like that, you will confuse him. Anyway there is nothing to watch out for." She turned to her father and kissed him on the cheek.

"Have a nice evening as well, and do not give all our

drink away in the bar to your friends, Papa, and do not flirt with Angel."

"Anything else my dear?" Vincente asked humbly.

"No.... just...behave please," and she kissed him again and got out of the Dodge.

She waited until Vincente had turned the truck around and was out of the drive before she knocked on the door. George answered almost immediately.

"Hola, Maria. Hola, Jorge, please come in."

Maria and Jorge walked into the lounge, Maria looking all around her. Jorge noticed the computer.

"Did you ever come when the previous owners lived here?" George asked, breaking the ice. He sensed Maria was looking a little tense. It was a warm evening, but she was rubbing her upper shoulder as if a chill had run down her side.

"Are you cold? I can close the patio doors." George asked with concern.

"No, I'm sorry, I am fine really, and no I have never been here before. Have you done much to it?"

"Yes and no. Mainly the decor colors and of course this room." He said pointing to the office. "This was the original dining room, but I converted it to an office... and games room... and music room."

Jorge looked around on hearing the word games. "What games has he got Mama?" Jorge asked his mother in Spanish.

"He knows the word game, George."

"Of course. Let's see what we can find." George opened a drawer under the desk containing several PC games.

Jorge's face lit up on spotting Mario Brothers and pointed to it. "Can I play that one please George," he said, not taking his eyes off the game.

"I think I understood that." George said, smiling at Maria. "Let's see if it works still, eh young man." George placed the DVD in the computer drive and Jorge let out a squeal of delight. "That will keep him amused for hours." George said, feeling satisfied with himself, and with the prospect of having Maria alone to himself all evening.

"Don't forget to stop to eat, Jorge." Maria called over her

shoulder to her son, as she and George walked onto the patio.

"Are you sure you are not too cold Maria?"

"No, no I am fine. It was just a silly reaction." Maria said, not sure if that was the correct word in English for nerves.

"Ok, if you are sure, we will eat out here."

"That would be nice. It's a lovely evening." Maria said, walking towards the iron railings. "Look George. I can see the bar from here . ," and she held on to the rail and stood on tip-toe ".... if I stand on tip-toe." George looked aghast and moved swiftly without wanting to panic her. "Yes it is a wonderful view, but I think a little safer a few steps back." He held her arm and moved her back from the rail. "It's probably OK, but I am having the railing checked to ensure it is safe. Part of it seems a little unstable... loose."

Maria looked puzzled, and just a little shocked to think she could have fallen.

"I do not think Papa would approve of you killing me on our first date," she said sternly, but soon smiled her wonderful smile, and George's heart melted just a little more.

"No, I would not want to upset *'Papa'*, first date or not. Is that what this is?" George asked hopefully.

Maria smiled back and put a hand up to George's face.

"He is not that bad really. What you say... he's barking is worse than his biting?"

"Yes, *his bark is worse than his bite...* but I am not so sure. I have been told it is the other way around."

They stood looking at the view a few moments longer. "I am a very bad host. I have not offered you a drink. Would you like wine or... what?"

"Wine would be fine thank you. Blanco please."

George went into the kitchen and took a bottle of Chablis from the fridge, and grabbed two glasses from the sideboard, at the same time glancing over to see that Jorge was still enjoying the game, which he was.

"Hope Chablis is OK. I still need to get into Spanish white wines. My knowledge does not go much beyond Rioja."

"I will have to teach you then George. But *Rioja Alavesa* is probably one you know. It is very dark and fruity. If you want a good Spanish white wine try *Bodegas Castaño*."

"Here ends the first lesson." George replied, smiling.

He wanted to continue on the subject of wine, but Maria wanted to know something. "What happened to the trout Papa gave you?"

"Ahh.... that's a very good question," he replied, seemingly pleased with himself.

"I ate one... simply grilled with lemon and salad of course, but I made tonight's first course with the other one... trout pâté."

Maria looked on with approval. "It sounds lovely. You do like to cook I think."

George considered this. He certainly did like to cook, but since he had been in Spain he seemed to have found a renewed interest in anything culinary. Was it the country itself, or where he was? If he lived in an inner city would he succumb more to 'instant' meals from supermarkets?

"Yes, I do like to cook," he said smiling. "But please reserve judgment until you have tasted it."

"I am looking forward to it." Maria said, looking at George with genuine interest, and considering how she really feels, if at all, about this Englishman.

They stared at each other for a few moments, not awkwardly, but as two people summing each other up and considering, albeit in a fleeting moment, if they are attracted to the other.

In George's case the answer is, *warming gently to her.*

In Maria's case the answer is, *has good potential, but not sure about the age difference.*

The cooker timer 'pinged', which brought each of them back to reality. "Ah... dinner is ready." And George went to the kitchen to finish preparing the meal, and Maria called Jorge over to the table.

After the pâté they had slow cooked chicken casserole with green haricot beans, butter beans and sautéed potatoes, cooked in garlic and basil, and plenty of *pan de horno* to soak up the sauce.

"Mama, can I leave the table?" Jorge asked eagerly. George did understand.

"He wants to go back to the game."

George smiled across the table at Jorge. "Of course he can. I have ice cream later if he wants some, or fruit."

"That was a lovely meal. I will have to be... on guard when you come to eat."

George understood, and was pleased with the compliment. "It is '*on my guard*' if you do not mind me saying."

"No, of course not, please tell me if my English is not correct."

"Your English is very good. Where did you learn it?"

"Some at school, but I did not have the chance to speak it much..." Maria was eager to talk freely and George was happy to listen, and to just watch her across the table. He liked the way she tilts her head to one side when she is thinking of something, and how she uses her long elegant arms to emphasis a point. He likes looking at her perfect lips and softly tanned complexion, and likes how she pushes back her thick black hair behind her ear when it falls over one eye. Her pretty perfect ears are adorned with oversized round silver earrings. "... so I am pleased to be able to remember my English again. Papa speaks it better than me. He was in England as a boy and learnt it there."

George realised he was only half listening. "Sorry, Maria, Vincente lived in England you say?"

"Yes, but it was long ago. He was about five years old. He does not really talk about it anymore," she said, reflecting on the memory and sipping on the wine.

Apart from Vincente, George also wanted to know more about her husband. "How did you meet you husband, was he local?"

Maria sighed and looked down, and then away to the horizon. Then she smiled a faint loving smile at his memory, one she may not have talked about to anyone for a long time. "We met in Barcelona at a food and drink Trade Fair. He worked for a food distributor in Rio and he asked me out for a drink. We were married six months later."

"Wow. .that's... fast." George said, with genuine surprise.

"Si, it was." Her smile was wide and full, she put her hand in front of her perfect mouth to hide it, as women often do.

"So, you married and he moved here."

"Yes, Juan gave up his job and we ran the bar, the three of us.... well when papa was around." The smile disappeared at that thought. Maria took a deep breath and continued without prompting from George. "We tried for children but it was not to be, or so we thought. Then it suddenly happened. I was nearly forty but the doctors did not have much hope and tried to persuade me to terminate." She looked over to Jorge at the computer. "I am glad I did not." She said softly.

"I agree." George said, and allowed her to reflect.

During the evening George had been playing a selection of his favorite 'chill out' tracks suitable for such occasions. He went over and changed the CD, and then to Jorge to show him the headphones. "Here Jorge, put these on, it sounds much better." Jorge knew exactly what he meant, and placed them over his head and adjusted the size so they fitted snugly.

"I think the music may have been distracting him." George said, as he returned to the table.

Maria smiled. "That was thoughtful of you," she said, starting to clear away the plates.

"Maria, please leave them, you are my guest."

"So! It is not so much to do." She said with some determination, so George let her clear the plates while he made coffee.

"Do you mind if we have this inside. I am feeling a chill now." Maria asked.

They each sat on a white leather sofa, opposite each other. George really wanted to sit next to her, but realised looking at her was even more pleasing.

"Maria, can you talk about how Juan died. Was he ill?" George asked respectfully.

She sighed, and shook her head as if remembering an awful episode in her life she wanted to forget. "No, not ill. Murdered."

George recoiled. "Oh, my God, I am so sorry Maria." He said, and instinctively reached out to take hold of her hand. She squeezed it, but let go and held her hands in a praying pose at her lips.

"I am sorry Maria, we can talk about something else..."

"No, it is OK George. I have not talked about it to any one for nearly eight years. I want to… I want to see if it still sounds. . the same." George did not understand, but reached out for her hand again, and this time she let him hold it.

"Juan was closing up one evening when a stranger came in asking for a drink. He refused, explaining it was late and told the man to go away." Maria took a deep breathe before continuing. "He started to shout abuse at Juan, I could hear it upstairs. I called to papa to go down and see what was going on. When he got to the bar, he found Juan lying on the floor, stabbed..."

"George moved to sit next to Maria and held her hand firmly.

"Please, do not..." George started to say, but she turned and smiled.

"It is OK, I promise.... anyway... papa called to me to call the police while he went to run after the man. I ran downstairs and cradled Juan in my arms, but he was already dead. There was blood everywhere."

George got up and poured two brandies. "Thank you, George," and Maria sipped on her drink thoughtfully.

"What did the police do, did they catch him?"

"No. By the time they arrived papa had taken Juan's car and a couple of his friends, and went to chase him. When they reached the main junction they did not know which way he had gone, so had to return, although it was some time... about two hours they spent looking." And her voice trailed off, as if considering another explanation.

"So no one was arrested."

"No. No one George, and never will now." Maria finished her brandy in one.

George sat in silence digesting this awful story, and wished he had not opened a can of worms.

Maria suddenly took hold of George's hand. "I have never told anyone this George, but somehow feel I can trust you."

"You can Maria. I will not tell a soul . ."

"No, its not that, its what I have not told you yet.... the next day I saw some blood on the front bumper of Juan's car, and the bumper was dented. Later, when I went back to check it the car had gone. I asked papa where it was and he said he had to take it to Martin as it was making a strange noise when he took it out. He said he drove it too fast and damaged the exhaust."

"Did you ask about the blood?" Maria sighed again and shook her head. "No. I was not 100% sure, and anyway I was too distraught to worry about it. I had to console Jorge and bury my husband."

"And nothing has been said about it ever since."

"No, nothing. It was just something... how you say... to get of your chest."

George gave a faint smile. *'Get it off my chest.'* He said, and rather embarrassingly glanced at her breasts before realizing it. Maria however had turned to see if Jorge was still playing on the computer and did not notice, or did not say anything even if she had seen George's casual glance. She half turned back to George. "Si, as you say George. Thank you for asking about Juan." And they sat holding hands looking out towards the night sky, letting their thoughts and memories settle once more.

Maria, too, wanted to know more about this new man in her life. Where he came from. What he did. What was his wife like? Were these questions she could ask? Or should ask after their recent conversation?

Over dinner they had talked mostly about her, and she liked the way he had included Jorge, wanting to know what he likes in sport and at school. She knew he had three children, but could not recall their names, or that of his wife... something beginning with A she thought.

The new CD George was playing was a little distracting. She was not used to having music playing so much at home, and especially during a meal, although Jorge would often watch TV at the table.

George felt her hand in his, which resonated a warm feeling he had not known for a long time. Not since Aimee died had another woman touched him in such a gentle and intimate way. He liked it. He liked remembering how it felt.

Each of them felt the connection. George wanted to lean over and kiss her. She wanted to be kissed. George moved closer and was about to kiss her long beautiful neck . when they heard a screem.

"Mama. I have finished this game... can I play another one?"

Perfect timing young man, George thought, and then realised his eyes were closed. Opening them he saw Maria smiling at him. She squeezed his hand even tighter.

"I think my young man has finished his game." She whispered, and went over to the computer.

"Well, if you don't mind him playing another one I do have a football game," and George loaded the game. "It is best to play with two people, but one person can play the computer."

"Are you OK with that Jorge?" Maria asked her son, but realised he had the headphones back on, and was already engrossed in the action of the players.

George watched Maria walk back to the patio doors. She swayed gracefully to the rhythm of the music, her long black dress fitted in all the right places and George could not help but notice her beautifully shaped rear.

"I know this one. It's a Tango, yes. Come on George, dance this with me."

It was indeed a Tango. The Gotan Project's Santa Maria – how perfect. George shook his head and waved a finger. "No, but I am happy to watch you though." Very happy, he thought.

Jorge had seen out of the corner of his left eye, his mother dancing and looked up to George still standing next to him, and shook his head in embarrassment.

"Don't worry, all parents do it." He said hoping Jorge would get the message.

Maria was in a good mood now, and felt she could take the advantage. Let's see how much he wants to please me, she thought. She danced, or rather swayed her way back towards George, who was enjoying the moment. She held out her hand for him to take, moving rhythmically to the accordion solo. "Let me show you. It's really easy once you get to know it," she teased, and grabbed George's hand pulling him closer.

"Now, hold me like this, and step once back and then forward." George was happy to have his arms, albeit one arm, around her waist, but he was not really listening to her, just staring into her beautiful dark green emerald eyes. Then the music stopped, and another song started.

"Oh no. Can we play that again? We just got started." Maria protested, with some degree of genuine disappointment, but the next song was more to George's liking. *Dance with Me* by Bobby McFerrin. An upbeat number which was also good to jive to. "OK, now you dance to my tune." And George proceeded to take the initiative and held Maria in a jive pose and twisted her around and back again before she protested. "No, I cannot jive George, please, I give in," and George stopped and held her around her waist, just as Bobby McFerrin sang the line, *I want to be your partner* which George mouthed the words to, as he knew them so well.

That moment, which he thought he would never experience again, had arrived. Still holding her waist he gently pulled her close. Maria felt something as well. She had not been with a man since her husband had died, and she too felt a most wonderful tingle of pleasure run down her spine. She had removed her shoes earlier before dancing, and now slowing elevated herself on tiptoe to meet his lips. Her arms reached around his waist and came to rest on his shoulder, preparing to urge him nearer in case he hesitated.

There was an even chance Jorge could have interrupted them, unintentionally, but it was not him this time. It was Vincente. Maria's mobile phone rang out with a most horrific melody that defies anyone to not answer it immediately.

"Hola, Maria, it's your Papa.' Vincente announced too cheerfully.

"Yes, Papa, I know that. It tells me on the screen. What do you want?" she said in Spanish, but George could tell she was not being subtle at all about the timing.

"Wanted to tell you I will be there in fifteen minutes, at

eleven. Remember? OK, see you soon my dear," and the phone went dead.

She turned to George who was sitting on the arm of the sofa looking forlorn.

"I am sorry, George. Papa is collecting us at eleven," and she called over to Jorge to stop playing and get ready to go soon.

"Do you have to leave so early?" George almost begged. "I could take you home..." he thought of saying, "eventually" but the moment passed to soon. Why did he hesitate?

"There will be other times George. I have had a really nice time, thank you so much," and she kissed him on the cheek, but not his lips, which had eluded her all evening.

"But, I think you should learn the tango," she suddenly said, looking pleased with herself at the challenge.

"Oh no. I like to dance but the tango is one dance too far," he said, holding his hands up in surrender.

"Oh come on, George. You want to dance with me again, yes?" George thought about this. Was she flirting again, or being sincere. Then he had an idea.

"Ok, I will, but you will learn to jive." He said, smiling broadly.

Maria looked deflated and stood there with hands on hips considering this.

"Si, senor. OK. I will learn to jive and you will tango. We have five months, OK." George looked puzzled. "Five months. I will probably need it, but why so long?"

Maria spoke to Jorge checking he had everything, and reminded him to say thank you to George for dinner and the games, which he did politely.

"Maria!" George called over as they reached the front door. "What happens in five months?" She turned to George just as the door bell rang. *'Columbus Day George, Columbus Day.'*

Chapter 4. June

George's mobile rang. "Hi Dad, I think we're lost. Where the hell are you?" It was Christopher.

"Chris... Hi son, where are you?" Silly question if they are lost, he thought. "Can you see any signs or landmarks?... Chris can you hear me. . ."

The line was silent, but George could see he was still connected.

"Chris are you there?" He called out again.

Then he heard a woman's voice, and for a split second it sounded like Aimee.

"Hi, Dad, its Alex, can you hear me?"

"Yes love, loud and clear. Do you have the directions I sent over? Do you know where you are?"

"I am sure we are very close Dad. We saw Calabaza sign-posted about five minutes ago, but we seem to be going in circles."

George heard Chris in the background protesting about not being able to read the directions.

"Alex, tell me what you can see." George begged in frustration, before the line went dead.

George had been up early making sure everything was ready, and in order, for his children's visit. Not that he usually worried when they came over to his house in England, so why was he fussing so now. He realised he was fussing, but he wanted to make a good impression. Let them see he was capable of looking after himself, albeit with a little help twice a week. Senora Torres was shaking her head so much yesterday, George thought about getting a neck brace for her. She cleaned, and cleaned again; the floors, the bathrooms, the sinks, the windows, until George was satisfied. Senora Torres could not make out what all the fuss was about. *They are family, not royalty.* In her experience, offspring hardly notice anything special around the home, they always expect it to look good and smell good. As long as the fridge is full, children are happy.

George surveyed his domain. Senora Torres stood like a schoolchild, waiting for her report. He smiled and nodded as he looked around. "Gracias, Senora Torres, Gracias."

Senora Torres looked on expressionless and shrugged. *"I am going now. You owe me two hours extra."*

"Si, Si." George said not really knowing what she had said. "Gracias again Senora Torres," and continued to rearrange the cushions for the tenth time as she closed the door behind her.

At 2.15pm the Renault Espace pulled up along the side of the house, opposite the old barn, and the first thing George knew of their arrival was the abuse being hurled at Christopher. "Damn you, Chris, I'm never getting in a car with you EVER again." *Unmistakably Bonnie's voice,* George thought. *Better prepare for the worst.* He opened the front door just as Bonnie was about to knock. "Bonnie darling, you are looking as beautiful as ever. Give your dad a hug."

Bonnie froze momentarily. "Dad," she said wearily "have you been in the sun?" and gave her dad a kiss on the cheek but could not hug on account of both her hands being occupied with hand luggage.

"You go in, I'll get the rest." George said and walked around the corner to the parked car just as Alex and Christopher had finished unloading the rest of the luggage.

"Blimey!" George looked startled. "How long are you staying for?"

Alex immediately dropped her case and hugged her dad. A good long hug and finished it with a kiss. "Oh, dad, it's so good to see you." Alex choked and turned away to brush away a tear. "Damn it," she said. "Sorry, didn't mean to do that."

"What! Hug me?" George joked.

"No" she said, sniffing, and searching for a tissue.

"Can a guy get a hug around here?" Chris came over and hugged his dad as well.

"You can kiss me. It is allowed. I am your dad."

Chris pulled back. "Hey, I only do hugs." Chris said jokingly.

"When you two have finished can we get this lot inside." Alex asked curtly. George thought she looked tired, but it may have been just from the journey.

"So what was your sister having a go at you for?" George asked Christopher, as casually as possible.

"Same old same-old. She wanted to stop every ten minutes. Either the loo, or coffee, or something." Chris hesitated. "Anyway, suffice to say she is not a good passenger on a long journey."

George was not convinced, but saw the frustration on Alex's face out of the corner of his eye. "Let's all go in and relax with a cool drink," George suggested, "and you can tell me everything."

"This is fantastic, Dad." Alex's face lit up when she entered the lounge. She stood there in awe, taking it all in. "Chris, you didn't tell me how great this is," she said walking over to the patio doors. "Wow dad, it's lovely. I had no idea. I know I've seen some photos, but this is different. I want to see it all," she said excitedly. "Come on, let's all have a guided tour," and grabbed her dad's hand.

George walked around the house, starting in the basement, with Bonnie, Chris and Alex in tow.

When they reached the first floor landing George said, "Well, one of you girls can have this one, and there's another next door. Chris, I thought you could have the basement as you have christened it already." All three looked at George with a puzzled expression. "Sorry, Chris, that didn't come out right, did it," and they all laughed, except Chris, who just looked hurt.

"Right. This is mine and I'm having a siesta." Bonnie announced. "I'm shattered." and she sat on the end of the bed and leaned back, kicking off her shoes. "Close the door on your way out."

"Siestas are after lunch." George corrected her, and lunch will be around 3 o'clock if you have recovered by then."

Bonnie waved an acknowledgement with eyes closed, and the others left her alone.

"I'll go and get the cases. I've seen the rest." Chris said, and headed back downstairs.

"OK, dad, just you and me. Lead on." Alex demanded with a smile.

"There's not really much else. Just my bedroom and a box room on the top floor, but the views are great."

"I want to see it all." Alex said, racing in front of her dad up the stone stairs, like an excited child.

The bedroom was just as she had imagined. Bright and light with wooden shutters on the windows. A pine tallboy and wardrobes, and a king size bed.

George opened one of the louvered shutters to let in more light. "I usually keep these closed during the day to keep the room cool."

"It's lovely dad, really lovely." She put her arms around her dad, and held him tight, with her head on his shoulder.

As she turned she saw a photo of George and Aimee on the bedside table. "I took that one." She said remembering the day. George smiled also at the memory, as he did every day he saw the photo.

She sat next to her dad and laid her head on his shoulder again. "I never thought you would survive a month. Was that bad of me," she asked, sitting up turning towards George with a sad expression.

He smiled. "No, of course not. You were probably not alone in thinking that. But thank you for telling me," and kissed her forehead. "Now, young lady, tell me what happened in the car from the airport." George asked quietly.

Alex sighed and shook her head. "I do try Dad, really I do, but she just won't... " Alex searched for the right words ".... try and relate to me." She put her arms around her dad again and cried softly. George sighed as well and closed his eyes and said a silent prayer. *"If you can hear me my love, please help."*

Alex sat up again and reached for a tissue from the box next to the bed. "Sorry, dad, this is supposed to be a happy weekend. It is your birthday after all," and she smiled her best smile.

"Quite right and I want no bad Karma from anyone."

George said with a laugh. "Come on, you can help me with lunch."

They tiptoed past Bonnie's door, but Alex stopped a moment to touch the door. She placed her left palm against the cool pine. "Sleep well." She whispered to the door.

George continued downstairs to the basement to see how Chris was getting on. "Want some lunch son?"

"Absolutely, and talking of meals, I hope you paid your debts to that lovely lady I met in town.... what was her name... "

"Maria." George said.

"Ha yes, Maria. Have you seen her again?" Chris enquired.

George smiled and Chris saw he was almost blushing. "You have, haven't you? You old dog."

"Hey, that's enough of the old... and yes... I have seen her. In fact we are having dinner with her and her father tomorrow evening."

"Wow," Chris looked at George with genuine surprise, "do the girls know yet?"

"No, I haven't had time. I'll tell them over lunch, or later on. Now get your act together and come and eat." George walked slowly back upstairs wondering how his daughters would take the news that he had invited another woman to dinner.

Alex had turned vegetarian soon after meeting Tom. She was not sure why exactly. Partly to impress him, partly because she knew it was right, partly because, at the time, it pissed George off. That was ten years ago when she met Tom at Uni. The first time she took Tom home she forgot to mention Tom was a 'veggie'. George and Aimee panicked quietly in the kitchen on hearing that news. "Why the hell could you not have mentioned it - or better still find a guy who likes meat." Until then the whole family enjoyed Sunday roast dinners. It was tradition, like turkey at Christmas and lamb at Easter.

She could not remember what they gave their prospective

son-in-law to eat, but it did not affect their relationship, and they eventually married - and had a full-on 'veggie' wedding breakfast as well. She did remember why she was at odds with her Dad at the time. She thought the twins had had more attention and love, and now she was away at Uni, she was missing out. None of this was true of course, but the first year away had been difficult, and she felt she had to have an outlet to blame for her underachieving.

"Hey you, daydreamer?" George said to Alex who was standing, staring out across the patio.

"No, err, yes, sorry. I was just thinking how lucky I am to have a wonderful Dad."

"That's nice... what's it going to cost me?"

"Dad, I mean it. No catches. I love you." She gave him a gentle kiss on the check and her eyes wept a little.

"Hey, why the tears. What's wrong? You and Tom got problems, because if you have you must..."

Alex put a hand to his lips. "No Dad, no problems. Just remembering how things were I suppose, I do miss her a lot."

"We all do my love. Even if your brother and sister don't show it as much as you, they do. . and they will remember her this weekend."

Alex wiped her eyes on a tissue and smiled, and turned to face her dad. "So, what have you got planned for us this weekend. Lots of sightseeing?" she asked with interest.

"Well, after lunch we could go for walk, and I can show you the town... or village... still not sure what it is. Then tomorrow I thought we could drive into Aranda de Duero, its only fifteen minutes away, and there's a wonderful Saturday market, not just food but a whole mish-mash of stalls selling antiques and bric-a-brac, and I need to do a food shop for tomorrow evening." George said, realizing he should tell her about Maria, but decided against it until later.

Of his three children, Alex would be the most concerned, and maybe upset, that he was seeing another woman. Although was 'seeing' the right word? He 'sees' Maria often in town and in the bar, but if he means 'seeing' her as a girlfriend, well... that is a little premature. George was frankly not sure how his children would respond if one day he announced he was getting married again. Maybe this weekend would be a good time to test the water.

Lunch was homemade gazpacho soup, prawn and chicken paella, cheese and fresh fruit. George smiled at Alex and at each of his children in turn, and raised a glass of wine. "To Aimee." George said quietly, and had trouble holding back the swelling in his eyes and swallowed hard. They all raised a glass and in unison quietly spoke the name. "Aimee", except Alex who said 'mum'.

The meal progressed through to the desserts, and they talked about everything and nothing, and George listened to them talking to each other - each trying to get their own point of view across - Bonnie, as usual, being more forceful than anyone else.

George realised it had been sometime since they had enjoyed a family meal like this, and he was feeling pleased and contented as he looked around the table. We have come through some bad stuff he thought, but we have made it out the other end, in one piece. Life does go on, not always in the same place with the same people, but it goes on nevertheless, and he knew Aimee would want that.

George put on a Keith Jarrett CD, 'The Melody at Night with You' which was Aimee's favorite.

For the past couple of years on this anniversary of her death, George wanted everyone to say what they remembered about her. It could be something insignificant, personal or funny - whatever. The first year all three thought it was not appropriate, and no one, except George, managed to say a few words about how he loved her and missed her.

At the second dinner, last year, he tried again. Chris actually said some nice things, and Bonnie read a poem, but Alex could not bring herself to say anything again. Not because she did not want to, but because of the fear of her emotions getting the better of her.

George asked if they would like to say a few words, and

he was pleased that Alex stood up to speak. "Alex love, you don't have to stand."

"It's OK, Dad, if I sit now I may not say what I want to say." She began slowly, slightly trembling and stuttering as if cold. "When Dad suggested this again last year I wanted to say something but I couldn't put into words what I was feeling. I now know why Dad has suggested this. It keeps Mum's memory alive, and it helps us to be a united family." She glanced at her sister who returned her a derisive smile.

"Go on love, if you want to." George said with some encouragement.

Alex continued. "I remember one day Mum and me went shopping for clothes for me to take to Uni. She was good at shopping. She liked clothes and she knew what B and I liked. Anyway, on that day we just ended up talking about how she wanted me to have a good time at Uni and not to worry. She told me all about her time at Bristol Uni, and what to expect - going over what I was studying, how the first year is the worst, for many different reasons, but most importantly to work hard and have fun at the same time. Anyway, that's my memory for now." Alex sat down and stifled a tear.

George reached over and took her hand. "Thank you Alex, that was lovely."

He realised the others were not going to say anything, so he put his head back and listened to the soothing piano of Keith Jarrett, and the memory that was his wife.

After lunch everyone seemed a little subdued, so George suggested they all go for a long walk, and let him show them something of the countryside.

As he suspected, Chris and Bonnie declined.

"Dad, I really need to send some emails and catch up on what's happening back at the office before they all go home." Bonnie shot in quickly before Chris could get out his excuses.

"Fine," George said, "I'll go alone."

"No you won't." Alex said, standing there holding a sunhat and sunglasses. "I want to see more of the village and do some shopping."

"Excellent, we can go along the river and end up at El Tango for a drink. You two can join us there if Chris can find it again."

Alex and George were out of the door before Chris and Bonnie had realised what he had said.

"Tango? What the hell is that?" Bonnie asked.

"Ah," Chris smirked, "that's where we will find all the gossip about dad."

George and Alex turned left out of the house and walked along the road for one hundred yards, before coming to a stonewall. They passed through an old wooden gate into the olive grove. "Not sure what to do about this." George said waving his arms around the orchard. "It's going to be too much for me to handle".

"It's beautiful," Alex exclaimed, "you must keep it, Dad. Someone must know how to run it."

The six-acre orchard was part of the sale, but George always thought he could sell it off locally, but Carlos could not find anyone interested in it.

"I will ask around. In fact I do know who to ask." George said, thinking Vincente would have an idea, or may even find it an interesting 'hobby' for himself.

They walked out of the orchard on to a narrow lane. They walked in silence for a while. The lane descended gradually, and as far as Alex could see just went on and on. "Where does this go Dad?"

"Wait and see." He said playfully.

They walked another ten minutes before turning off the lane into a thinly wooded area that did not seem to have a natural path. The woods were in fact a large copse separating the road from the river. A few yards more and they exited the copse into lush green open ground, with a river beyond.

The wide Rio Arandilla ran from the nearby mountains and parallel to the village, and continued for well over one hundred miles to the west.

"Do you really think you will settle here Dad and be happy?" asked Alex, thoughtfully.

George thought for a moment before replying. "I am

happy my darling and I *am* settled as far as I know. I can't see me moving anywhere else now."

"Not even back home?"

"I don't want to start thinking of what might happen - I can't plan my life anymore. I just take one day at the time, and to be content with what I have. After all, I am financially comfortable, reasonably healthy for my age, and have work and hobbies to keep me busy - what else could I ask for, apart from Grandchildren one day. . ," and immediately regretted saying that.

Alex stopped walking. "Dad." she said, almost desperately.

"Sorry darling, that wasn't fair on you. I just meant... well... most parents hope to be grandparents one day, and it's not just you either. Your sister may surprise us."

Alex smiled a little. "More likely Chris will surprise us," and she laughed a guilty laugh.

They walked on a little further in silence, Alex with her arm in George's.

"Dad, between you and me, and I mean *you and me,* we are trying."

George's face beamed. "That's wonderful news darling," and he hugged his daughter as if she was already pregnant. "I won't tell a soul, I promise."

They continued to walk along the river path then turned left through another small copse and up a slope to meet an old stone bridge over the river, and join the main road heading back to town.

They walked into town and out the other side, avoiding El Tango. George had decided it would be better for them to meet tomorrow evening, on home turf.

George had gambled that Chris and Bonnie would not be bothered to venture into town to find the bar, and he was right. Chris had fallen asleep on the patio, and Bonnie had been writing emails all afternoon.

That evening no one really felt much like another large meal, so they picked on bits and pieces, and sipped wine or beer. Chris played on the computer for a while, and then challenged Bonnie to a game on the Wii. Alex sat on the patio reading. George, well George felt uncomfortable. He had never had so many people in his house at once, and although they were family, he was not sure how he felt about his space being invaded now they were here. Living without children at home, once they have left for whatever reason, the home becomes something else; *Quieter, Tidier, Cheaper.*

He decided to read a while, and joined Alex on the patio. They sat silently reading and occasionally looking up at the landscape, and were captivated by the setting of the sun over the distant hills to the west. "It's going to be another beautiful day tomorrow." George sighed.

***

The floor tiles were cool on her bare feet so she knew she must be in the kitchen. The lounge had rugs which she had just covered on tip-toe, taking about ten minutes to do so due to the lack of light. *'Trust me to pick a night when the moon is new instead of full.'* She cursed to herself.

Having memorized the layout of the lounge between the bottom of the stairs and the kitchen, she had grabbed a dressing gown and opened her bedroom door as quietly as possible.

She had not expected the outside to be as black as it was. But even in blackness the eyes become sensitive to form, and aided by the memory of the geographical layout, she descended the stairs in a crouching position holding on to the hand-rail. She tiptoed across the lounge using the office wall and patio doors as guidance, and slipped into the kitchen. She worked her way along the right side of the utility drawers, eventually touching the coolness of metal, and locating the unmistakable large handles of the Smeg fridge. She breathed a sigh of relief.

Alex opened the fridge door and the light was almost blinding. She closed it again. *'Why can't a fridge have a dimmer switch for occasions like this?'* She mumbled to herself.

She opened the door again and scanned the shelves for her quest. There it was, covered neatly in foil.

Like a thief trying not to touch an alarm wire, she

carefully removed the foil with her left hand while still holding on to the door with the other hand.

The prize was the leftover chicken from the Paella. She had eaten as many prawns as possible, and George had done extra for her, but she really wanted to bite into the succulent chicken, with all its tasty juices from the dish.

She thought about warming it in the microwave, but that would make too much noise. *'Sod it',* she thought, *'they look good enough.'* She picked one of the largest pieces and took a bite. It has been said, some food experiences are better than sex, and she had to agree, it was, but on the other hand, most things in her life were just now.

Feeling triumphant and relaxed, she closed the fridge door so it was still ajar, allowing some light into the kitchen. Still in her world of food ecstasy, she stepped back two paces and sat on the breakfast barstool.

If she had not taken such a large mouthful of succulent chicken, she would properly have either screamed or choked, or both. She looked up to see George standing at the kitchen entrance, arms folded and looking bemused.

George sighed, and shook his head as he walked over to the bar and sat opposite his daughter. Alex chewed slowly and purposefully, not for wanting to spit out the meat, but buying time to think of something to say.

Having swallowed the prize, she spoke first. "Dad, I'm really sorry," she whispered, but he interrupted her, raising a hand.

"Darling, it's not for me to comment, let alone be judgmental. I just wished you told me earlier. I brought a ton of extra prawns just for you."

They both laughed, and she leaned forward and kissed his cheek.

"It's just that Tom is getting even more obsessed with food. He's even talking about not eating fish now. I know he has a point, but if we do have children soon I am not sure it's the best diet to raise them on. They can make up their own minds when they are older, the way it should be."

George held Alex's hand. "I think it's something you need to discuss together before it gets too far down the road. You are a levelheaded girl and you know how to put forward an argument. I've heard you often enough," and smiled to try to ease her tension.

She smiled back at him, and picked a piece of chicken from a tooth.

George stood up and kissed his daughter on the forehead.

"Knock yourself out kid. There's plenty more," and George turned to leave.

"Just a minute Dad, why did you come down to the kitchen in the first place?"

"Ah yes," George said thoughtful... "I had a dream which woke me up with a very dry mouth, and I needed some water." George sat down again, remembering the dream. Alex fetched a bottle of water from the fridge and took a swig before passing it to her dad.

"Come on, you can't stop there," said Alex. "Tell me, what was it about?"

"Well it was strange. It was about me and you're Mother."

George then started related to Alex what he remembered. She was mesmerized, and took the foil-covered plate from the fridge. She was past caring now.

"It was like an out of body experience. I was watching your Mum and me on a screen. We were walking and talking, but I could only see us from behind. There was no sound so I could not make out what we were saying, but it seemed we were in deep conversation. Gradually however, the angle of view changed and I was seeing less and less of her. First I saw her in silhouette as she turned to talk, but gradually I could only see her shoulder and arm, or a wisp of hair as she turned to face me again. Then the angle moved even further away, so all I saw was a hand touching my shoulder as we walked. All of a sudden the image pulled back into a wider view, and all I could see finally was myself walking and talking... to no one, she had gone completely."

George stopped and stared, as if trying to remember more. "That's when I woke up panicking. I had lost her Alex, I can't see her anymore." George said with tears in his eyes.

"Dad, dad, listen to me." Alex reached over and held his hand with her free one. "It means nothing of the sort. It means she wants you to let her go and move on... if you want to... with someone else... if that should occur...." Alex looked curiously at her dad. She tipped her head slightly to one side.

"Why are you looking at me like that?" George asked.

"No reason. I was thinking it was a nice dream and well meant, and if you want to be with someone else, mum...and we do not have a problem with it."

"We, as in all of you? You've discussed this have you?"

"The subject did come up on the drive over here, and we agreed we want you to be happy, and if that includes another partner," Alex could not bring herself to say wife, " . .then that is OK. And it seems OK with Mum, because that is what your dream was about - moving on. The fact you saw yourself still talking to her when you could not see her, means you will never forget her or stop loving her."

George smiled and sighed. "Thank you Alex. You may be right. I hadn't thought of it that way."

They stood up and gave each other a long hug.

"Goodnight my love, don't eat us out of everything," and kissed Alex on the cheek and turned to walk away.

"Dad, about the meat thing..."

"It's OK love, your secret is safe with me." And blew her a final kiss goodnight.

As soon as Alex closed the fridge door the rooms were thrown into total blackness again. At this very point a figure moved swiftly and silently away from the side of the kitchen entrance to the downstairs spare room. That same figure was smiling and thinking. "Yes my dearest sister. Your secret is safe with me, ho,ho,ho."

***

The next morning they drove to Aranda de Duero as George had suggested. The market was buzzing. Chris and Alex soon found themselves looking at old books and paintings, and Chris was delighted to find a DVD stall. He looked through every DVD he came across looking for rare or interesting film musicals having collected hundreds over the years, and traded them on eBay, with very good results.

Bonnie, on the other hand, found markets noisy and dirty places, and would have preferred to have stayed at home, but George insisted she came as well, so she reluctantly agreed, just to keep her dad happy as it was his birthday weekend. She sat at a pavement café and ordered coffee and Danish.

"Will you be OK here while I go shopping? Shouldn't be too long." George said hovering next to her.

"Dad, I'm a big girl now. Run along and shop," she replied with a wave of her hand, while thumbing her iPhone with the other.

George wandered around the market with a list of ingredients in hand. Looking at the list he realised he had not told Bonnie or Alex about tonight's guests. He also recalled last night's conversation with Alex about his dream. What she had said about it 'being OK' to see other women or to have a 'partner' pleased him, and was sure the evening would be a success. He was brought back to reality by being pushed and shoved around the crowded market aisles. "Sorry. Perdone," he repeated often to bewildered faces. They had agreed to meet back at the café at one o'clock, in half an hour. "Damn" thought George. "Must hurry." and he refocused on his list of ingredients.

He eventually joined the others, and arrived carrying four large shopping bags.

"Are you stocking up for something?" Alex asked, intrigued.

George sat down exhausted. "I could do with a cold beer," he said avoiding the question.

Alex called the waiter and ordered beer, coffees and Tapas. "On the wagon, sis?" Chris observed, looking at his other sister with a grin.

"No, I prefer drinking coffee during the day," Alex replied sourly.

"Hey, please. No bickering. She can have what she likes." George said firmly.

"Anyway, drinking alcohol is all too easy over here. I've had to watch my consumption." He said patting his stomach.

They sat in silence until the drinks arrived.

"I meant to tell you all about this evening." George said, apologetically as possible.

All three looked at their dad with interest, but Christopher was grinning.

"I have invited Maria and her father, who is also the Mayor of Calabaza, over for dinner, hence the large number of carrier bags."

"Guests! Dinner! Tonight!" Alex and Bonnie said in unison, and then looked at each other with a look of horror.

"It's no big deal guys. I wanted you to meet some of the people I have got to know... and like. And I want them to meet you. My family." George said in justification, and with some pride in his voice.

"OK dad, but tonight. That's only five hours. How on earth is a girl to get ready?" Bonnie asked in panic. All three looked at George for what he thought was forever. Alex's face was the first to break into a grin, then Bonnie following with a smile she tried to hide behind her hand. Chris just shrugged.

"You told them, you..." George stumbled for the right words but soon saw the funny side.

"So, what's she like, this Maria?" the girls wanted to know, they asked in a probing manner. George was not sure how much they knew already.

"I'm sure your brother has told you about her, and the bar... and everything."

"Everything!" they exclaimed together, looking shocked.

"I mean the episode with the money - or lack of, on the first time we went there to eat.. that's what I meant... there's nothing else to tell." George stated factually.

"So, you haven't been seeing her since Chris left, and what's that old jukebox doing in the basement?" Bonnie asked.

"No, well, yes." George stuttered. "Of course I see her. In the bar. . and she's been to dinner."

"Really! So it's serious then?" Bonnie quizzed, but Alex could see her dad was getting a little agitated. "OK, stop teasing now. Remember what we said, if dad wants to see another women then it's OK by us, and I for one am looking forward to meeting her." She reached over and took her dad's hand, and gave a gentle squeeze.

The other two just shrugged and finished their Tapas. "Whatever makes you happy old man." Chris said, taking the last of the tortilla.

George ignored the 'old' and suggested they head for home if everyone was ready, but Alex said she wanted to pick up some toiletries from the chemist, and she would see them back at the car.

"What are you two whispering about?" George said, looking in the rear view mirror at Bonnie and Chris.

"Nothing," came the obvious reply.

George had heard Alex's name mentioned. "Give your sister a break wont you. You're old enough to get along like grown-ups now," he said, feeling he had sounded too stern. But perhaps that was how he wanted to sound. Individually they each get on OK, but Chris and Bonnie together seem to bring out the worst in each other when it comes to Alex.

"I was just saying it was a shame you have to cook separately for Alex.... I mean, as she doesn't eat meat." Chris said with a straight face. George realised he must know something. Perhaps he saw her last night in the kitchen. He hoped not, as she would be taunted forever and a day.

"As it happens, we will all be eating the same tonight." George said with some satisfaction.

His two offspring looked at each other in horror. "Not nut roast, please dad, anything but that." Bonnie said fearfully.

George smiled inwardly, and told himself he was looking forward to this evening.

Much to everyone's relief Maria and Vincente arrived at 8.30pm. George had become use to eating later, but the others were starving by seven, and had started raiding the fridge for tit-bits, or picking at the prepared evening food.

He would probably have said something under normal circumstances, but he could see they were hungry. To avert their attention from food, George assigned each a task.

"Chris, check the BBQ for me and see the charcoal is stacked and that we have matches to hand."

"B, would you set the table for me, and don't forget the napkins."

Alex looked at her dad with raised eyebrows. "Can't think of anything for me to do dad?"

"Not at all my love. Would you open some red wine, and check we have chilled white in the fridge."

He knew these tasks would not keep everyone occupied for another hour, so he would have to think of something else. However, for now, looking around, he smiled and thought how good it was to have them all here this weekend.

Seeing everyone was occupied, George went over to the laptop to organize the evening's music. Some people he knew, not very far from him right now, felt very strongly about music playing at a dinner party. "It spoils the conversation" or "It's too loud" or "What the hell is this music George?"

He and Aimee overcame these objections by pre-selecting music that would not detract from the conversation, but allowed their guests to experience new sounds, and, they hoped, the pleasure of listening to them.

"If that's music you're sorting out then we need to have a say as well," came the statement from Bonnie, "need something other than your usual..." George waited for the abuse - he was used to it, ". . .rubbish."

George sighed and looked surprised. "That was mild for you."

"I know. Must be losing it. It's working in this heat," and fanned herself with a napkin.

"OK, a compromise. What do you want until they arrive?" George suggested, knowing they would never all agree.

Alex stood at the sideboard and opened one of the drawers housing a selection of CDs. "How about this. Mum liked this one." She passed the CD to her dad who popped it in the laptop. "Yes, nice choice," he said thoughtfully.

The distinctive guitar opening of 'Only When I Sleep' by The Corrs filled the room, and Chris, Alex and B gathered around the sofa and sang, karaoke style, on the chorus. George could get bleary-eyed at the drop of a hat, so it was no surprise he had to suppress a wave of emotion running through him at the sight, and sound, of his kids actually doing something together. He could not help it. He went over and had a group hug, which no one objected to. Bonnie however, suggested thirty seconds was long enough and anyway, said she had to finish the table, wiping a tear from her eye without anyone seeing.

The Corrs sang out their greatest hits, and the Morton gang got on with preparing for their guests.

"So dad, what's Vincente like?" asked Chris. His sisters looked on with interest for the answer.

"Spanish" George offered.

"Not funny," quipped Chris.

"OK.... he's erm... I suppose a grizzly bear."

Everyone looked shocked.

"You've all heard the phrase 'gentle giant.' They all nodded. "Well he's the opposite... so do not annoy him please."

"That's hardly a description dad." Bonnie objected.

"I think we will have to make up our own minds - that was a car I just heard arrive." Alex announced.

"OK gang - don't let me down... you know the drill by now..."

"Dad!" Alex almost shouted "Its fine. We're fine. Calm down."

She was not sure if the others had noticed it, but Alex had never seen her dad acting like a boy with crush... was all she could think of. Were he and this Maria an item? After only three months - surely not. Not that she would mind - they all wanted their dad to find someone - either a soul mate or close friend or... lover? Yes, as long as he is happy. The three of them had touched on the subject on the drive down. Chris was the only one to have seen Maria, and his recall of women is not always 100%. He did however tell of the overly long time George had held her hand when they first met.

"Oh my God," Bonnie exclaimed. "He's in love already."

"Don't go around saying that B," her sister suggested. "you know dad - he's a... sentimental type, and likes tactile situations..."

Chris and Bonnie raised an eye to each other, accepting their sister 'knows best.'

"Chris!" snapped Alex, "keep an eye on the road will you. My husband wants me back in one piece."

"Sorry sis." Chris replied. "But are we agreed we do expect dad to find someone - one day."

The question lingered in the air as they drove on, each pondering the possibility.

George showed Vincente and Maria into the lounge.

Chris, Bonnie and Alex just stared at Vincente. He was more or less as their father had described him. Tall, over six foot. Rugged features. Broad shoulders. Thick black wavy hair. He was wearing black slacks with a black Oxford style cotton shirt and a dark green casual waistcoat. His tanned complexion and blue eyes were not lost on the girls either.

George broke the silence. "Kids, this is Maria and Vincente," and as they shook hands, George introduced his children. "This is Alex, my eldest, and this is Bonnie and Christopher, who are in fact twins, but you can't tell."

All three held their breath and prayed George would not finish that snippet of information with his usual tag line, *"unless you see them naked..."*

Thankfully George did not embarrass his children - not then anyway.

"Hola." Vincente and Maria said to each of them in turn.

"*Hola, encantada de conoceres,*" replied Alex in Spanish.

Maria and Vincente smiled. "You speak Spanish. George did not tell me that. I must be careful what I say." Vincente said with a smile.

"I hope you three won't be leaving us out of the conversation all evening." George said making light of the fact he, Bonnie and Chris could not understand Spanish.

"OK, we will let you in sometimes George." Maria said, and touched George's arm, which did not go unnoticed by Bonnie.

"Good. How about some drinks. Chris can you do that, and everyone, please sit down."

Alex broke the silence. "I hear you have a restaurant in town, Maria."

"More of a bar. We do not serve food in the evening."

"Yes." George interrupted. "I have been meaning to talk to you both about that. Perhaps later tonight or over lunch this week."

Maria looked at George and smiled. "That sounds interesting. What do you think Papa?" she said turning to her father.

Chris came back in to the lounge with a jug of Sangria and six glasses.

"I think El Tango has potential as a restaurant." George continued, trying to expand on his suggestion.

Vincente looked at him with interest. "Why do you say that," he asked.

George poured the Sangria without asking who wanted any, and gave everyone a glass.

"I have walked around town a few times now, and apart from the bar, El Toro, the other end of town, I did not see a good restaurant. Did I miss one?" he asked smiling, looking at Maria.

"But first," George raised his glass, "a toast, to new friends."

Everyone raised a glass, and in unison, if not with enthusiasm from his three children, repeated the toast.

"Thank you George," Maria said, "we hope you will like it here, and your children will visit you often."

"I feel very welcome already Maria." George replied with a warm smile, probably staring too long at Maria.

Vincente stood up and broke George's thoughts. "Have you done anything to the place since I was here last?"

George blinked and refocused on the big man standing next to him. George did not have to look up to Vincente, but the sheer presence of the man standing next to him made him stand back to answer.

"Err. . no . .I don't think so Vincente. It's more or less as it was when you last came."

George saw Vincente was looking around at the now open office entrance, which was closed when he had brought George back with the jukebox.

Alex moved over and sat next to Maria. Bonnie and Chris sat alone sipping their drinks, and feeling like wallflowers at a wedding. "This is going to be a long night brother." Bonnie whispered in his ear.

"Then we must make it enjoyable, sis." He whispered back, and they touched glasses as if to bond their mischief making.

"What are you two hatching?" Alex called over.

"Nothing," they replied in harmony, looking a little guilty.

Alex smiled and was about to ask Maria a question when she asked. "They are close, being twins, even if they are brother and sister."

"Yes," Alex looked across to the twins again, "yes they are close, and mischievous," she added with extra venom.

Maria looked puzzled. "What is that mis . ."

"Oh sorry Maria. In Spanish it's like... err... naughty... err... *malo* si, very *malo*."

Maria smiled. "Of course, but I am sure they are not that bad."

Alex let the question hang for a few seconds. "No," she said turning to face Maria and smiling, "no, not all the time. Anyway, tell me all about Calabaza. Have you lived here all your life?"

"No, we came here when I was young, just after my mother..." She stopped and looked at Alex. "Oh so sorry. This is very hard to say," and looked around for help, but everyone was talking. "What Maria, it's OK, in Spanish if it helps you."

Maria took a deep breath as if she needed fresh air, and touched Alex's hand.

"Si, gracias," she almost whispered, "my mother died suddenly, she was ill. We came to Calabaza to start a new life I suppose, just like your Papa." She looked up at George who had turned to see the two women holding hands. Vincente had heard Spanish being spoken and looked at his daughter as well. "I think we should practice our English tonight Maria as we have the chance to do so."

"Si, sorry, yes Papa, of course, it was rude of me."

"Not at all." Alex came to her defense "She was just telling me of a good bar to go to," and winked at Maria, who blushed.

George was not sure what was going on but was pleased to see the two women getting on. "OK, talk amongst yourselves; I have to go to the kitchen. Bonnie can you help me please, and Chris can you check the barbeque is on."

"Alex, entertain our guests - I won't be long, I promise."

Vincente waved a dismissive hand. "Not a problem George, you carry on," and turned his attention again to the office. He walked the few short steps gingerly to the entrance, and looked in tentatively, as if he were on the threshold of a room with a dark secret.

"OK everyone - take your places please." George announced with some authority.

He was not too concerned where everyone sat, as long as he could maneuver Maria to a seat next to him. Luckily, she seemed to have the same idea. The table was rectangular, and ran parallel to the opened patio doors, which provided a cool breeze against the warm evening air. Two seats ran each side of the table, plus one each end. George stood guarding the end seat nearest the kitchen. "Sit wherever you like, but it would be convenient for me to be here nearer the kitchen."

Maria and Vincente approached the table and George pulled out the chair to his right for Maria. Vincente sat next to her. Bonnie and Chris virtually tripped over each other trying to take the other two seats next to each other, but Alex slipped into the chair next to her dad and opposite Maria. Chris grabbed the chair next to Alex as if it was a lifeboat. Nothing was said but the look on Bonne's face told Chris he was in trouble. George sensed the commotion even if their guests had not.

"Enough you two. Please behave." He said as calmly as possible.

Bonnie shot him a look and was about to reply but thought better of it. Instead, she gave her sister a sarcastic grin and sat down. When George was happy, everyone was settled he gave out instructions. "OK, wine. Chris, please do the honors. Bonnie, would you help me with the starters."

Alex, being left at the table with their guests again, smiled politely. Maria smiled back but Vincente looked at Alex as if choosing a tie. "You are married I see." He gestured to her wedding ring.

"Yes I am." Alex replied.

"So where is your husband tonight?"

"Papa!" Maria intervened, but Alex held out her hand to Maria.

"It's OK Maria. There's no mystery, he is at home of course. He couldn't get time off, but I will bring him next time."

Vincente nodded to indicate he understood.

Silence.

"So, Alex, do you work?" Maria asked with interest.

"Yes, I work in the library at Bristol University."

"Ahh." Vincente interrupted. "A student of literature. I too, read a lot. We must compare."

"Papa, when did you last read a book?" Maria interrupted.

"I am not talking of modern books - paperbacks - I mean history, factual works."

Maria shrugged and smiled at Alex, whilst shaking her head.

"It is the first time I heard of this, so be careful what he tells you," and winked, but Vincente ignored her.

"She does not know everything," he added, just as George came in with Bonnie carrying plates of warm chorizo salad, and warm goats cheese salad for Alex.

"I am glad to hear you are getting on well." George remarked.

"Si, George, I was just saying it is not possible to know everything about someone, no?" leaving the question hanging. George set down the plates and did not respond to the rhetorical question, hoping it was not as probing as it sounded.

Everyone ate in silence. The only sound was from the music George had selected. A collection of soft background music called Chillout Acoustic Sounds, which would not easily offend anyone.

"So, Vincente," George decided to open up the conversation. "where did you learn your English?"

Everyone looked at the big man with interest, although

Bonnie kept 'forking' her salad, still undecided if she really liked chorizo, and secretly coveted the warm goats' cheese.

"I was taught most at school in England." Vincente announced as if he was proud of the statement.

"Wow, when were you in England and for how long?" Alex asked with genuine interest.

Vincente knew he had a captive audience, and looked around the table to see if everyone was being attentive. Even Bonnie was a little curious by now.

"Well, my parents worked for the Royal Household in Madrid before the war, the civil war that is. My father ran the stables, and my mother looked after the *Infanta,* a daughter of the Royal family of Alfonso XIII. In 1938 we came to England. We stayed at Ham House near London for a while, and other various 'guest houses' of the English Royal family." He paused for a sip of wine and a mouthful of salad. No one spoke. Everyone was transfixed by this most surprising story.

Alex was trying to work out how old Vincente was. "How old were you when you came to England?" she asked.

"Not very old," is all he offered. "However, I attended English school and grew up speaking English. My mother and father spoke Spanish to me, but I had to speak English if I wanted friends." He paused, to revive some distant memory.

We stayed in England through the Second World War for some reason. It would have been safer to have gone back to Spain," he mused. "We were neutral after all."

More wine was consumed, and most, by then had finished the starters.

"Very good chorizo George. You are full of surprises," Vincente said, looking directly at George, hoping for an unguarded reply.

"I like to cook, as my children well know, and I'm not afraid to try out new recipes too. I am glad you liked the chorizo salad."

Alex collected the plates and George went to check on the main course, out on the patio BBQ. "Wait until I get back - I want to hear the rest of that story Vincente," he called out from the patio.

"There is not a lot more to say really, George," and looked

back at his remaining audience. "We returned to Spain in 1946 and continued our lives."

"So you played with royalty when you were young." Bonnie asked.

"Yes I did. But I did not really know they were anything so very special for a long time. They were just other children my age, playing together."

"Do you keep in touch still with the Royals in Madrid?" Chris asked.

Vincente took some bread and chewed on it thoughtfully. Maria looked a little pensive and turned to see what George was doing.

"No, not really." Vincente answered thoughtfully. "We go on different paths when we get older, so no, I do not." Hoping that would close the matter. However, he remembered well the reason he had broken his family ties with the royal household. He had married a Basque girl, Maria's mother.

Maria touched her father's hand. "No more stories Papa." She said softly in Spanish.

George came in with a large plate holding a shoulder of lamb. "Another of dad's specials." Chris announced with glee, and then remembered something.

"So Alex, lucky we are eating all the same tonight."

George just smiled and ignored the comment, as did Alex.

Vincente and Maria looked at the meat with interest. "You are clever George. You will make a wonderful hus..." and stopped in mid sentence "... Oh George I'm so sorry. I am silly. . I . ." Maria kept apologizing.

George seemed unflustered by the remark, and took her outstretched hand.

"It's OK Maria, its fine, really." Smiling all the time to assure her he was not offended. He leaned closer and whispered. "I hope I will one day," and squeezed her hand again. She wiped a tear away quickly to hide her embarrassment further.

Vincente looked at his daughter with a piercing glaze. He considered this an embarrassment, and as a guest felt inclined to say so, but he could see George had the situation in hand - in more ways than one, seeing he was still holding Maria's hand.

"Dad," Alex interrupted, "meats getting cold."

"Yes, sorry. Of course. Alex, Chris, veggies please, and yours is in the oven." He said turning to Alex, "Unless you want to convert."

Now it was Alex's turn to have all eyes on her. Chris smirked. Bonnie was aloof. Vincente and Maria just looked on not knowing what was going on.

Alex sighed. "It does look good dad... but you have cooked for me and I appreciate that."

George knew he would be safe with a roast of any kind. It is a universal favorite, and although cooked in different ways to produce different flavors, the result was the same. George had impregnated this shoulder of lamb with cloves of garlic and sprigs of rosemary, and spit roasted it over the barbeque for forty-five minutes - medium rare - as it should be.

"This smells good George." Vincente said, eyeing the cuts of meat George was carving. "Another of your specials George?"

Bonnie, this time, came to her dad's defense. "Actually dad is a good cook. We had the most perfect paella last night, didn't we Chris, Alex?" She said with a flourish of excitement, looking to her brother and sister for confirmation.

George was smiling modestly, and did not notice Vincente's eyes squinting, almost quivering.

"Are you OK Vincente, do you want some water?" Alex looked at him with concern and at the redness in his cheeks.

"Si, please, that would be good." Alex poured him some water.

"Thank you, Alex." He tried to smile. "If you do not eat meat, did you not have the paella?" he enquired.

Alex handed plates of meat around the table. "Ah, I forgot the gravy, dad." And went to the kitchen."

"Did I say something wrong?" Vincente shrugged.

"No, not at all. I think she... is..." George hesitated.

"Confused..." Suggested Bonnie, sarcastically.

George gave one of his looks but Bonnie looked away, whilst raising her head high.

"Alex eats fish, so paella was appropriate. Tonight I cooked her salmon," he said, looking at Bonnie again.

"George..." Vincente was about to say something that had to be said.

"Papa... no please, not tonight." Maria retorted in Spanish.

Maria looked at Alex because she had understood what had been said, but continued in English. "I know what he is about to say and think he should not. We are guests here, remember please Papa." She finished in Spanish.

George was intrigued, as were the others. "Come on Maria, it cannot be that bad." He said encouragingly.

Vincente took the invitation in a second. "You see," he waved an arm in George's direction. "George is a grown man. He can take criticism."

Maria leaned back in despair and closed her eyes.

Vincente tucked into his plate of food and considered his next sentence carefully. How tactful should he be? He is a guest after all, and George is not going anywhere. Yes this lamb is good, and maybe he can cook, but when it comes to paella he is treading on sacred ground. Damn it. It has to be said. "George," Vincente finally said, "so, this paella of yours, what was in it?"

George smiled. He wants a recipe from me, wow that is a compliment.

"Well let's see, paella rice of course, red peppers, chorizo, chicken pieces, tiger prawns, onion, garlic, paprika, saffron, peas, tomatoes and my secret ingredient, mussels... and that's about it." George beamed and relaxed, savoring the expected praise.

"George, I do not mean to be rude... "

Maria nearly choked. Everyone looked at her. "Are you OK?" George asked.

She nodded, holding a napkin to her mouth. Vincente looked at her unimpressed.

"As I was saying... paella is made using locally found produce, and the meat is always from the region; rabbit, boar, venison etc. Where do you think we get prawns and mussels from in the middle of Spain?" He left the question floating in mid air.

"If we cannot get local fresh produce for the paella, we do not make it. And when we do make it, it is a ritual, not a recipe to come from a cook book."

"Papa... please, enough. I am sure George knows that." Maria interrupted, looking embarrassed at her father's outburst.

George shrugged. "More wine needed," and went to the kitchen to fetch the Rioja Vincente had brought. Damn, what was that all about? It's only a bloody paella for God's sake. George was thinking fast. How do I appease the man? I don't want him for an enemy.

George retuned with the wine. "Yes, I have made paella many ways, but usually with produce our family like." Hoping that would satisfy the big man.

Everyone ate in silence for a while longer.

"You really must try it Vincente, dad's paella, it's the best ever." Bonnie suddenly declared, seeing an opportunity for further mischief.

Alex shot her a glance that should have turned her to stone.

Maria stopped eating midway from plate to mouth.

Vincente turned to George. "That is a good idea young lady."

Bonnie grinned.

Alex frowned.

Maria almost fainted.

Chris smiled - "How about a cook-off. You each make one and we judge it!"

George considered this.

Vincente considered this.

Maria choked. She leaned over to George. "You do not know how competitive he is. He has a passion for making paella. Please do not do this." She was almost begging.

"Oh come on. It is just for fun, eh, Vincente." But the big man just sat and grinned.

"Can we change the subject please?" Maria suggested.

"Good idea." Alex agreed, and nodded to Maria. Alex liked this lady. She was smart, attractive and assertive when necessary. She looked at her dad. He was enjoying this evening. It felt like a new beginning she was a witness to, and tried not to become too emotional. Unfortunately, she was not strong enough and had to excuse herself.

"Not used to real food, sis." Chris whispered to Bonnie, and they both laughed too loud.

"Hey, that's enough please." George said on hearing the interruption. "Make yourself useful please and clear away the dishes for me."

Maria excused herself too and went upstairs to the bathroom. The door was locked. "Sorry I thought you went downstairs." She called through the door.

The key turned and Alex opened the door. Her face was flushed and she had obviously been crying. "Alex, what is it. Can I help?" Maria asked with sincere concern.

"So, George, while the..." Vincente searched for the right words, but George was ahead of him.

"*Spoil sports* we say in English Vincente."

"Ah yes, spoiled sorts have gone." Vincente corrected.

George said nothing. It would take too long. "What do you have in mind?" George continued.

Chris and Bonnie had disappeared in to the kitchen, and the *'spoiled sorts'* were nowhere to be seen. "Come George, let us get some air."

The two men walked onto the patio, all of two yards away, and sat at the mosaic coffee table.

"Tomorrow we will each cook our own paella and let our families choose the best." Vincente suggested.

"That will not work. They go home tomorrow. We will have to think of another way." George said, thinking this may be a good way out of an awkward situation.

Vincente shrugged. "Well, we start early, eh?"

The two men sat in the cool of the evening air pondering the question. George wondered if it was too soon for brandy.

Alex opened her bedroom door opposite the bathroom.

"Please come in a moment, Maria."

The two women sat on the bed, each unsure of what to say.

"Alex, have you been crying?"

Alex looked down at her feet. "I do get emotional, Maria. I'm so sorry, it's not your fault, I promise." She took Maria's hand for reassurance.

"It's OK to remember, Alex. Memories are good. I think about my mother all the time."

Alex smiled and tried not to choke again with emotion.

"You are very kind, Maria. Thank you."

Alex looked at Maria and smiled. "Are you and dad..." but Maria put a finger to her lips. "Let's go and see what those men are up to, yes?" And kissed Alex tenderly on the cheek.

"Any chance of pudding Dad?" Came a cry from inside.

"OK, Bonnie. It's all under control." George called back. "Well, we will have to decide later Vincente," and the two men walked back to the table.

George laid out chilled oranges in wine, a large bowl of crème caramel and glasses of lemon sorbet."

"Wow, George, I am impressed." Maria said, as she and Alex rejoined the others."

"Had a good chat you two?" Chris asked, grinning at Bonnie.

"Yes thank you, Chris." replied Maria, which he was not expecting. "We talked about everyone."

"Impossible. You were not gone long enough." Bonnie replied, as quick as lightning.

"OK, dig-in, as we say in England." George looked at Maria. "Are you OK?" he asked as she sat next to him. "Si, I am OK. Are you OK George? What have you been talking about with my Papa?"

George looked at Vincente. Vincente tried to narrow his eyes to tell George not to say anything, but Alex was staring at him. "Something in your eye Vincente?" Alex asked in Spanish?

George's mind was racing. Why had Vincente suggested cooking tomorrow?

Answer: Because he knew the kids were going home.

"Alex." George almost snapped the name out and made her jump. "Sorry dear, didn't mean to do that. What time do you leave tomorrow?"

Vincente looked up from his bowl of crème caramel, and half an iced orange, and eyeballed Alex.

"Well, the flight is at 10.30 tomorrow evening, so we would have to leave by seven at the latest."

"Yes!" George said triumphantly. "We can do it tomorrow."

"Do what?" Came a chorus, but Maria already knew the answer, and turned to her father.

"Papa, no, it's not fair. Where will George get the ingredients on a Sunday? And you - what do you have?"

Vincente looked his look, and shrugged. "I have some things in the store cupboard," and leaned to whisper in Spanish to Maria," do not worry my lovely, all is in hand. Do not say any more." He winked with his left eye hoping again no one noticed.

Maria shook her head slowly, and looked at Alex. "Ay ay ay!" she said in despair.

George and Vincente were, in fact, the only two around the table having fun. "Why is everyone looking glum? It's only some fun." He said, hoping to get a response.

"Vincente, tell them, it is only in fun - it is not a competition after all." George's voice trailed off as Maria caught his eye, and raised her eyebrows.

"You are both acting like boys. This is a silly idea. I told you papa is serious about paella."

George was concerned about Maria's concern. Had he gone too far? Just what were the logistics of cooking a fish and chicken paella tomorrow? He had some frozen prawns but not the large tiger variety he preferred. He also had no chicken or mussels left thanks to Alex. Perhaps he was a little hasty. On the other hand where would Vincente find rabbit, venison or fresh boar?

"Can I suggest," George asked in a calm manner, not wanting to sound the pessimist he was becoming, "we wait until the shops are open and stock up on essentials during the week."

"Ah, no dad, we will miss all the fun," Chris said. "And I thought you wanted our support." He added for extra weight.

Vincente looked at George with raised eyebrows. "He is correct George. Where will you be without your 'team' for support?"

"Papa," Maria shot in, "that is not fair. Can we drop this until next week? George is correct. We... he... needs time to prepare." Maria agreed.

"Ah, so you are in another camp." Vincente said without any apparent concern.

"No... papa... that is not fair. I will be... referee."

George smiled. "Well in that case I accept. Tomorrow is fine by me." Everyone looked at George.

"What! How... dad, are you going to be able to cook... " Alex tried to ask, but George put a finger to his lips. "Trust me. Now, anyone for a brandy?"

"Chris, Bonnie, please clear away the plates and put the coffee on. Alex, entertain our guests please for a moment. I will be back in a minute." And George left the table with a straight face, and headed for the upstairs bathroom. He took the iPhone out of his pocket and pressed the speed dial number before he reached the first stone step.

"Hello old friend. Hope I did not wake you."

"George, is that you. What's wrong?"

"Wrong, nothing. Just need to ask a favor. Have you eaten yet, Carlos?"

"George, it is nearly 10.30, of course we have. Why?"

"I need you to go to a restaurant and order the following... have you got a pen?"

The first thing George noticed when he returned to the lounge was the music.

"Who's been playing with the CD player?" He asked, looking first at Chris and then Bonnie.

"Why do you assume it was one of us? Alex knows how

to change a CD as well." Bonnie replied in defense, but not convincingly.

George was about to say something but he heard his name being called.

"George!" Vincente called over from the table. "We need to confirm the time for the cook-off tomorrow."

"OK, how about 2 o'clock. Ideal for lunch, and just before siesta."

Vincente looked at him with suspicion. "George, you are starting to think Spanish."

George smiled and nodded, acknowledging the compliment.

"Dad, are you sure about this? Maria and I think it's foolish." Alex said, adding "and a bit childish."

"Stop worrying. It's fine. Now let's talk about something else." He said, looking around the table for support.

Realizing the conversation needed a kick-start, George told one of his favorite anecdotes, much to the moaning chorus of his offspring.

"My dear old dad always said there were three things you should never talk about at dinner." He paused for effect, and to ensure everyone was listening. "Religion, Politics and Sex, and we haven't, so far, have we?"

Vincente took the bait, but not as George had expected.

"My friends," he started, and then too, paused for effect, to ensure everyone was listening. "Spain is 99% socialist so there is nothing to talk about. We are also 99% catholic so again we do not talk about it, so no argument there. And as far as sex is concerned," he paused again, but avoided looking directly at Maria, who was about to blush, "we do not need to talk about it," and leaned over the table as if to whisper to Alex, Chris and Bonnie, "we just get on with it," and leaned back with a roar of laughter.

George actually appreciated the joke and laughed as well. Chris joined in and the girls just smirked. "I am sorry for my father tonight. He is usually very quiet." Maria said, shooting a killer look at her dad.

"Oh, George, I am in trouble I think." Vincente suggested, with another roar of laughter.

The atmosphere was back to normal, but both George and Vincente were going over in their minds the program for the next day's cook-off.

Chris decided to try something. "OK, no religious sex," he grinned.

"Chris," George tried to look fatherly. "That's not what I said."

"Oh, sorry pop. Anyway,... I know something about bullfighting."

Bonnie let out a long moan and buried her head in her hands. Chris ignored her. "She's just jealous." He added, to no one in particular. "Did you know bullrings were not always round. They were once square," and sat back with a wide satisfying grin, as if he had just delivered a world shattering announcement.

Maria and George looked at each other and smiled politely. George was not sure if Chris was talking out of his backside, but was keen to hear what Vincente had to say.

"Actually he is correct." Vincente confirmed. Everyone seemed surprised. Chris tried to hide poking his out tongue at Bonnie, but not successfully.

"Several hundred years ago, the military officers' and noblemen were bored between fighting, so they practiced chasing bulls in fields with lances. This developed into a sport of sorts, and was moved to town squares for ordinary people to see." Vincente took a sip of brandy and saw everyone was glued to his tale. "However, because there were no barriers, many people were killed by the bulls, so they designed barriers in a square to protect the people."

Chris smiled. "Yes," he said, and clenched his fist in the air, "knew it," and leaned forward to hear more.

Vincente continued, ignoring the interruption. "One problem with a square is that a bull, or a person, can be trapped in the corner, so after a while the 'square' became round. In fact it is slightly oval, and the modern ring was designed by one of history's most famous bullfighters, Juan Belmonte, who died in 1960 something. . I can not remember the date."

"Well done Chris," George said, "and thank you for the

most interesting history lesson. In the words of a famous English actor, *'not many people know that.'*

"Oh, dad, no please. You are rubbish at voices." Bonnie called over, which prompted Chris to have a go at the phrase, followed by Bonnie. George surrendered and raised his hands in the air. "I think our guests think we are mad."

Maria smiled and touched George's hand. "No, not at all, just err... different, but in a nice way."

"I think that was a compliment." George replied, still letting Maria hold his hand.

"Well, I still think bullfighting is horrible and you will never get me near one, and it should be banned - but that's just my opinion." Bonnie announced, feeling left out perhaps at not knowing the language, or just jealous of her sister. She folded her arms in an act of defiance.

"Bonnie, please, you are in Spain and must respect the culture." George said hoping Vincente had not been offended. He was still getting to know this man and he did not want to upset him, especially tonight, and by one of this own children.

However, Vincente smiled and waved a hand, as if to dismiss the comment. "George, an opinion is like a . ." and paused to ensure he found the correct word he was searching for in English.... " a... navel, si, a navel."

"Belly button, you mean a belly button." Chris suggested

"Ah, si, if you prefer, a belly button. That is what an opinion is like - a belly button - we all have one." And shrugged with smile at his own pearl of wisdom, as the others analyzed the significance of the observation.

"Not unless you have an *'outy'*!" Bonnie said immediately, looking directly at George. "Does that mean you don't have an opinion either dad?" she added with a triumphant grin.

"What is the *'outy'* " Vincente asked in all innocence.

"It is when a belly button has been pushed out." Alex explained.

Everyone, except Maria, had a look of concentration on their faces whilst considering George's *'outy'*. Maria, however, was smiling to herself, head down, caressing her brandy glass, and gave out an almost whispered "Si".

The room went quiet. Maria lifted her head and saw the audience. "What is so funny?" someone asked.

Maria, in all innocence, was remembering the time she had seen George's unusual naval, and had commented on it then. "It is true, he does have one," she said in all innocence.

Vincente coughed.

Chris and Bonnie looked on in amazement.

Alex raised an eyebrow towards her dad.

George seized the moment. "Don't look at Maria like that. As if she had committed a crime. She has seen me in shorts. There's no great mystery." He explained with a touch of authority, hoping that was the end of it.

Vincente said nothing, but gave a questioning look at his daughter.

"I think on that note we must leave. Thank you George for a wonderful meal."

Vincente stood up and offered his hand to George.

"Oh come on, the evening is still young. Must you really go?" He directed the question to Maria.

"Si, I must get back for Jorge, but thank you. It was a wonderful evening," she said, touching his arm."

Vincente was saying goodbye to the others when George guided Maria to the kitchen area. "It was good to see you again. I hope we can do this again soon, without your papa," he whispered. Maria smiled and took his hand. "That would be nice." She whispered back.

"What are you two planning over there?" Chris called out, alerting everyone.

"Just planning our strategy for tomorrow." George responded, and winked at Maria, "and trying to bribe the referee." He said quietly, squeezing her hand.

"Ah yes George, tomorrow. Are you sure you want to make a fool of yourself." Vincente called over.

"Papa!" Maria snapped, "That is not fair. You started this."

Vincente smiled, and shrugged at George, looking the innocent.

"It's OK. I am looking forward to it. What did we agree? 1.30 at El Tango."

"Si George. 1.30." Vincente nodded and waved as he headed to the door.

"Will I see you all tomorrow?" Maria asked the others.

"Yes, we will be supporting dad." Alex said, and locked arms with him, to show her support, at the same time eyeballing her brother and sister.

"Can you all clear the table while I see our guests out." George asked, and ushered Maria to the door.

He leaned forward and kissed her on the cheek. "Thank you for coming. I hope you did enjoy it."

"Of course. Your children are lovely George. See you tomorrow," and she got in to the big man's car, which cruised slowly down the drive to the main road.

Back in the lounge Chris, Bonnie and Alex were all standing in a line, arms folded. "Didn't that go well?" Chris said, with hardly any sarcasm at all.

The next morning George was up early. Well, early for a Sunday, and started to make notes about the day's forthcoming events. In the light of day it did seem a little childish, but both he and Vincente wanted to prove a point. George however realised that by proving that point he may well embarrass Vincente, which was something he wanted to avoid - he needed him as a friend, not an enemy.

George looked up from his notes when he heard whispering coming from the hall.

"Happy Birthday to you,
Happy Birthday to you,
Happy Birthday dear daddy/dad
Happy Birthday to you."

George met all three of them in the middle of the lounge and gave them all a hug and a kiss. "Thank you gang - that was lovely, I wasn't expecting anything."

"What makes you sure you have something." Chris asked.

"Well, maybe something to do with that rather long wrapped thing you are trying to hide."

"We tried to think of something to give a fussy guy... "

"Very fussy." Bonnie underlined "...but decided on

something meaningful and lasting." Chris said, handing the gift to his dad.

George looked at them all with intrigue. "That sounds very... deep, thank you, thank you all."

George tore the paper gently. It was heavy and solid. It had the feel of a cricket bat. George's heart skipped a beat as he saw the wooden object in his hands.

"I hope we have done the right thing." Alex said. "We thought about it for ages. Even asked Grandma and Grandpa, but they said you wouldn't mind... "

"Alex," George interrupted, "its fine, it's wonderful, it's beautiful," he said turning to Bonnie and Chris. "All of you, it's the most wonderful present you could have given me." George ran his hand over the smooth varnished pine, touching each of the deeply engraved letters spelling the name *Malinye*.

Malinye was the name of their house in England. George had persuaded Aimee to name their house after falling in love with the piece of music of the same name by Jan Garbarek. It is a simple haunting melody, made distinctive by Garbarek's soprano saxophone, and reminded them of some wonderful weekends in Paris. George also remembered how they loved to make love to that tune.

After a breakfast of toast, marmalade and coffee, George started gathering his utensils and ingredients for the paella cook-off. "Dad," Alex asked in a puzzled tone. "Where are all the other ingredients? Chicken, prawns, mussels etc. You have nothing here."

George smiled back. "Don't you worry - it's all under control my love. I just need to drive over to Aranda and should be back around 12.30."

"But all the shops are closed on a Sunday. Where are you going?" Alex insisted, but George was out of the door and climbing into the Espace. Alex followed. "Can I come as well? I don't want to sit around the house for a couple of hours, and Chris and Bonnie will probably go back to bed."

George looked at his daughter's pleading eyes and could not refuse. "OK, go and call out we are taking the car and will be back in a couple of hours."

The drive to Aranda took only fifteen minutes on a Sunday morning. The roads in Spain are quiet at the best of times, but even more so on Sundays. They found Carlos's house easily from his directions.

"Hola, George, what have you been up to now my friend?" Carlos asked as they walked up to the front door.

"Carlos, good to see you too. This is my daughter, one of them, Alex. Alex this is Carlos."

"Hola, Carlos, good to meet you at last. Dad has talked about you."

"Ah, really, I must find out what he says." Carlos replied giving George a sly look.

"Come, come in and have some coffee. We have just finished breakfast."

Carlos and Alyce had a small bungalow style house on the outskirts of town, on a new development. Not much land but it was a good size with two bedrooms, L-shaped lounge/diner and kitchen, and a bathroom/shower room.

"Hola, George." Alyce came over and kissed George on both cheeks.

"Hola, Alyce. This is Alex my eldest daughter."

"Hola." Alex said and continued in Spanish. The two women walked off into the kitchen, talking as if they had known each other for years.

"She is lovely lady George. You are very lucky. Does she miss you being over here?" Carlos asked.

George frowned and was still looking in the direction of the kitchen. "Yes, I think she does, but over this weekend she and her sister and brother have made it clear they want me to be happy first and foremost, and if that includes another partner, then I have their blessing."

Carlos shrugged. "That is all you could ask, no? And who then is the lucky lady?" He added out of curiosity.

George smiled. "Watch this space." Is all he offered.

"So George, tell me about this cooking challenge you have got into with the Mayor. Do you think it was wise?" Carlos asked with friendly concern.

"It started over dinner last night. I think one of my

children said I had made a great paella the previous day, and one thing led to another, and before I knew it he had challenged me to a cooking competition."

"Excuse me!" Alex called out as she and Alyce came back into the lounge with coffee.

"I remember YOU suggesting a cook-off. It was Maria and me who thought it was a silly idea." Alex sat next to George and smiled. "Remember now dad?"

"Ah, well... I may have said something to defend my honor. I cannot remember the details. Too many brandies." George sipped his coffee trying again to remember the previous night's events.

"Well, George, taking on the Mayor, especially Snr. Vincente, it is a brave thing, and you should have all the support you can, so we have decided to come over and give you our support, plus some friends are visiting us from Barcelona, so we will bring them as well." Carlos said with some pleasure.

"Really! That is wonderful. Thank you both." George was really touched that he would have this extra support and secretly thought it would even out the odds. "So, Carlos, how was your shopping trip last night?" George asked.

"Well, come and see," and they went to the kitchen to see what Carlos had brought from the local restaurant.

"So, that's why you were so confident last night." Alex said looking at the produce Carlos had laid out on the kitchen table; tiger prawns, two red and green peppers, two chilies and several large chicken portions. "The only thing I could not find were the mussels, but I think you can work it OK without them."

"Carlos, this is fantastic. Thank you so very much. I really do owe you."

"Well, how about a good lunch today? One more thing you can use my friend..." Carlos opened the fridge and took out a covered dish. "We use these in our paella, calamari."

George's face beamed a wide smile. "That's fantastic. Thank you again, both of you."

Alyce said she would pack all the food in a cool bag with ice packs, and bring it out in a few minutes.

"Do you have everything else, paella rice, olive oil..."

"Yes, yes, I have all that thank you Carlos. We are meeting at El Tango at two. Is that OK for you?" George asked hurriedly.

"Yes, of course, we will be there to give support - and my friend, you will need it. The locals really know their paella, and the Mayor will not want to lose face... you understand." Carlos said with some concern.

George smiled and shrugged. "I understand Carlos, and appreciate your concern, but I think, hope.... the good people of Calabaza will see it as some fun."

Carlos was not so sure, but remained silent. The girls reappeared with Alex carrying the cool bag. They said their goodbyes and said they looked forward to seeing them later in Calabaza.

George was quiet on the journey back. He kept going over and over in his mind how to cook the damn dish, one he had cooked so many times before, but now, in front of an audience he was not so confident. Carlos was right - Vincente would not want to be made to be embarrassed. What was he to do? Make an inferior dish?

Alex sensed her dad was deep in thought. "I hope you are concentrating on the road home and not on anything else." She asked, touching his arm.

"Of course, my love. What could I possibly be thinking about?"

They arrived back home at 12.45 with a smile. "OK, time to gather the rest of the ingredients and get into town. Find your brother and sister please and see they are ready on time."

"Yes, sir." Alex mocked with a salute and went into the house.

George smiled, and was glad he would have at least seven people in his camp.

With everything packed in the car George called out. "Time to go everyone..."

Bonnie and Alex appeared and sat in the back seat. "Where is your brother now?" George asked in frustration. But before he could get an answer his mobile rang.

"Hola... Maria... yes we are still coming, why, has Vincente changed his mind... good... no don't worry, it will be fun... yes fun... OK, see you soon."

"So Vincente is not backing out. That's a shame Dad." Bonnie said, catching his glance in the rear-view mirror. George was about to respond when Chris opened the passenger door and sat next to his Dad. "Sorry... had a serious buyer on E-Bay. Hey lets go, I'm starving."

As they approached El Tango the streets were empty, and apart from some children playing in the side streets, it was very quiet. "Maybe no one's heard of the gun fight at the 'OK Corral' today." Chris mocked.

George parked the car and tried the front door. Locked. He walked to the side street entrance. Locked. He went back to the front entrance where by now Chris and Alex had tried to raise anyone inside the bar. Bonnie remained seated in the car. George took out his mobile and was about to call Maria when she opened the door.

"Sorry, I had been seeing to Jorge, he has a temperature." Maria informed them.

"Oh no, is he OK, should you call a doctor?" Alex asked with concern.

"No, he will be fine. Probably just a cold," she said, "and how are you George. Ready for battle?" Followed by a kiss on each cheek.

"Bring it on, as we say in England." George announced, looking around the bar.

"And where is my opponent?"

Maria sighed. "He will be down soon. He has been on the phone all morning getting everyone he knows to come along," she said looking exhausted.

"Maria, why don't you go and stay with Jorge and leave us to get on with it. You don't have to be here." George suggested, as tactfully as he could.

"Would you like some company, Maria?" Alex asked.

"Si, that would be nice, thank you." And the two women left to go upstairs.

"Great, so what do we do chef?" Chris asked, looking lost.

"We, young man, go to the kitchen. But first, fetch the cool bags please and ask Bonnie to bring in the other box of goodies."

Just as Chris left the bar, Vincente came down stairs. "Hola, George, I did not think you would go through with it. Do you still want to do this?" He asked half-heartedly.

"Of course, if you do. I have everything I need to get started.

"Do you?" Vincente said, hoping George was backing out. "Do you really have all the ingredients? And where did you get if from so quickly?" he asked rather sternly.

George allowed himself a wry smile. "Don't you worry about that, I have all I need. Now, what is the plan?"

Vincente realised there was no going back now without losing face. "OK, we each cook our paella here, and let our friends and customers be the judge. We have some disposable plates and plastic spoons we can give to everyone to sample each dish. You agree?"

"Sounds like a plan to me, Vincente. Let's cook."

Upstairs, the two women sat on the edge of Jorge's bed. "Hola, Jorge, I am George's daughter, Alex. How are you feeling today?"

Jorge looked at Alex then at his mother. He had never heard an English person speak Spanish to him.

"You speak Spanish!" he whispered.

Alex smiled. "Si, I learnt it many years ago at school, and on holiday with my parents in Spain."

Alex felt his forehead. "What is his temperature, Maria."

"An hour ago it was one hundred and one. Do you think I should call a doctor?"

"Does he have any rashes on his body?" Alex asked, thinking back to how she nursed Chris when he was young with a temperature.

"No, nothing I saw. He just feels hot and sweaty." Maria confirmed.

"I used to keep a warm towel or face cloth on my brother's forehead. It seemed to help, and let him sleep a while." Alex offered. "I am no doctor, but take his temperature in another hour, and if there is no change then perhaps call someone."

Maria touched Alex's hand. "Thank you. It is good to have someone to talk to. Papa is good with Jorge, but not so good with illness, like many men."

"I understand. It must be difficult sometimes, being alone to bring up a child."

Maria looked at Jorge and gently brushed his fringe away from his eyes as mothers do. Jorge was either too tired or too weak to object as he would normally have done.

"Si, it is lonely sometimes, but that is why I like the bar. I meet many people and talk to locals and strangers about their lives, and mine does not always seem so bad."

Maria went to the bathroom to fetch a warm face cloth.

"So," Alex said to Jorge, "you like computer games I hear. What is your favorite?"

Jorge thought about this for a moment. "Mario Brothers," he answered with a nod and a smile.

"I like that too. I will play you next time I visit my papa, OK, so get well soon for me," and she leaned over and kissed his forehead.

Maria returned with a small bowl of water and a facecloth.

"I will go and see how the other two 'boys' are getting on. See you later Jorge."

"Thank you Alex, and make sure they do not burn down the kitchen please."

Maria sat next to her son and gently squeezed out the warm cloth and placed it on his forehead.

"Mama?"
"Yes my angel."
"I like her."
"Yes, so do I."

Alex heard the raised voices before she entered the kitchen. She stopped to listen and peered through the glass square in the door. She could make out Spanish and English, so this was not a two-way conversation. She took a deep breath and pushed open the swing door.

"Excuse me, gentlemen, *escuseme* Vincente," she called out assertively. Both George and Vincente froze.

"Alex, hi. What's the problem?" George asked in all innocence.

"Problem!" she said trying not to raise her voice. "The problem is I could hear you two upstairs. There is sick child up there trying to rest!" She said with as much assertiveness as she could.

The two men looked suitably guilty and George turned away as naughty boys do when being told off. "Is Jorge OK? I thought he had a cold." Vincente asked, looking a little annoyed at the interruption.

"He has a temperature and is trying to rest. Now what is all the shouting about?" Alex asked trying to move away from her little white lie about Jorge, but it was the only thing she could think of. True, he is not very well, but she had no idea if they could be heard from the upstairs bedroom.

"George does not have all the ingredients, and wants to use what we have here. I say that is cheating." Vincente exclaimed.

George turned to Alex and shrugged. "I only want some seasoning and paprika. It's not too much to ask, is it?"

"Maria was right. You are acting like school boys," she said walking up to Vincente.

Although he towered over her, Alex calmly raised her head to meet those piercing steel blue eyes.

In a quiet voice she spoke in Spanish. "Vincente, you have the whole town behind you. What have you to worry about? Papa knows you will win. He just wants to do the best he can."

George was straining to hear but could not make out anything except the word 'papa'.

"Are you talking about me?" he called over.

"No." Alex shot back without turning, waiting for Vincente's answer. "Si, OK he can have what he wants." He agreed with a shrug, and nodded towards the cupboard where the seasoning is kept.

"Gracias senor." Alex said, and found what George wanted.

"What was that all about? What did you say to him?" George asked suspiciously, but with just a touch of pride that a daughter of his could make a giant quiver.

Alex just winked and walked out of the kitchen, just as Chris came rushing in. "Hell, Dad, there must be fifty people out there. All wanting a piece of paella," he blurted out.

"A portion son. You cannot have a piece of paella." George said, correcting him.

"OK, whatever, but you had better make a ton of it." Chris replied, and left the kitchen as fast as he had entered it.

George and Vincente looked at each other and nodded. "She is a handful your daughter." Vincente said in a matter-of-fact way.

George smiled. "Yes, she can be," he agreed.

"Well, we do have something in common, my friend." Vincente said, laughing.

Alex could not believe she was hearing laughter from the kitchen. A few moments ago they were at daggers drawn with each other. Just then, Maria came into the bar and was taken aback by so many people seated and standing around talking with anticipation.

She saw Alex talking to Angel. "Hola, Angel." They kissed hello. "I am glad you have met each other."

"Si, Alex was telling me what is happening here. Is George mad!" Angel asked. Then realised what she had said "Sorry Alex, you know what I mean?"

"Yes I do Angel, and we all agree, but it is too late now," and they looked around the bar again to take in the number of people there.

"As you are here Angel can you help with the wine?" Maria asked, and they headed for the bar.

"Maria," Alex called out. "I am just going to find my brother and sister," and headed out of the front door.

The temperature outside was just as hot as in the kitchen. She looked up and down the street for her brother and sister but could not see any sign of them. "Deserters," she thought to herself, but just then saw Chris appear from around the corner. "Where have you been brother?" she said, sounding too much like a schoolmistress.

"Just seeing the sights, sis," he said, but not with much conviction.

"And where is Bonnie? I think we should all be supporting dad no matter what we think of this whole stupid stunt." Alex exclaimed in frustration.

"Wow, sis, calm down. It's only some fun, and dad seems to be in control."

Alex looked up at her brother and sighed. "Sorry, Chris. It's just that Dad has to live here, and I don't want him to be a laughing stock."

Chris gave his sister a hug. "He will be fine. He seems to have new lease of life - don't you think so?" he asked calmly.

Just then Bonnie appeared from nowhere. "Ok, what is all this about you two, what's happened, is Dad OK . ." She asked earnestly, seeing her brother and sister hugging.

"Just moral support, sis." Chris replied, letting go of Alex.

"OK," Bonnie said slowly, "but don't expect me to join in," and she walked passed them into the bar.

Chris and Alex were about to follow when a car horn sounded and a car and pulled up in front of them.

"Hola, Alex." It was Carlos and Alyce, and they had another couple with them.

"Glad you remembered where to find us," Alex said greeting them with a kiss.

"These are our friends Christos and Lucy, who is English. They live in Barcelona but came down to see us for the day so I thought we could have more numbers for support, yes!"

"That's very thoughtful, Carlos, dad will be pleased." Alex replied, and after introducing herself and Christopher, they all went in to the bar to join the mêlée.

It was more organized chaos than a mêlée. Maria and Angel were serving wine, or rather giving it out freely. Chris went behind the bar to help, but Alex could not see Bonnie anywhere.

Just then the kitchen door swung open and Vincente and George appeared both wearing chef's aprons. A loud cheer erupted and the chattering stopped. Everyone turned and looked at the two contestants - summing them up, as if they were boxers preparing for a fight. Vincente surveyed the room. His bright blue eyes seemed to touch everyone in some telepathic way, urging them to make the right choice when voting. How could he lose? So many locals who know and love the Mayor, and just a handful of friends and family supporting the outsider. George did not stand a chance.

Vincente moved further down the bar, causing a nervous Chris to move an equally further distance along the bar until he reached the end.

"My dear friends... and family," he started to say, looking around to catch Maria's attention. "Thank you all for coming to this hastily arranged... contest." He was choosing his words carefully, as he knew he was also speaking to someone who knew Spanish. "Last night, Maria and I had the pleasure of dining with our new resident Snr. George Morton and his family." Vincente raised his right arm in George's direction just to make sure everyone knew who he was talking about. George, on hearing his name, nodded nervously to acknowledge the room full of eyes now piercing through to the back of his skull.

Alex maneuvered herself to stand next to her dad just in case he wanted an interpreter. George did not say anything, but appreciated the gesture.

"At dinner we talked of many things, but one subject was the cooking of our national dish - paella." Vincente paused again for this to sink in. "It seems my friend George here, according to his children, cooks a great paella - but my friends... ," another pause to ensure they all know he was their friend, "... the debate focused on the ingredients of our national dish. We all know it can be made in many different ways, but always with local ingredients." Vincente was on top form. You could hear a pin drop. "Now, George here prefers to use the tourist's version, seafood and chicken." A soft murmur suddenly developed. Whispers of shock and disbelief filled the room. Vincente stayed expressionless, trying to remain as neutral as possible, but Alex and Maria especially, could tell he was working the crowd.

"So, we came to a decision... over a few brandies I agreed..." and his 'gentle-giant' smile came into play, and the whole room breathed a sigh of relief and laughed with him. "...we would have a 'cook-off' this morning." Everyone clapped and started talking. "I know it is short notice..." Vincente raised his voice to bring everyone back to his attention. . "but it seems George has found his ingredients from somewhere, or someone, so we have prepared two large helpings which we want you to judge in a few moments. Thank you."

More applause and the chattering grew louder with anticipation.

Vincente moved back to where George and Alex were still standing. "Well, George, did I say that fairly?"

But before George could answer, Alex replied on his behalf. "Si, you said it all OK, thank you... now let's get this over with."

The two men returned to the kitchen to finish their respective masterpieces. Alex looked around the room and joined Carlos and his friends. "So it's a friendly fight." Carlos asked cheerfully, accepting another glass of wine Angel was offering from a large tray. Alex took one as well.

"Free wine Angel?" she enquired. Angel smiled. "Si. Maria thought it... appropriate," and winked before moving on.

"What did she mean by that?" Carlos asked with interest, but Alex was on the look-out for Maria. She spied her in the corner. She also was carrying a tray of red and white wine and handing it out *free gratis*.

"What's with all the free wine Maria?" Alex asked touching her arm. "Hello Alex. Chris has been helping. He is really good behind the bar," she said, avoiding Alex's question.

Alex was about to press her further when another loud cheer went up in the room.

The smell of paella filled the bar quickly and everyone surged forward to see what was being brought out from the kitchen.

George and Vincente each carried a six litre catering cooking pot into which their respective dishes had been placed, after being prepared in a large paella pan, which would not have been so convenient to serve from on the bar.

"OK, this is what we will do. Everyone take a portion first from one of us, then come back for the other one, OK... come and get it." Vincente announced.

Queuing was not the order of the day. Most people however gathered around Vincente's end of the bar, probably out of respect for the Mayor, but more to do with preferring the locally made recipe than George's concoction.

George however did have seven eager customers, and his face lit up on seeing Carlos. "Carlos, glad you could make it. Hope it is worth the trip." George said rather unconvincingly.

"Dad!" Alex raised her voice "Stop worrying and enjoy it. It's not over until the fat lady sings, that's what you always told us."

George smiled and was glad they were here. "Thank you for your confidence. . all of you. Now tuck in, I think there is a lot to finish."

"Save me some." Maria said, appearing next to Alex and putting her arm around her.

"It smells wonderful," she said loudly, so others waiting for Vincente's serving could hear her.

Several moved over and took a plate for George to fill. Now, whether this was because Vincente was slow to serve everyone, or because Maria, the patron and giver of free wine was endorsing George, no one could tell, but Alex liked to think it was the latter.

Gradually, as the afternoon wore on, the mood became more congenial. Others started to sample both dishes on offer, and expressions such as *muy rica* and *la mejor de todos*, could be heard throughout the room. Eventually all the food was eaten, and the only two people to have gone without were George and Vincente. People started to drift off home by four o'clock, well past siesta, but as it was Sunday no one would be put out too much.

Vincente suddenly realised everyone was leaving, but no voting had taken place. "What about the vote? What do you think?" He called out to no one in particular. They came and shook his hand. "Thanks Vincente." or "Thank you Senor

Mayor. Very good lunch, and for the wine." This was repeated several times, not only to Vincente, but also to George. Alex was on hand to translate when needed, but George could see from the expressions on people's faces they had enjoyed the day.

Vincente came over to George's table where he was sitting with Carlos and his wife and friends, plus his children. He stood, hands on hips, towering over the table. "Well," he said, and smiled, "I guess we can call that a draw, yes." Everybody not only laughed, but breathed a sigh of relief. George rose to his feet and shook Vincente's hand.

"It was..." George searched for the right words... "an honor to work with you." Vincente just shrugged as if it was of no consequence, but inwardly he told himself it was not over, not yet... he would have the last word on the subject. Vincente was about to elaborate on his thoughts for a rematch when the kitchen door swung open, but no one could be seen standing there. Little Jorge appeared from behind the end of the bar standing in his pajamas, looking very sleepy. "I'm hungry Mama. What's for lunch?"

Chapter 5. July

George decided it was time to revisit the music festival at Cáceres, in western Spain. An annual event organized by WOMAD, a UK organization promoting World Music, who put on festivals in many countries. George and Aimee had visited Cáceres every year for the last six years, where they delighted in discovering new artists from all over the World.

This particular festival has several attractions. It is set in the magnificent medieval old town in and around its many plazas and squares, and all the events are free. The fortified town was built on several levels, and every year George and Aimee found new areas to explore and new bars and restaurants to discover.

George reflected on the times they had visited the festival. Over the years they had made friends with many other regular visitors from home and abroad, as well as vendors selling jewellery, clothing, carvings, musical instruments and of course CDs.

The 'stalls' had an appearance of nomadic tents, and were colorful and approachable, while nearby, continuing the theme, were many food and drink sellers offering freshly made pizzas, Moroccan kebabs and spicy curry, washed down with local cider, beer or wine.

How would it feel to go back alone? George asked himself. The friends they had made there saw them once a year and did not know of the circumstances of the past three years. They were just another couple who had not returned. Forgotten in time to become a distant memory.

George was not sure he wanted that. The people they had met and befriended needed to know what had happened to his life. Aimee's death. The move to Spain.

The problem was the festival is held during the 3rd week in July. Today was the 2nd July and the hotel they always stayed at would surely be full. George sat at the computer and checked his Outlook history folders under 'WOMAD

Spain'. He clicked on the sub-folder 'Hotels', and there it was - Hotel Alfonso XII. He sent a short and somewhat begging email, asking if any accommodation was available for two or three nights over the festival period, or could they recommend any other hotel that may help.

'Muchas gracias, George and Aimee Morton'.

'No,' he sighed, and corrected the sign-off - *George Morton*.

It would be several hours, if not the next day, before he would have a reply as only one of the receptionists spoke and wrote English. George thought about looking for other accommodation, but decided that if fate dictated he would go, then it would only be to the Hotel Alfonso XII. There was always next year and many other places to visit in the meantime.

He poured a beer and sat on the patio lounger under the sunshade. It was Sunday and nothing was stirring in the small town. The church bell struck 11 o'clock, calling its flock to Mass.

He closed his eyes and returned to Cáceres, and imagined the two of them running up the old cobbled steps to the Plaza San Jorge to buy crepes and beer, with the sounds of new and exotic music being carried in the warm breeze.

George's interest in world music came about almost like an epiphany. He and Aimee shared some musical interests. They had both enjoyed listing to the greats like Ella, Sinatra, Basie, Charlie Parker and Miles Davies, and the 'songbooks' of the 50's and 60's. All legends, and all excellent in their time. Then one day he was listening to JazzFM radio in London. This music station had gone through many changes over the years trying to adapt to listeners' demands, and trying to satisfy the entire 'genre' that makes jazz what it is. They eventually failed in this task, resorting to 'East Coast' easy listening 'smooth jazz'. *More suited to the elevator,* thought George. Therefore, he was surprised when one Saturday evening a forward thinking presenter named David Freeman played an hour of *'World Music/World Jazz'.*

This program was unusual in one major way - he played nothing from the USA. The thinking behind this unique program was that the USA had, and still has, too much of an influence on what is played on mainstream radio. Be it Jazz, Rock, Pop, it is still predominately USA driven, and far too retrospective - too many stations insist we want to hear nothing but *'old favorites'*, and neglect new bands and musicians, especially if they are not known in the UK.

Not everyone agreed with his thinking, including some of his own colleagues at JazzFM, but they, and everyone else, were missing the point. Freeman wanted to bring some of the world's most beautiful and exciting music to a new audience - an audience like George, who was ignorant of other 'genres' beyond the bounds of commercially controlled local radio.

This had been the turning point for George - his epiphany.

He was fascinated by what he was hearing for the first time. Bands and artists from around the world, but never played on mainstream radio. He discovered in a matter of weeks, Jan Garbarek from Norway, Abdulla Ibrahim from South Africa, Rabih Abou-Khalil from the Lebanon, and many, many others. These people, in most cases, had been around for a long time and had built a successful international career, but George could not understand how he had never heard of them. He researched all the names he could find, and his CD collection (before iTunes) changed almost overnight.

Aimee, also, was eventually drawn into the new music that was played in their house, and car, and at every opportunity.

What George could not know however was the kind of following any of these musicians had in the UK. One day he saw Rabih Abou-Khalil was playing at the Barbican in London. They bought tickets, and still not knowing what to expect, took the train to London. They could not believe what they experienced that night. The Barbican was full to capacity - *'where had all these people come from'* they kept asking themselves. Thousands of people coming together to see a Middle Eastern band he and Aimee had only heard of a few weeks earlier. It was eventually obvious why they had come. Rabih himself was a most engaging musician. He played the oud, and was an excellent orator and leader of musicians. This particular band consisted of over twelve international musicians playing drums, French horns, saxophone, tuba, flute, harmonica, tabla, violin and double bass. The sound of Middle Eastern fused with western influences was, and still is, so intoxicating.

They were hooked. More and more concerts followed, and then, another way to see, and experience new artists was discovered. The Music Festival.

After much research the Brecon Jazz Festival in South Wales was selected. This was more to do with location and timing than anything else, but as it turned out it was one of the best decisions' they had made. More discoveries were made and treasured; Richard Bona from Cameroon, and Heroni, originally from Japan, were among some of the new artists they came to love and follow.

Bona was one of the few exceptions George was happy to include in his collection. Since his 'conversion' to World Music, his preferred artists had predominately been instrumentalists. Bona sung only in his native tongue - a most beautiful, almost angelic sound. His band was also exceptional, playing great instrumentals as well. The lineup of electric keyboard, soprano saxophone, guitar and horns, with Bona on bass guitar, was a tight-knit sound of funk-jazz and fusion. Some of what is known today as Nu-jazz.

The solo performer, or band, playing without vocals, was in George's opinion the single most enjoyable sound to be heard. He never tires of hearing soprano saxophonist Jan Garbarek or pianist Keith Jarrett, or multi talented all-rounder Gilad Atzmon.

"It takes far more concentration to listen to instrumentals than it does to a singer, thereby appreciating every sound of every instrument you are listening to - and furthermore, it is the listening, not the hearing that is important in appreciating music."

This little sermon was the basis for many a debate in the Morton household when his children visited. But with Christopher advocating 'rap' and 'new soul' as the only music worth listening to (which was odd considering his liking for musicals), and Bonnie turning her nose up at anything that wasn't Britney, Lady GaGa, or Adele, George was not getting any converts. Alex stayed neutral. She really did not have a set view on music. It was one of those things that she was just not passionate about – *"there are too many other things in the world to worry about than music,"* was her contribution to the debate over dinner. George would watch and listen to the conversation to see who could put forward a counter argument - but it never really materialized. He would say to Aimee after they were alone, "No one seems to have a passion for anything anymore."

"Are you becoming a grumpy old man?" she would taunt him. And whisper in his ear, "I still have a passion for something." Taking his hand and leading him upstairs.

George brushed away a tear, and got up to refresh the now warm beer he had left in the sun, and put on a Sigur Ros CD.

Over the years the genre had opened up to encompass electronic music and chill-out sounds prompted on the excellent ChillFM station. George now searches for new artists; he does not wait to hear them on radio anymore. The use of computer based sites like LastFM and Spotify allow endless opportunities to search and discover. And most, still to this day, can be attributed to the 'World Music' program which David Freeman happen to play one Saturday night when George just happened to be listening, all those years ago.

He was about to return to the patio when the email notification bell sounded on the PC. It was a reply from the hotel in Cáceres.

Hola Snr. Morton

We are pleased to hear from you and to inform you we have a room available, but only one twin bedroom. It is only available for one night on Saturday 23rd

Please let me know very soon. Price is still same as before Euro49.00

Regards Sophia
Hotel Alfonso XII

George was pleased about the room, but one night only.

Still, better than nothing he conceded. He sent a reply and accepted the booking. He would have a whole day on the Saturday, and could enjoy the Sunday closing parade and festival, so not all was lost. He did not mention he would be alone as the booking was for the room, and not how many people occupy it.

He leaned back in the office chair and listened to the haunting, ambient sounds of Sigur Ros, and closed his eyes and imagined he was dancing with Aimee, but when she turned he saw Maria's face. He opened his eyes and sat up. "Maria," he whispered. "Of course, she would love Cáceres. A break will do her good. Angel and Vincente can cope for one weekend."

He looked at the photo gallery of Aimee on the screensaver. "I still love you my dear, but Cáceres will not be the same alone."

George was keen to ask Maria about Cáceres, but needed to approach the subject carefully. Vincente would surely object, especially with only one room available. Could he persuade her that sleeping in a twin room was perfectly fine and proper? He would be a perfect gentleman. George thought about that again. It would be difficult, but for one night - who knows what might happen. The music, the sangria, the stars - they might get swept away on a sea of romance and find that one single bed is just as comfortable. . .

George snapped out of his thoughts. The telephone was ringing.

"Hola," he grunted.

"George is that you?" It was Maria.

"Sorry Maria. I not did mean to sound grumpy. I thought you would be at church."

"George, it is three in the afternoon. More the time for a siesta."

"Is that an invitation?" George smiled.

"George, behave. It sounds as if you have been sleeping already - or drinking - are you OK?"

George hesitated - was it the right time to ask her about Cáceres?

"Maria, I need to ask you something. How do you feel..."

Maria interrupted with some urgency in her voice. "George, I am sorry but I must tell you first.... " There was silence.

"Maria, are you there, what's happened?"

"It's Papa. He has gone again."

George was almost relieved. He was expecting *'little Jorge is unwell'*. *'George, can you help me in the bar tonight?'* or even *'George can you take me away from all this.'* But to hear Vincente had gone AWOL again was perfect.

"Maria, he always comes back, eventually. What can I do?"

"I do not know really George. I just want to know where he goes. You heard him say its just business. If it is business why can he not tell me?"

George could hear the concern in her voice, coupled with anger at her dad for not confiding in his daughter.

"Would you like to come over? Or I can come to you. Have a drink and a quiet night in."

"That would be nice George."

"OK good." He took the initiative. "You and Jorge come to supper then. I want to talk to you anyway, and we can see what can be done about your Papa."

"That sounds lovely. You are a good friend George. Around seven o'clock OK?"

"Perfect, see you then."

Good friend! What did she mean "Good friend". Good friends do not go away together and stay in one room. Good friends do not hold hands under the table like the time she came to dinner last month, with his children and Vincente.

***

Two days previously, or to be precise, an hour before sunrise on the Friday morning, Vincente woke up. He did not need an alarm clock; his body clock knew exactly what time to get up. After all, he had been doing it for many years. He slipped on grey tracksuit trousers and a navy blue sweatshirt - it might be July but it was still chilly at that time of morning, and there was no heating on in the house.

He gathered his keys and some change off the dresser, and pulled out a black holdall from under the bed he had packed earlier. He picked up his trainers, and took one last look around the room before he opened the door. He nearly let out a scream at what he saw. Jorge was standing directly in front of him. Was he staring at him, or into space? Vincente could not make out in the dim light of the hallway. He waved his hand in front of Jorge's eyes. No response. He quickly tried to assess the situation. If Maria came out of her room and saw her father standing there dressed, and holding a case she would. ., well, Vincente did not want to contemplate that. He took Jorge gently by the right arm and turned him towards his bedroom at the end of the hallway. "Jorge. Back to bed - there's a good boy," he whispered in the boy's ear. To his surprise, and relief, the boy started walking slowly, still staring upwards, but walking towards his room.

Now, Vincente was not sure what to do next. Should he see him to his bed or leave him to make his own way back. He decided to leave him and headed for the stairs, after all, he seemed to know where he was going. He descended the wooden stairs, ensuring he missed the creaking ones. He knew these off by heart and had never ever made a sound as he reached the ground floor. As always he stopped to listen just to make sure all was as it should be. Then he heard it. The stairs creaking, and creaking. He turned around to see Jorge on the third from bottom step, still staring upwards, just a few inches from Vincente's face.

He had never known the boy to sleepwalk. Maria had never mentioned it and as far as he knew, there was no history of it in the family. Why would he start now? He did wet the bed when he was very young, but that was after his father had died, and the doctors said it was a reaction to the trauma of losing his dad. It did not last long - six months or so. But never sleep walking.

He felt like picking the boy up and bundling him into the Dodge, but that was definitely not a good idea. "Jorge, what do I do with you?" he whispered. Vincente gently put the holdall on the floor and maneuvered the boy until he had turned 180degrees. He thought of carrying him upstairs but that might wake him, and start him to panic. Then the whole house would be awake, and Vincente's little escapade would be discovered.

"Come, Jorge, come with Grandpa," and taking his hand led the boy back upstairs. The floorboards creaked but Vincente had to chance that Maria did not hear them. That was where he made his mistake - mothers all over the world know when their offspring cough, sneeze or get up to go to the bathroom or go downstairs to get a glass of water. Maria was no exception. Since the bed-wetting episode, she knew when Jorge was in need of something. Her motherly instincts now detected a noise on the stairs, and assumed someone was either going down stairs, or coming back upstairs. Now she was awake she had to get up to check. Vincente and the boy were just one yard from the boy's room when he heard Maria's door start to open. He did what he did not what to do and picked the boy up around the waist and opened the bedroom door, and was inside within three seconds.

By now Jorge was semi-conscious and crying out for his mother. The only light was the moon seeping through the open window between the slightly parted curtains. Vincente put the boy on the bed and covered him with the quilt. "Hush my lovely boy - sleep". Vincente straddled the single bed in one bound and lay prostrate on the floor between the wall and the bed. Instinctively he reached up and pulled the curtains so they met, causing a shadow to cover him, and darken the room. He had just enough time to bring his arm down to his side when Maria opened the door. The light from the hallway lit the room enough for her to see Jorge without turning on the bedroom light.

"Jorge my darling - have you had a bad dream. What is it?" She was now sitting on the edge of the bed with her arm around her son. Without letting him see, she slid her right hand under the quilt to check for any wet. Relieved, she looked at Jorge again. "What was it my little one?"

Jorge blinked, and blinked again - "Grandpa," he whispered.

Vincente closed his eyes and held his breath.

"Grandpa?" Maria replied. "What about him?" she said, looking inquisitive.

"He, he... took me to bed..."

Maria smiled. "Yes my love, he put you to bed last night and he is asleep as well. Now you lie down and close your eyes and go back to sleep, OK?" She kissed him on the forehead and walked towards the door, turning once to look at her son again as she backed out the door.

Vincente let out a breath of air slowly and as quietly as possible. He now had to get out of Jorge's room, retrieve his holdall and get back to his room. He could not possibly go now. If he were found to be missing Maria would add two and two and realize Jorge may have in fact seen him sneaking out. He could still have had a good few days away, but he could not face another inquisition on his return. He lay on the floor for another twenty minutes until he was sure Jorge was asleep, then slowly got to his feet and tip-toped to the door. He retrieved his holdall and went back to his room.

He sat on his bed and wrote a text. *'Will be one day late. V xx'*

***

Maria and Jorge arrived soon after 6.30pm. "He could not wait George. He wants to play on the computer again. Is that OK with you?"

Maria looked tired. Not just from the walk to the house, but physically tired. If Vincente knew what effect his secrecy had on Maria, surely he would be more honest with her. George gave a reassuring smile. "Of course my favorite nine year old can play." And he lifted Jorge above his head until he could reach the ceiling with outstretched arms.

"George, careful please." Maria insisted. George brought the boy down to earth and sat him at the computer. "What's it to be Jorge?" Jorge looked at his mother for help. Maria gave a faint smile. "I think George knows which one by now."

The boy let out an excited cry. "Mario, Mario, Mario," he repeated.

"Ah, yes." George said thoughtfully, "I think I have that one, unless someone has taken it," and George pretended to look in all the compartments and drawers under the desk.

Jorge however was not to be outdone, and thought he knew exactly where it was.

He reached under the desk and pressed a button. The desk moved slowly away from him, and George, who was on both knees, stared in astonishment at first, and then in horror.

Maria was not sure what was going on but thought it was part of the game. George reached under the desk and pressed the button again, and the desk retracted to its original position within a few seconds.

"What made it do that, George?" Maria asked, still not sure what had happened.

"Ah, it's nothing my dear, just part of the equipment. I did not know he knew how to work it himself." George said, trying to defuse the incident. "Come outside and have a drink while the sun is still up."

The game was in fact already setup, as George knew exactly what the boy would ask for. He pressed play and the screen lit up, as did Jorge's face.

Maria, bemused, patted Jorge and said to have fun, adding. "You know where I am if you want anything." Jorge nodded without taking his eyes off the screen.

George went to the kitchen and poured two glasses of white wine. "How on earth did he know about that button?" He kept asking himself. He was sure no one had ever seen him open the safe, let alone know one was there. Senora Torres had strict instructions not to go in there, and his own children knew nothing of it.

Maria came over and kissed him on the cheek. "What was that for?" asked George.

"For being so good to Jorge," she replied

He leaned closer to Maria and whispered, "Can I be good to you as well now?" Sliding his hand along her hips.

"George behave, not now," she was serious. George raised his hands in surrender. "Sorry." He sounded hurt. "I forgot we are just friends."

"Si, we are friends, but nothing else in front of Jorge. It may confuse him."

"Confuse him!" George checked himself and bit his lip.

"We have a word for that back home," he said under his breath, but Maria picked up on it.

"I thought this was your home."

They looked at each other in silence. "I'm sorry." George eventually said. "I thought, hoped, we were more than friends," he said, looking as humble as he could.

Maria sighed and touched his check with those long perfect fingers. Eyes met eyes. She leaned forward and kissed George on the lips. A long, but not heavy kiss. The kind of kiss that is remembered for a long time, as first kisses are. A warm and tender loving kiss.

"We have a word for that as well," he whispered.

"What is that?" she whispered back.

"Bloody marvelous," he sighed, he eyes swelling with emotion.

"That is two words I think," she teased, not taking her eyes off him, which was just as well, as she saw in George's eye the reflection of the room behind her, and an arm raised in the air holding a triumphant 'thumbs up'. Maria smiled a warm gratifying smile that only she knew why. George smiled as well, but out of sheer pleasure.

"I think we need to go outside before we get an audience," she whispered. "And you did promise dinner."

George picked up the glasses and they went on to the patio where George opened up the barbeque and turned on the gas. Within half an hour they were eating spicy chicken legs, corn on the cob, sausage and salad. As soon as he was able, Jorge rushed back to the computer.

"You haven't mentioned Vincente yet." George enquired when they were alone.

Maria sighed deeply. "I am too cross to talk about him. How could he keep doing this to us? Going off without a word. Not phoning or leaving a message with anyone." She paused for breath. George listened with a smile on his face.

"Why are you smiling?" she asked. She held up a hand. "No, do not answer that - I know what I sound like." Her eyes' swelled with tears and she could hold it in no longer. "I don't want to make a fuss in front of Jorge, but it's not fair. He has this other, secret life and expects everything to be normal when he gets back. What about my life, George? When do I start to have one again?" She was looking at George in earnest for answers.

"Do you have *any* idea where he goes?"

"No, not exactly. He could go anywhere." She shrugged.

"You must have some idea after all this time - what friends does he have? Family – anyone?"

Maria hesitated. "What is it, Maria? What do you know?"

"My mother and her family originally came from the North, where I was born."

"OK, that's a start. Where from?"

"The North, George." emphasizing the North.

"Yes, you said, but can you be more specific. Where from?

Maria sighed. "You don't understand George." Maria lowered her voice and looked around to see if anyone was listening. Of course, there was not, and Jorge was too far away and engrossed in his computer game.

"Maria, what is it? We are alone."

"My mother was from Pamplona. We lived there until she died when I was sixteen, that's when we came down here, to start a new life."

She looked at George for understanding but he still said nothing. Her eyes looked tired and anxious.

"During the time we lived there Papa got to understand the Basque people and what they had been striving for."

"So," George interrupted, "you think he is... was, a sympathizer?"

She shifted on the chair and looked down to the floor.

"Ok, so he had sympathy, err... an understanding of the Basque movement. There is nothing wrong in that, is there. You are half Basque aren't you?"

Maria nodded without speaking. "Si, of course, but I think he may be visiting some of his friends who were active in the old days, in ETA, which is very different. I have no evidence, just a... ," she was lost for the right word.

"Gut feeling." George helped out.

"Si, gut feeling George. You do understand don't you?" She held his hand and squeezed hard.

He lifted her head. "Maria, the short time I've known Vincente I have never thought him a political animal. He is stubborn, argumentative, opinionated, proud, strong willed, and not a very good father... but a political terrorist?"

Maria looked puzzled but could not find the right English words. "I did not say he is a terrorist," she snapped.

"I understand, I am sorry, and I know you are concerned Maria, but I think the political connection is..." now he could not find the right words. "...is... just wrong."

They sat in silence for a while. "Would you like a coffee?"

"Si gracias"

"...and perhaps a brandy."

"No, George, thank you. I have to think clearly, and I have Jorge to take home."

"You can always stay here," he suggested. "I have plenty of rooms," he added quickly in case she got the wrong idea, which he hoped she would, had they been alone.

She smiled at last. "Thank you George. I know."

George made coffee and took Jorge another orange juice.

"He's really doing well with the game. I will have to get some more."

"I am glad you like him, George. He likes you to, he says so."

George knelt beside her and brushed her beautiful black hair away from her eyes. "Thank you for listening George." She leaned forward and kissed him again on the lips. "That's what friends are for," he said touching her face gently, wiping a stray tear away.

He got to his feet and pulled her up from the dining chair, and they sat on the more comfortable sofa in the lounge.

"I have two... no, three things to say to you, Maria." She looked at him with interest. He took her hands in his again. She leaned back a little, pre-empting what he might say and whispering his name in an inquiring sort of way.

"George, what are you...?" But before she could say another word, a loud scream of delight filled the room.

"Si. Si, Si Si gané gané, Mama, Yo gane."

George and Maria hurried to see what all the excitement was about. "He won the game again. I will have to find a more difficult one I think." George declared.

"Si that is what he says."

"*Well done, bravo!*" and she kissed Jorge on the head.

Jorge turned to George and said slowly in English, "I won, George."

George knelt down to look the boy in the face. "You did win young man. Congratulations. Do you want another game or watch a film?" George asked in English, hoping he would understand.

Jorge turned to his mother for help, but she felt the rhythm of the evening had been broken and decided it was time to leave.

"No no, not yet, please please Mama." Jorge begged.

George did not need a translation. "Maria it's still early. Let him watch a film and let us talk for a while more. Please."

Maria looked at George, and then at Jorge who was smiling the widest smile. "OK, but only half an hour," which she translated to make sure Jorge understood.

"Thank you, Mama thank you, I love you." Jorge repeated excitedly.

George took out the DVD of Shrek. "It's in English but it should keep him amused."

"He knows the film so I think he can follow." Maria said, and they walked back over to the sofa and sat down next to each other.

"I remember you had three things to say, George."

"Three?" George looked puzzled.... "I am sure it will come to me soon, but I do know I want to say this." He paused, not for effect but to see that Maria was in fact listening and following him. Satisfied, he continued.

"Firstly, I will try and find out where Vincente goes, I promise." Maria's face brightened. "Oh, George, how?"

"I will tell you the details when I have them, but I think I know how to do it without Vincente being suspicious." He paused, this time for effect. She squeezed his hand tighter. He did not resist.

"So, what else do you need to tell me?"

"Ask you, Maria, not tell you."

"OK, ask me, George."

He took a deep breath. "Did I ever mention how Aimee and I went to the Cáceres music festival each year?"

Maria looked thoughtful. "I think you did mention it once."

"Well, I was thinking of going again later this month."

"That's good, George. You should go." Maria said, trying her best to sound positive, but instead sounding a little anxious.

"Well, I was wondering if you would like to come with me," and before she had a chance to answer he continued with"... but there are a couple of considerations err, points to... err, talk over."

Maria frowned. "What are the points, George?"

"Well, because I have only just thought of going, I could only book for one night. It is at the same hotel I always use, a lovely hotel, Alfonso XII, very close to the action.." Maria put a hand on his shoulder. George paused. "George, slow down. I cannot keep up with you always."

"Sorry. I was trying to say in my clumsy way, I could only get one room." He looked her straight in the eyes - those beautiful green eyes. "She wasn't going for it," he kept repeating to himself.

Maria looked away towards Jorge watching Shrek, and knew he would be disappointed very soon as they must go. It was still a school week after all, even if it was the last one before the summer holidays; end of term meetings, end of terms plays, end of term presents to buy. It was going to be a hectic week. And when did she last have a few days away?

Two years ago visiting relatives in Pamplona, and trying to avoid comments like, "So, Maria when are you getting married again?" and "little Jorge needs a father", and "Vincente won't be around forever".

Answers: *'When I decide I want to.' 'He's doing fine so far,'* and *'He is hardly here anyway.'*

Well, those were the replies she actually wanted to say,

but being a good niece she always gave the answers they wanted to hear, avoiding any unnecessary arguments.

George thought he had made a terrible mistake and misjudged her. She had not spoken for several minutes. "Maria, are you OK?"

She turned to him and smiled. George's heart pounded. "Si, George," she said quietly.

"Yes, you are OK, or yes you want to come?"

She laughed out loud. "Sorry, George, yes to both," and kissed him tenderly on the lips.

Jorge turned around to see what the noise was about, looking unhappy at the interruption.

Maria called him over. "Jorge, come quickly, I have some news." Jorge ran over and sat on his mother's lap. *"What news Mama?"*

"How would you like to go to a music festival in Cáceres with George and me?"

"Si, Si a holiday..."

"Well not a long one, just one night, but it will be an adventure."

George was listening carefully, but was getting mixed signals which he could not translate entirely.

"Maria," he interrupted with a tone of caution, "why is Jorge sounding excited?"

"Ah, he is happy about the music festival," she replied smiling, and before George could reply, she stood up and picked the boy up.

"We really must go now George, it is the last week of school and lots to do. Say thank you to George for dinner and the film."

"Thank you, George." He managed in good English.

"You are welcome young man," and turned back to Maria. "But Maria, what do you mean, *he's* happy about the music festival. Are you saying you want to bring him as well?"

"Of course, George - I must have a chaperone - especially as we are all in one room."

She leaned over and kissed George goodbye. "Come and have coffee tomorrow and we can talk again. I want to hear what you have planned for Papa."

She seemed a different person - ten times happier than an hour ago.

"At least let me walk you home."

"No. It is fine, really. Good night, George, and thank you for dinner."

George was left wondering whether to be elated or disappointed with her answer.

Little Jorge waved as they walked down the road, and George could swear Maria was almost skipping.

***

The Dodge pulled into the gravel driveway at 9.30am on Saturday 3rd July. At the same time the door opened to the impressive villa, and Rosanna Maria stepped out to greet Vincente. They embraced and kissed. "You are a naughty boy. Keeping me waiting a whole day."

"Then let's go in and make up for lost time." Vincente replied, with his devilish smile.

***

The following day George walked into town. It was nearly 1.30, much later than he had intended, but he had been up for several hours the previous evening with a few brandies, working on a plan and sending e-mails.

He entered the bar and saw Maria look up from serving a customer in the far corner and smiled at him, then looked at her watch as if to say *'where have you been?'*

Angel was behind the counter and gave a huge grin on seeing George.

"Hola, Angel, buenos días," adding, "you look happy." Although he knew she did not understand him.

"Buenos días, George," she replied, still grinning madly.

"Hola, George." Maria greeted him joining them at the counter. "How are you?"

"I'm fine, but what's up with her?"

Maria waved Angel off. "Go and do some work and stop staring." Angel walked away whistling a tune George could not make out.

"You told her didn't you, about Cáceres?"

Maria blushed ever so slightly, but with her Spanish complexion it was not easy to spot. She bit her lower lip.

"Sorry, George, but we tell each other everything."

"Wow... I must remember that," and adding, "do you mean everything?"

Maria looked at George for a moment. "He is handsome," she thought, "and nicely tanned now he's been here a few months. Intelligent; good with Jorge; good cook; gets on with Vincente, Christ, I'm ticking boxes..."

Maria blinked once. "Si, everything, but do not worry George," she leaned over and whispered in his ear, *"not until it has happened."*

George looked unconvinced and confused. Is she saying something will happen between them? Certainly not in Cáceres with her chaperone.

They were two friends sitting at the bar having a private conversation. She leans over and whispers in his ear. Something very personal. Something sensual. Something she should NOT be saying to him. *She should be saying it to ME.*

Ricardo Sanchez sat unnoticed in the corner, having just finished lunch. Unnoticed that was by Maria. He has been coming in two or three times a week for over a year now, and she had not even had a conversation with him. True, he had tried on several occasions to talk to her.

"Hola, my name is Ricardo."
"Hola, Maria. How are you today?"
"Hola, Maria. Can I buy you a drink?"
"Hola, Maria. Can we go out together?"
"Hola. Maria. Will you marry me?"

In truth he did not get past *my name is Ricardo*, but now felt content to admire her from afar. That was until four months ago. Ricardo had been in the cafe the morning George and Christopher had come in that first time, with no money. He had recognized George from the solicitor's office where he worked. His boss had carried out the procedure of sale, when George had come in last November to sign the papers. In January when Vincente was made Mayor, after the old mayor died suddenly of a heart attack, Ricardo sought favor, and told him of the new owner, and the work that was being carried out by 'imported labor' at the old farmhouse.

Vincente seemed not to care too much, or at least gave

that impression to Ricardo. He also did not encourage his support or his undeclared love for Maria. Vincente was sure his daughter could do better than a solicitor's clerk, or stay unmarried forever, which he would prefer. Ricardo now watched and waited for a new opportunity.

"Go and sit down and I will get us some coffee." Maria suggested to George. She returned shortly with two coffees and some tortilla. "I thought you may not have had breakfast."

"That is very kind but you must let me pay this time." - the laughing resonated around the bar and everyone looked at the couple. Especially Ricardo.

"So, George, about last night."

George nearly choked. Looking around however, he realised no one actually understood English. "Can you keep your voice down just in case you are misunderstood," he whispered.

Maria looked genuinely hurt. "George, look at me." He turned back to meet her eyes.

"George, this is a small town so whatever we say or do, the very fact we are talking together, will have tongues wiggling."

"Wagging. Not wiggling, that's something different."

"Thank you, George. Wagging. I remember that."

"Anyway, you don't mind that?" George asked seriously.

She reached out and took his hand. "No, I do not. Do you?"

"Not in the least," he said, staring into her beautiful emerald eyes.

The few customers, if they did notice, just carried on eating or drinking or reading the morning papers, except one.

"So, George, about last night."

They smiled and shared the joke again, and George went over the plans for Cáceres. The date, the hotel and what to expect. "Jorge will love it. There is a children's parade on the Sunday morning we can go to before heading back. The kids make their own costumes during the festival, but I am sure we can get him in on Saturday if he wants to go." George explained enthusiastically.

"I think we will have to wait and see, George. He can be insecure on his own sometimes, but it sounds a lovely idea," Maria agreed.

George raised the question of Vincente. "What will Vincente do... ?" but before he could finish the sentence Maria came back with a sharp reply.

"I do not care, George," she said, raising her voice, which made George feel uncomfortable.

"He leaves me and Jorge for weeks at a time whenever he feels like it and never explains where he has been - no George, I do not care what he will say. I deserve a break."

"Of course you do. I was wondering what he will *do* to *me* when he finds out." He said half smiling.

"George, we are adults are we not. We can both stand up to my Papa, no?" she said slightly unconvincingly, but smiling. "But tell me George, you said you had a plan for finding out where he goes to."

The previous evening George had contacted his old friend in the security business. He had arranged for George to receive, on loan, a vehicle tracking system, or as known in the trade, an Asset Tracker.

He explained to Maria that he would need to 'plant' an electronic device on the Dodge near to the time when he was preparing for another 'trip'. They could then follow him at short notice, tracking the vehicle on a laptop or iPhone.

Maria looked impressed. "You arranged this yesterday? You are wonderful. Will it work?"

"Yes, to all three," and they laughed together again.

"But to be serious, Maria, if he finds out about the tracker we are in a lot of trouble."

"Do not worry." She reassured George, "It is a wonderful idea." And leaned over and kissed him on the cheek. "Thank you George."

Just then a customer ran out of the bar, almost knocking into George's chair.

Angel came out shouting after him. *"Maria he has not paid."*

"It's OK Angel. Its only Ricardo, it must be an emergency. Make a note will you."

On the following Thursday Vincente returned, and life went on as normal. In fact, too normal Vincente thought. Maria had not chastised him or quizzed him this time. Angel and Jorge were of course pleased to see him, but Maria just carried on as if nothing was wrong. Well, as far as Vincente was concerned nothing was wrong. He had always believed what he did was his own affair. Nobody got hurt (maybe cross, but not hurt) and he always came home. So what was wrong this time? A few days had passed and he was still troubled by Maria's reaction, so one mid-morning he drove up the hill to see George.

"Hola, George, how are you? Is that coffee I can smell my friend?"

Vincente walked on in. "Do come in Vincente. You are in a good mood today. What brings you here?"

"Oh, I just wanted to see how you are. It has been some time since I last saw you George. How is the family?"

"That may have something to do with you being away again for a week or so, and thank you, they are all fine."

George made some fresh coffee and took it to the patio while Vincente was inspecting the contents of the fridge. George had become used to this, and in a strange way almost thought of it as a compliment. He and Vincente had got to know each other over the past months, and one thing they shared was a passion for food.

"You must buy more chorizo, George," he called out.

George ignored this, and waited for Vincente to join him, which he did carrying a plate of bread, Comte cheese and gherkins. "Glad I have something you like, Vincente," George said sarcastically.

"You are getting better with the fridge. You are starting to think Spanish George," and commenced to devour some of the cheese.

"The cheese is in fact French, as you well know."

"Si, but I mean you are building up a good stock cupboard for someone who lives alone."

Vincente sat quietly eating most of the tapas, making George a little uncomfortable.

"I think I have something you like as well, George." He eventually said with a grin. Now George was uneasy. "What is that?" he replied, sounding as calm as he could, reaching for the last of the cheese.

"You and Maria seem to get on well, George. Are you just friends?"

This was not a conversation George was expecting. His mind was racing. Has Maria said something about Cáceres? Has she said she likes me more than just a friend? How should he react? "Yes we are friends. You and Maria were the first to welcome me here, and I hope we are friends too, Vincente," George said, putting the onus back on him.

Vincente sipped coffee and looked as if he had the troubles of the world on his shoulders. This larger than life Spaniard with thick shoulder length hair and rugged features looked suddenly vulnerable. George felt some empathy towards him. They were both widowed, had unmarried children, and loved life, food and freedom. He hoped they were friends. George felt they had something to share with each other, but what that was he was not yet clear about.

"Si, George, we are friends. And as a friend I want to ask you something."

George relaxed a little, but kept his guard.

"George, since I got back from my err... trip, Maria has been strange."

George then realised he had the advantage. What luck he thought.

"Strange in what way?" he asked casually.

"When I return home from my... trip, she always. . how you say... *has a go* at me, but this time she has been all smiles and happy. It is not right George."

"Do you mean you want her to be mad at you for not being honest? For not telling her where you go. . .where do you go by the way Vincente?" It seemed a good opportunity to ask.

Vincente knew he had walked into that, but as always was able to dismiss the question in his usual "that is my concern" reply.

George felt he still had the upper hand and pressed him. "Vincente," he lowered his voice, "Maria would be more sympathetic if she just knew you were... " he paused to choose his words. ". . are, not *involved* in anything,"... he paused again... "that would embarrass her." George leaned back in his chair and waited for a hostile response.

Vincente turn to face George full on.

"Is that what she thinks? I'm involved in something, what, illegal?" He looked hurt.

"I did not say that Vincente. She is concerned that you may be following an agenda dating back to your wife's family and your friends... in the north... there I've said it."

Vincente raised his voice. "She thinks I am involved in ETA matters?. *¡Dios mío!* how can she!"

"Vincente, she does not think anything - she is confused about what you are doing. For God's sake man, tell her the truth and end this."

Vincente stood up to go. "Tell her I am not concerned with any political matters. That was a long time ago – it is finished with. The rest, however, is my concern." He said vehemently.

George stood as well. The two men now facing each other, eye to eye, more or less. "Listen to me. I like Maria very much and do not want to see her cross with you every time you go away. She is hurt. Do you understand Vincente?" He paused, but Vincente said nothing. He just stood staring at him. "Please sit down again. I have something else to say to you."

At this, Vincente blinked, and then barked out loud. "What else can you want to say? I think you have said enough." And headed for the iron steps leading down from the patio before George had time to block his move.

On reflection, George said what he thought was right and truthful. Not the best timing maybe, but it just came out. "I think I am in love with Maria."

Vincente froze. "Well that got his attention," thought

George, and immediately sat down before he was knocked down.

Vincente slowly walked back to the table, giving him time to take in what he had just heard. He sat down again and picked up a gherkin. George leaned back as far as possible in his chair.

"Do you mean what you just said?" Turning to face George, and popping the gherkin in his mouth.

"Yes, I believe I do. Is that a problem for you?"

Vincente looked at him with no sign of emotion showing through his aged bronzed face, just his bright blue eyes piercing into George's head.

"If you said that just to keep me here..."

"No, I would not do that, I promise." George interrupted sincerely.

"Good.... then..." his lips turned up very slowly to form the faintest of smiles. "You can bring out that good malt you keep trying to get me to drink."

George went in and quickly returned with a bottle of Dalwhinnie, and two glasses. He poured two moderate shots and passed one to Vincente.

"Does this mean you approve of me?" asked George, raising his glass, and his hopes, with a faint smile. 'Salute'

"Not at all." Came the swift reply, which nearly caused George to choke on his drink.

Vincente sipped the drink. "Don't you need Maria to approve of you? I do not think you have told her your feeling of love, have you?"

George was taken aback. "She knows how I feel. Why do you question my sincerity?"

"Because she would have told me, and she has not." He said forcefully.

"You arrogant... *culo* ." George could not for sure remember what it meant, but knew it was not a kind word.

Vincente was not ruffled. He just sat there and sipped his drink, staring at George.

George was ruffled, very ruffled. "You expect your daughter to confide in you after the way you are treating her!" George finished his drink and poured himself another, but not Vincente.

"You had better know now, I have asked Maria to come away for a weekend with me to Cáceres, and she has said yes, so I guess that answers your question whether she approves of me!" and downed his refill in one.

Vincente blinked and smiled slowly, "Cáceres? What is there you say?

"It's a festival of music - music from all over the World. My wife and I went there many times," George explained solemnly.

"How long for and where do you stay?" Vincente asked mildly.

"It's usually for four days but as I only recently thought of going, and I could only get a room for one night, Saturday the 23rd July. And before you ask, Jorge is coming as well. It's a great family weekend."

Vincente raised an eyebrow and grinned. "You do not need my permission to go on holiday George, but as long as you take care of my family, I hope you have a good time." He then looked down frowning, as if to think what to say next, but instead put the empty glass on the table and stood up.

George stood as well, not sure what to expect next.

"George. . ." Vincente spoke slowly. "I do not mean to upset Maria, but please know I do not intend to tell her where I go or what I do." He paused to reflect again. George said nothing. "You can tell her however I am not doing anything...bad." He then held out his hand." George looked perplexed but automatically took the handshake.

"I hope we are still friends George."

George relaxed and grinned widely. "I would like that very much Vincente. Would it be better for you to tell Maria what you just told me?" he offered, as Vincente walked into the lounge, "I mean, at least you can put her mind at rest."

The big man stopped opposite the office doors thinking. George had not shut the louver doors as he was not expecting anyone. Vincente glanced around the office area from where he stood. His eyes darting from wall to wall and over the floor. After a minute without turning his head he replied. "No. I think you can tell her George," in a quite calculating tone.

George had an idea. "Please. . ." He gestured towards the open door. "Have a look at my inner sanctum. I've added a few things since you came last." Vincente cleared his throat. "Thank you, I would like to." And walked pass the desk into the small room. The walls, which were bare on his last visit, now displayed two rows of framed posters and pictures of concerts George and Aimee had seen over the years.

Twelve on one side and eleven on the opposite wall. "One space left here." George pointed out. "Perhaps I can fill it after the visit to Cáceres."

Vincente was only half listening "Yes, maybe." he replied glancing at the framed memories. "You have seen all these people? Most I have never heard of. In fact only Paolo Conte, and I thought he was dead."

George smiled. "That is the great thing about World music - so many artists to discover, and I will go on discovering them until I die." But Vincente was now standing at the top right corner of the room looking at a poster of Rabih Abou-Khalil and nodding to indicate he was listening, but was at the same time gently tapping the wooden floor with his shoe.

He turned to see George staring at him. "This is a good floor you have here George, it's a nice room."

Seeing Vincente tapping the floor like that, George smiled to himself, as he recalled Carlos telling him of the stranger, who claimed to be the Mayor, looking over the house, and in particular this room, where he saw a workman laying the new floor.

This stranger had also noticed a three foot square hole in the floor in the top right corner of the room. George now knew the stranger was Vincente, but was disturbed as to why he still thought there might be a false floor there. After Carlos had related the visit to George, George instructed the floor to be covered, and planned a more expensive secret safe under the desk. He had brought over a specialist team from the UK to install it at great expense. A secret, that was, until little Jorge had discovered it last week. He was sure Jorge had not mentioned it, otherwise Vincente would not still be interested in that corner of the room.

"Is there anything else I can show you?"

"No thank you, George, I must go now. Thank you for the drink and our talk."

Just as he was at the door he turned to George. "Did you mean to call me an *Ass* or an *Arse*?" He smiled, and left George pondering the question.

"Either would have worked for me," he called out after him. George watched as he drove the monster Dodge down the dirt road, and wondered when he would get the chance to plant the tracker.

***

It was mid July with a week to go before the music festival and George realised he had not seen who was performing. He opened up the website *www.womad.org* and clicked on Cáceres and printed out the line-up of artists' appearing this year. He looked down the list in anticipation but as in many years gone by did not recognize one performer, not one.

On his next visit to town, George had to arrange transport to Cáceres. It wasn't that he could not afford whatever he wanted, within reason, but one of the expectations of starting over, especially in the idyllic area where he lived, was not to damage the fragile eco system any more than necessary. One of the pleasures of living in Calabaza, and leading the life he now aspired to, was the lack of *'in your face'* statistics and reports on how the world is in constant peril. Not having to see every day reminders of 'turn-off the lights - save electricity', 'drive less', 'exercise more', 'stop smoking', 'save more', 'help the economy - spend more', was a relief.

The UK, George believed, was one big contradiction. Governments, he thinks, set out to confuse the population, and then, when the time is right, take control of their lives - the foretold Big Brother State.

He was not even tempted back by the recent General Election result. "Give them a couple of years and see if they have fared any better," he thought, but deep down he knew he had left England for good.

George was also a realist. Spain has its own problems, but somehow they are not magnified in the same way. Not understanding the language also helps. A sort of natural defense to his indifference to the outside world, *'more your head in the sand attitude'* he could hear Alex saying. "I'm not apologizing for wanting to leave. I have done my share and contributed to the Inland Revenues coffers since I was seventeen, and for what, to be judged guilty until proven innocent." He got cross just remembering the conversation he had with Alex before he left - the weekend he stayed with her and Tom to say goodbye. If Alex and the others thought he was running away, then fine, perhaps he was, but he had no regrets whatsoever.

His thoughts had strayed slightly from cars, but that is the beauty of living the life he lives. More time to rationalize, more time to think things through, more time to daydream.

"Hola, Martin."
"Hola, George, how are you today?"
"Same as yesterday and the day before that," he said with a smile.
Martin laughed. "This new life of yours is good for you I think. But we mortals still have to work for a living."
"Yes you do, Martin, and I am here to help in some way."
Martin stopped what he was doing and looked at George with interest. "That sounds interesting."
"I need a car of my own. Cycling is fine, but limited. So I want you to find me a car with these features." He handed Martin a list;
Seat Leon
Audi A3
Ford Focus
2 to 3 years old.
Auto, Diesel. CD player. Air con.

"I've given you a wide scope so hope you can find something covering most of what's on that list."

Martin grinned. "I assume you do not want all three cars, my friend."

George replayed that phrase again, 'my friend' - that made him feel good.

"George... something you have forgotten?" Martin asked, since he could see George was thinking.

"Oh no, sorry... but there is something I need to ask you to do for me, Martin, in confidence."

After leaving Martin, George called into the bar to see Maria. "Hola, George." Angel called out from the back of the restaurant. *"Maria in kitchen."*

"Gracias, Angel." He called back, and headed behind the bar and into the kitchen where Maria was working. He walked up behind her and put his hands around her waist. "Hola, Maria," and kissed her neck.

"George, no! Someone may see." George looked hurt. "Oh sorry, I thought we were. . err. "

Maria turned around and kissed him. "Si, we err . are." She replied sarcastically, but smiling.

"Very funny.... but good to see you happy my dear," and added. "Is Vincente here?" looking around, and trying to sound indifferent.

"No, he has taken Jorge out fishing." She replied in a frosty tone. "Just when we are getting busy he goes out. I think he does not want to work, or be with me. George what can I do?" She pleaded, looking to George for answers.

George realised she was reaching out. His reason for visiting would have to be abandoned.

"OK, what do you want me to do?"
"Do? What do you mean, George?"
"Let me help. You are busy, I am not," he said, shrugging his shoulders.

"Oh, George, thank you... thank you...err...oh... can you help Angel outside serving?"

"What? I cannot speak enough Spanish to take orders."

"You take the food out first. I can tell you which tables. And clear tables please."

George spent the next two hours serving dishes, clearing

tables, wiping tables, washing up, making coffee and feeling exhilarated.

With only one customer left, Angel went outside for a cigarette. She did not have to, (smoking in bars is at the discretion of the owner as long as a notice is on display) but it gave Maria and George an excuse to sit down and relax. "Oh thank you, George. You were great. I could really scream at my father sometimes for not being here, again."

"I'm sure he had a reason." George offered, trying to be neutral, but he knew after his talk with Vincente, he had to tell Maria what he knew.

"Maria, Vincente came to see me this week." Maria looked surprised, but still cross.

"What did he want?" She asked, coldly.

George coughed, still not sure how to play it. "Well... he was concerned about you and how you have treated him this time when he came back..." he paused for a reaction, but none came. He lowered his voice and looked around, but still there was only one diner, Ricardo, sitting in the same corner as always. "By the way..." On seeing Ricardo, George said. "Did he pay the last bill?" nodding in his direction.

"Si, do not change the subject." Maria insisted without turning around. "What did he say?"

"First, since our plan to..." George mouthed the word 'bug' the car. . you have been different towards your Papa. You have been 'happy.' Maria just stared at George.

"He feels uneasy about you not being cross with him when he came back the other week."

"OK, I can be cross with him, in fact, George I am cross now..." she raised her voice, which made Ricardo look up from his paper.

"OK, OK, I know you are, we talked a lot but he would not tell me where he went or what he did, but he did tell me one thing you should know."

Maria waited. Her eyes focused on George. "Well, tell me..." she insisted.

"He is not doing anything...err dishonest... do you understand that?"

"Si, si, I know the word but he is doing something that we

are not to know about, and that is dishonest." She exclaimed, and sat with her arms crossed and with a look of despair on her face.

They sat in silence for while until Angel came in and announced Vincente and Jorge were back.

As she stood, she leaned over to George and whispered. "This is not over. You must put that thing on his car soon," and walked over to greet her son.

George sighed and sat back in the chair to watch the reunion of mother and son.

"Hola, Mama, we caught a big fish and Grandpa let me reel it in," the boy related excitedly. Vincente followed him in carrying what George saw to be a decent size trout.

"Hola, George," he called over and kissed Maria on the cheek. Maria smiled and told him to put the fish in the fridge. George waved back in acknowledgement and Jorge ran over to him to say hello.

Vincente and Angel disappeared to the kitchen and Maria came back to the table. *"Go and get washed now and have a siesta, Jorge."*

Jorge frowned, but obeyed, and said goodbye to George.

"I must go too, but I wanted to talk to you about Cáceres. I have the artist list and thought you may recognize some of them. I can't say I do."

"Perhaps during the week, George, when I feel up to it. I need to rest now."

"Of course. But working here today has given me even more reason to talk to you and Vincente about the restaurant ideas I have, so let's have dinner one evening."

"That sounds nice. Call me tomorrow and I will see when I can get a sitter for Jorge." They kissed goodbye and George left the bar. The heat of the July afternoon hit him immediately he stepped outside. He paused for a moment and breathed in the fresh summer air before continuing his walk home, feeling elated.

He did call Maria the next day but she said she was too busy that week, and besides, *'on Saturday we have two days together to talk.'* So George tried to keep busy for five more days, pretending he did not mind.

7.00am Saturday 23rd arrived, and George walked over to Martin's workshop as arranged to collect the hire car... well, car was too kind-a word. All Martin could find was a thirty-year-old clapped-out Citron 2 CV. "Perfect Martin. This will do nicely."

Martin still was not sure about it, but he had found what he had been asked to find, and George seemed pleased.

George drove slowly, although he had no other choice - the old car seemed only to have two gears working. He covered the short distance from the workshop to the bar in ten minutes - most people can walk it in three minutes - and parked next to the gleaming Dodge.

If Maria and the family had not been expecting him, they would certainly have known he had arrived from the noise the exhaust was making. Maria came out of the side door carrying an overnight case and immediately dropped it. Before she could take in what she was looking at George was out of the car and almost jumping towards her with his finger to his lips.

"Please, Maria, trust me," he whispered and kissed her on the cheek. As if on cue, Vincente came out of the building carrying Jorge who was decidedly not a morning person.

"Hola, George, lovely day for a drive. Where do you want this little bundle?" he asked, looking up and down the street for George's car.

Maria was finding it hard not to say anything, and could only think this situation would end badly.

"In the back please, Vincente," and George opened the driver's door of the Citroen and tried to bring the front seat forward to gain access to the back seats.

Vincente froze and almost dropped Jorge. In fact, he put the boy down. "Maria, take Jorge please," he requested without taking his eyes of the antique vehicle. "George, tell me you are not taking my daughter and grandson in THAT!"

"I agree it's a little small, but these Citroens go on forever," he replied with a smile.

"George... ," he turned to his daughter, ".... Maria!" He was getting frustrated. "George... you are not driving my family all the way to Cáceres and back in that. . that...thing," he blurted out, finding it difficult to describe the car more colorfully.

"It is all Martin could find at short notice. If we start now we can be there before dark. Martin said something about the lights not being 100%..."

The three adults stood staring at each other for what Jorge thought was a lifetime. "Mama, are we going?" he said, tugging on his mother's jacket.

"Si ,si, my love, in a minute," she said without looking at him.

"This is not for discussion, George. NOT in that car, is that clear?" Vincente was getting near boiling point.

"Vincente, what can I do now. It's too late to find another car." George replied sounding determined, without trying to overact his situation.

"OK, OK I am thinking." Vincente said pacing the pavement.

George looked sideways at Maria and winked out of Vincente's sight. Maria nearly choked.

"Are you OK? Get some water," George suggested opening the door to the back of the bar.

"I hope you know what you are doing." Maria whispered hastily, as she was ushered in.

"Trust me," he whispered back.

"George!" Vincente called out, turning on his heel from where he had walked to. "There is only one thing to do. You will have to take my car."

George looked surprised. "I cannot do that.... can I?"

"It is the only way you will go to Cáceres today."

"This is very kind of you, Vincente," and hugged the big man, much to Vincente's surprise and displeasure, and just as Maria and Jorge reappeared.

"Oh, what is this?" she asked tentatively.

"Good news. Your very kind Papa has suggested we take his car, the Dodge. Isn't that kind of him Maria? I think we should get going now. Have you got everything?" George wanted to leave before Vincente changed his mind. Vincente swung open the rear door and put in the two overnight bags while George retrieved his bag from the Citroën.

"That is good news, thank you, Papa, thank you."

"OK, OK, just make sure he brings it back in one piece."

"Oh Papa, of course we will. Now take care of the bar and do not stay open all night with your friends, drinking the profits," and kissed her father on the cheek.

Vincente handed George the keys. "Have you driven one of these before, George?"

"To be honest, no, but how hard can it be?"

"It is a smooth ride. Remember it is automatic and diesel, even Jorge could drive it, but do not let him." He almost smiled.

George put the transmission into reverse and looked around to check the road. As he pointed the car in the right direction, he opened the window and called over to Vincente. "I will take the hire car back on Monday."

"No problem. I will do it for you George," and waved his beloved car goodbye, "besides, I want a word with Martin," he said to himself through clenched teeth.

A few yards down the road the Dodge stopped. Vincente jogged over.

"Oh, I almost forgot, can you please feed the cat. Here are the keys. The alarm code is 19475. Thank you, Vincente." And before Vincente had time to confirm what he had just been told, George put the car into drive, leaving Vincente looking much bewildered. "Cat, what cat!" He called out after them, but they had turned the corner and were heading for Cáceres.

Maria gave a playful slap on George's leg. "That was naughty - you do not have cat."

"Well, no... but I am thinking of getting one," and they both laughed aloud.

"Also, you planned all this, did you not George?"

"I do not know what you mean, Maria."

"Getting Papa to give you the car! That old thing Martin gave you was rubbish. I would not have gone one yard in it. How did you know Papa would agree?"

"Oh really, Maria, you are so suspicious," he replied with a grin. "Now you must navigate. I have a map in my rucksack on the back seat." He looked in the rear view mirror. "Hola, Jorge, how are you today?" Maria translated. "He is fine, but tired. He will sleep for a while."

"Also in the bag are some CDs. Take one out and put it in the player. Shame he does not have an iPod connection, but beggars cannot be choosers," he said still grinning.

Maria chose one not knowing what it was, and the CD player sucked it in. "Ah, you will like this, it's a Spanish band called Matinalsystem," and the speakers came alive with Nu-jazz.

They stopped for lunch near Salamanca, and arrived at Cáceres just after 4.30pm.

It was hot, very hot. Many of the streets had canopies strung high between each side of the buildings, giving much needed respite from the sun. The canopies were very colorful, depicting the national flag, and contemporary art.

After checking in at the Alfonso XII, and arranging a spare folding bed for Jorge, they quickly changed and went to explore the old city.

***

Vincente drove the old Citroen to Martin's workshop, feeling like a sardine in a tin. The Citroen was not built for six-foot four, seventeen stone men.

He came to an abrupt stop pinning Martin against the garage door.

"If you ever do something like that again I will see you are burnt in hell!" He was inches from Martin's face.

Martin shrugged and tried not to grin. He thought of denying any involvement, but for some reason it seemed good to leave Vincente with the knowledge that he was also George's friend.

***

George, Maria and Jorge entered the Plaza Mayor from Paneras Street, only a few hundred yards from the hotel. The Plaza was crowded with young and old, locals and tourists, all there to enjoy the splendor of the events, and to appreciate the wonderful surroundings.

To the south of the Plaza there was a large stage. No seating, but plenty of room to view and hear the performers. The stage was being set for the first act of the day, but the trio wanted to see more of the old city so they climbed the steps leading to Estrella Arch. Mostly people just follow other people, who themselves were following the tourist street map of the old city. "Let's just go with the flow," suggested George "but hold on to Jorge." The narrow Arco de la Estrella Street was full of people walking single file - going up on the left, and down on the right. Well, most people did. Eventually they spilled into the much wider and busy Santa Maria Square. This square was full of colorful Nomad style tents selling everything the tourist needs; T shirts, Kaftans, hats, shoes, jewellery, musical instruments - mainly the popular frame drum, but also flutes, guitars and other exotic instruments, some even George could not recognize.

One of the stalls was selling beautiful Jade jewellery. George knew the owner well. He had brought Aimee many pieces over the years from here, and from his London workshop in Camden Lock.

John Capel had the appearance of a 'free spirit'. Dressed in a Kaftan and sporting dreadlocks, he could have just stepped out of Woodstock. "George, good to see you my friend." And they hugged for several seconds. "So, you old devil, you did it, you actually moved here."

"Good to see you too, John," ignoring his last remark for now. "I never got a chance to thank you properly for coming to the funeral."

John held up a hand. "I wanted to George. I seem to have connected to you two over the years, and she had a wonderful 'aura' about her. She was a lovely lady." George tried not to show any emotion in front of Maria. He knew it would be hard for him, but Maria stepped forward a pace and held out her hand to John. "Hola." she said to John. "I am Maria, and this is my son Jorge."

"Oh sorry, Maria, yes John this is Maria and Jorge. Maria owns a lovely bar in Calabaza where I now live."

"Pleased to meet you, Maria." John shook hands and felt a

little uneasy, but he was not judging the situation. George had to move on and he was bound to meet someone, he told himself.

"This was a last minute decision. I thought it time to come back, and Maria needed a break, so we have come for one night, and hope to get little Jorge here in tomorrow's procession."

"That sounds a good idea. Have you been here before, Maria?" asked John.

"No never, but I love it already. It is so full of life and colour."

John could see the sincerity in Maria's eyes, and knew George had found another soul mate.

"Mama, look, look." Jorge was tugging on Maria's hand. *"Over there!"* Jorge was pointing to a group of street entertainers, jugglers and fire-eaters.

"Ok Jorge, just a minute."

"I think he is getting fed up now, we must move on, but nice to meet you, John."

"You too Maria, but just a second before you go."

John reached over to his display and picked up a leather friendship bracelet with a beautiful Jade clasp. He went to place it on Maria's wrist. "Please accept this as my welcome to Cáceres."

"Oh no, John, I could not." She looked at George for help.

"It's lovely, but you must let me pay for it," George insisted, but knew what the answer would be. "Sorry, George must go - lots of customers - have a great day and see you later perhaps for a drink." And he slipped back behind the counter and was in conversation with another customer before Maria and George could blink.

"You must let me pay him, George." Maria said as they walked away, admiring the unexpected gift.

"Maria, he won't take my money so there is no chance of him taking yours."

They walked arm in arm into the centre of the square where a crowd had circled the entertainers. George lifted Jorge on his shoulders for a better view, and Maria squeezed his hand. It was a good day.

***

Vincente had persuaded Senora Torres to come with him to see about feeding the cat. He wanted a witness in case anything got damaged. "There is no cat, Senor Mayor. I would have seen one by now," she insisted, climbing out of her husband's old Honda.

"We will see. If there is not, someone will pay for this night," he said in a cold tone.

Vincente unlocked the front door and entered the house. He keyed in the security code on the alarm panel behind the door, and Senora Torres walked through to the lounge, calling out for a non-existent cat.

***

George and Maria had had a good day. They had seen several acts during the afternoon after they left Jorge with the festival class. Here the children worked on making costumes, masks and other colorful accessories to use in Sunday's procession through the old city to mark the closing of the WOMAD festival.

Maria was apprehensive at first, but as soon as Jorge saw the other children working away with paint and glue and glitter, he wanted to stay and join in. She smiled as he ran towards the group, and all her fears evaporated.

She and George then headed further up the old stone steps to Plaza San Jorge and followed the cobbled stone road to Plaza Veletas, where the food and drinks tents were situated. They choose thin crust pizza with cheese and anchovies, and a cool beer each. They sat in the shade under a large old olive tree and ate in silence for a while.

"Thank you." George said, looking directly at Maria.

"For what?" she asked.

"For being here. It means a lot to me that you came today. It would not have been the same alone."

George thought she was going to tenderly touch his face or embrace him, but she picked up a tissue and wiped away some cheese from the corner of his mouth.

He smiled and whispered, "Thank you," and was about to say, *"That's just what Aimee would have done,"* when he realised he was comparing Maria to Aimee in so many ways.

Did he bring Maria as an Aimee substitute? He closed his eyes and dipped his head.

"What is it, George? What is wrong?" She asked with concern in her voice.

He raised his head and struck the back of it on the tree several times in frustration. "I'm sorry, Maria," and reached out and took her hand. "It may not have been a good idea asking you to come here. I don't want you to think I wanted to relive this weekend doing all the things Aimee and I did..." He wiped a tear away and looked down again.

Maria put a hand under his chin and lifted his head gently. She leaned forward and kissed him long and tenderly.

"I came with you because I wanted to be with you," she said. "It is natural to have memories, and no one can take those from you - or should want to." Maria spoke softly and sincerely, and George realised a feeling in him he had not experienced for a long time. "Come," Maria whispered in George's ear. "I want a siesta." And they kissed again. "But I am not sleepy." She added, with a warm smile.

Later that afternoon they laid in each others arms after making love, realizing the future was about to change for them both.

***

The next day, after breakfast, they took Jorge back to the festival workshop. The children had made colorful masks and costumes. The theme had been storybook characters, and Jorge had made a wolf's head. Well that's what it looked like to Maria who remembered he had always liked the stories of the little boy who befriended a wolf. The colorful and musical procession wound its way down from the highest point in the old town, through the plazas and narrow streets, eventually reaching its conclusion in the Plaza Mayor. George and Maria followed the crowd trying to keep up with Jorge. They held hands tightly so not to be separated, and George was determined that would not happen, not then, or ever.

Jorge slept most of the journey home, and Maria and George talked about the future - not the past. George told her of his idea of investing some money into El Tango and opening it as a restaurant a few evenings a week. He felt sure there was good business to be had if the adverting and marketing were right. Maria, for her part, relished the idea of something new in her life so she too could draw a line under her past and move on, with or without Vincente.

A few miles before they reached Calabaza, George pulled over and attached the asset tracker to the underside of the car. "Now let's see where he takes us."

Chapter 6. August

"What shall we do with him, George?" Vincente asked in a menacing tone.

Vincente was standing behind Peter Barnes who was trussed up on a wooden chair in the middle of the barn. The chair was facing George, and he was somewhat surprised, and confused, to see this mild mannered man in this predicament.

As luck would have it, or not, Peter Barnes had found himself in El Tango, craving some cold refreshment, and shelter from the heat of the August sun, and asking directions to El Pino Farmhouse.

Vincente of course played the innocent. He wanted to know why he was looking for George. Vincente said he wanted to phone a friend who may be able to help, but instead called George.

"George, there is an Englishman here in the bar asking for you. He is looking very suspicious."

"Who is he, Vincente?"

"I do not know his name. He is not a tourist. He is wearing a jacket and tie, and about to have a stroke if he goes out in the sun."

"Can you describe him a little more, Vincente." George asked with some frustration at being disturbed.

"OK, he is about sixty five, under six foot, sand colour hair, going bald, he . ."

"Stop!" said George, almost in a trance. "That sounds like Peter Barnes. The man who accused me of a very serious crime, and was partly responsible for me coming to Spain."

"You mean the bank robbery?"

George was silent for a moment.

"How did you know about that?"

"George, I have many friends, and when a stranger wants to take my daughter out, I find out everything about him -

and I mean everything. Do not worry my friend, I have not told Maria you are a thief."

"I am not... a thief, Vincente... it's complicated." George knew he had said too much.

"I believe you, George, I do, but what of this man? Has he come for revenge and to get even, yes?"

"I cannot see how. Anyway, he was never convinced I was guilty, but never actually stood up and said so."

"What shall I do with him, George? Send him on his way or 'question' him?"

"Not sure if I like the tone of that, Vincente. Send him up to the house. I am sure he is harmless."

Thirty minutes later George got a mobile call from Vincente. "We are in the barn George - I have him as you say."

Before George could utter anything, Vincente caught his eye, and winked before saying, "I could take him into the woods. No one will find him after the boars have finished." Which on reflection, George thought, was said in a more menacing way than was necessary.

Peter went redder and redder, as if about to burst.

"For God's sake, Vincente, untie him please."

Vincente removed the handkerchief from around Peter's mouth.

Peter gasped for air. "George, please help me - this man is mad. He wants to kill me. I only wanted to talk to you. I mean you no harm."

George and Vincente untied him. "Peter, what exactly are you are doing here. How did you find me?"

"I will explain everything, George." Peter said breathing deeply, and wiping his brow.

"Of course, Peter, come in the house and I will get us some drinks."

Peter moved close to George and said in a low voice, "Who is this mad man? Does he have to come?"

George gave Vincente a scornful look. "You did not have to tie him up. I said bring him up to the house, not string him up."

"Sorry, George, sorry Senor," Vincente said, looking as apologetic as possible. "It is my English, it is not so good on the telephone, I must have not heard right."

Peter turned away and Vincente gave a shrug to George as if to say, "What did I do wrong?"

Peter came into the living room refreshed. He had even removed his jacket and tie, and George had a brandy waiting for him.

"I was just telling Vincente here - sorry by the way, this is Vincente, part owner of El Tango, where you met - was telling him who you are, but I have no idea how you found me."

Peter, still suspicious of Vincente, gave a nod of recognition and sat down opposite him, not wanting to be too close to him in fear of any sudden mood-swings Vincente may have.

"If he is your friend, George, you have questionable taste." Peter said as he sat down.

"On the contrary, Peter, he was looking out for me. We are closer than you imagine.

Peter looked up from his brandy. He looked at Vincente. Then at George. Then back to Vincente.

"I had no idea, George, but if that is want you want over here, then good luck to you both, I am a broad minded man," and raised his glass in a toast.

"What is he saying, George?" Vincente asked, not sure of what Peter had just said.

George winced and shifted on the sofa, not sure how to respond. He could get his own back on Vincente, and go along with what Peter was thinking.

"Yes," he said coyly, "we have been seeing each other for a few months now."

Peter almost choked on this drink.

Vincente was looking bewildered, not understanding all of the English, but knowing something was not right.

"Ah si." Vincente said at last. "He and my *daughter,*" with the emphasis on daughter, "have been seeing each other."

Peter was confused again for a moment, and then saw George grin.

"Oh, well done old boy, you had me there for a moment."

They all laughed a nervous laugh, except Vincente, who laughed the loudest, and was pleased with himself for understanding the joke.

"George, I hope you have some food in the house, it is lunch time," Vincente enquired.

"Go help yourself, Vincente, and bring us something as well."

"No, not for me George, I did not mean to intrude for long."

"Now you are here, Peter, you will have to eat - it's a ritual here in Spain. Where are you staying?" asked George, wanting to change the subject to help him relax more, and open up as to what he wanted.

"I have a room at a hotel in Aranda for two nights. I hired a car from Madrid airport, but came straight to Calabaza, as it seemed easy to find on the map."

"But who told you I was here?" George asked with interest.

"I must confess it took me a while to find out, but I remembered you used to go to the 606 Jazz Club in Fulham regularly."

George looked surprised that he remembered that, and had a flash back to some good times there. He had been a regular for several months before he moved to Spain, and remembered Gilad Atzmon was the last musician he had seen there.

"When I asked about you, the club secretary said they were supposed to send your *'What's On'* program to Spain. They kindly gave me your address, after I told them I was an old friend who had lost touch - which is not totally untrue George."

George stared in bewilderment. "I must speak to Helen about giving out my details to anyone."

"I am sorry George - I don't want to get her in trouble. She did give me these for you". He opened his briefcase and took a brown envelope and gave it to George.

"She said you would appreciate these by hand, and she could save on the postage."

George smiled. He had the last three months, and next month's programs for the 606 Jazz Club. There was not much chance he would be going back regularly, but he liked to keep in touch, and to see who was playing there. His taste in music had evolved sometime ago - shifting away from the mainstream artists appearing at the club, but he loved a live band whoever they were, and if they played Jazz, they were worth seeing. George instinctively went over to the music centre and put on a CD by Acoustic Mania, an excellent acoustic guitar duo, which he had seen several times live.

"So, Peter," George asked, feeling more relaxed, "tell me why you are here."

"George," he whispered, "do you want me to talk with him here?" Nodding in Vincent's direction.

"He seems to know more than I realised, so please continue Peter." George replied, giving Vincente a passing glance.

"Well, George, I never really felt you were responsible for the theft. I have known you for ten years and I am usually a good judge of character." He took a sip of brandy.

"You were happily married, and it was a dreadful thing that happened to your wife. You have three supportive children and good friends, and a successful business." He considered his words carefully. "After your wife died you stopped working for six months, which was understandable. Some say you had a breakdown and turned to drink, or worse, drugs."

George sighed deeply. He glanced over to Vincente who had been listening in, but continued to prepare the lunch when George looked in his direction.

Peter continued, "It was six months later the theft happened. It is said you had been planning it all that time, and then carried it out. The police, however, could not find any concrete evidence to convict you, no matter how hard they tried - and believe me they tried. You were the only suspect they had, and after a year had to let you go. The Crown Prosecution Service did not have enough evidence, thank goodness, to continue."

He took another sip of brandy.

"You even gave me the name of a company to do some... shall we say... covert investigations, but they too seemed unable to find any new evidence." He paused to remember. "However, you should know my son, Oliver, has retained them again to investigate you further."

George listened with interest without commenting, and let Peter continue.

"Most of this you know of course. Then you sold up and moved to Spain. Questions were raised again." George did not look surprised, but was thinking about Jackson Security investigating him.

"I have nothing to hide Peter, let them look all they want, they will not find anything new."

Vincente was still listening with one ear. Is this man really innocent or very clever? Did he steal five million pounds and really get away with it, he thought to himself.

"The thing is George, I believe you. That is why I am here. I retired from the bank..." Peter paused mid-sentence. . "Well, actually I was asked to stand down with a handsome handshake. The board gave me a vote of no confidence. My son was voted in as Chief Executive."

"I am so sorry Peter... I had no idea. It's not something I would expect a son to do to his own father," George said, with genuine sympathy.

"I must admit it surprised me too. I thought I knew the board of director's better, but Oliver convinced them he could recover the money, and he knew who took it - you George, and he is totally convinced of that."

George, of course, knew this since he had received caustic phone calls from Oliver Barnes, and it was he who was probably guilty of harassing Alex. George realised then something needed to be done, and soon, if he was to have a long and meaningful life again.

Peter was still talking, but George was only half listening. . "George, are you OK, did you hear me..."

"Yes, sorry Peter, do continue."

"Well, since I retired I have been thinking more and more about what happened, and thought you may have some answers. Surely you have considered some possibilities as to who did it."

"I've been over the whole episode in my head many times," replied George, "they took away my computer so I did not have access to all my bank work, but yes, I thought it through and came to the same conclusion every time, whoever did it was very clever, with a good knowledge of banking security and computer analysis."

"So, it could have been you." Peter said cautiously, with a nervous smile.

The statement hung in the air. George could not see where this was going, and was relieved when Vincente announced lunch was ready.

"It's not much, but I am limited to what George keeps in the fridge," he said, giving George a knowing grin.

George and Peter walked over to the table, and Peter stood there in amazement. "You made all this, just now?"

It was only a light lunch, but Vincente had made; potato omelet (a quick version of tortilla), chorizo in red wine, chili prawns, sautéed mushrooms in garlic and a wonderful tossed salad.

"It's one of the things he does, Peter. He cooks at El Tango, *when he is there*. He and his daughter run it."

"Well," said Peter, still taking in the array of plates in front of him, "who would have guessed the man has such hidden talents. After all - no offence Vincente - but you do not look like a chief."

Vincente was not sure if this was an English compliment or not, so just shrugged and said "Enjoy please." And they sat down to eat.

Vincente ate heartily as usual. Peter picked tentatively at the prawns, and tried the chorizo. George started to eat, but then almost went into a trance.

He wanted Peter to relax more and enjoy the food and wine, and more importantly not upset Vincente. So they talked generally about life in Spain, life in England, the weather in England, the weather in Spain, etc.

Eventually, George brought the talk back to the Bank.

"So, how is Oliver handling the Bank? Has he made many changes?"

Peter looked at George for a moment before answering. "He is doing OK I guess. The Board of Directors have confidence in him."

"That is not what I asked, Peter. Is he as good at it as you were?"

Peter looked uncomfortable with this question.

"I still keep in touch with some of my old colleges on the Board, and my old PA, Christine, who was very good and loyal, and was sorry to see me leave."

He took a sip of water.

"At the Board meeting after the robbery I just hung on to my position. The investigation was still on-going and I assured everyone the money would be found, and the culprit sent to jail." Peter sipped more water. "After a year without any charges being made, and no money recovered, a 'vote of no confidence' was carried, and I resigned. Oliver was voted on the Board and made Chief Executive. I wish him well, but... " He hesitated to find the right words. ".... but, the atmosphere inside the bank is not the same. He has his own staff, and he brought in a new computer analysis at an exorbitant cost, not that you George, were underpaid, but these costs have spiraled, according to what I hear."

Peter was more relaxed now. It seemed a weight was off his shoulders, and he was relieved to have shared his thoughts.

They sat in silence for what seemed a long time, until Vincente's mobile rang. "Si, OK I will be back very soon my love. It's Maria, she wants me to collect Jorge from a friend's house. I must go."

"Thank you, Vincente for your help, in the kitchen I mean, not the other thing." George gestured toward Peter.

"Si, sorry about the confusion, Peter. You must come to have dinner with me at El Tango so I make amends."

"I don't think I will be here that long, but thank you." Peter held out a limp hand, which Vincente shook.

George saw Vincente to the door and said his goodbyes.

When he returned, Peter was on his mobile. "I was trying

to get hold of Oliver but his PA said he is on holiday in the South of France."

"Very nice, does he go there often?"

"I'm not sure. He likes sailing, but the young 'jet set' people he mixes with are not my cup-of-tea."

"Maybe not, but they were probably your best clients."

"He worked hard to get where he is. I started him on the shop floor and made him work up through the ranks. I don't believe in nepotism. It's not fair on the other staff, and it can cause morale problems and resentment." Peter sighed deeply. "He earned a good wage and has his own property, but he does mix with city high flyers that are on a different financial level all together."

Peter sat down on the sofa. "Could I have another brandy, George?"

George poured two large brandies.

"George, I am sorry. You have suffered greatly over the last couple of years. Coping with your wife's death, and then this affair. How have you survived it?"

"Simple, Peter, by knowing I was innocent." George smiled weakly.

Peter raised his glass. "I believe you, George."

George was almost humbled by the man's concern, and his sincerity. After all, he did not have to come here and find him. Their paths would never have crossed again, but Peter could not have known how George had turned his life around, and was 'reborn' and getting on with life.

Peter was tired. "George, can I lie down for while before I drive back."

"Of course you can, but I think you should not go to the hotel. You can call and cancel it. You can stay here so we can talk some more when you feel up to it."

"Maybe, George, let's see later how I feel." George helped Peter up the few stairs to the first guest bedroom, carrying his jacket and briefcase. He helped him off with his shoes and laid him on the bed. George hung the suit jacket in the wardrobe and left the briefcase on the chair. Peter Barnes was asleep before George had closed the door.

***

Oliver Barnes was enjoying the high life in the South of France. He was staying at the five-star George Hotel in Nice. His suite had two bedrooms, a lounge, dining area, bar and a wonderful view over the Mediterranean. It was Saturday morning and his mobile was ringing. The local time was 6.30am.

It took him a while to realize where the sound was coming from, but eventually he located the phone under a pile of clothes on the floor. Clothes that included a skirt, blouse, bra and a G-string.

He found the phone and crept back into bed, and leaned over to look at the body lying next to him. He smiled and answered the call. "Yes."

"Oliver, your father has gone to Spain."

"How nice, was that really worth a call at this time of the morning."

"He has gone to see George Morton."

The statement suddenly focused Oliver's attention. He stood up and walked over to the sofa.

"Are you sure. How do you know this?"

"Mr Barnes, you asked us to investigate. This is what you are paying for. I thought you should know who your father is meeting with."

Oliver tried to clear his mind of the previous night's excesses. He noticed traces of white powder on the glass coffee table and pressed his forefinger into it, and slowly placed it on his tongue, as if savoring the most succulent foie-gras.

"Mr Barnes, are you still there?"

"Yes, Jackson, just sampling breakfast." Oliver replied coolly. "OK. You need to send someone over there, under cover, so to speak. Can you do that?"

"Of course. I will make arrangements and let you know..." but he was cut short.

"NO! I do not want to know your arrangements. You do not contact me until we have a result. I cannot condone this. . arrangement, until I have a result to put before my board of directors. Is that clear? "

"Perfectly, Mr. Barnes." The line went dead.

Oliver fingered up what was left of the powder, smiling to himself, and starting to rehearse his victory speech to the board of directors for the recovery of the five million pounds. Something his father could not achieve.

The body in the bed stirred. "Hey lover, what time is it?"

"Time for breakfast." Oliver said thoughtfully. "Let's have some Tutti-Frutti."

***

The next morning George tapped on the guest room door. "Peter, are you awake?" Peter was lying motionless, on one side, facing away from the door. George walked around the bed and put a mug of tea on the bedside table.

Then he saw the expression on Peter's face. The man was dead.

George quickly checked his pulse and listened to his heart, but there was no sign of life.

"Shit," George said aloud. "You poor man. You could have told me you were ill."

George went down stairs and called Maria.

"Hi, Maria. Sorry to call early but is Vincente there?"

"Si, yes, he is. Is anything wrong George? You sound strange."

"I need your father's advice on a matter." And left it at that.

Twenty minutes later Vincente was at the house, looking over the deceased Peter Barnes.

"What did you do to him after I left?" he asked, nonchalantly.

George was defensive. "What do you mean? We talked some more. He had a brandy and went to bed. Said he felt tired from the journey. It had been a long day for him. That is all. Are you saying something else, because if…"

"No, no George, but the police will want to talk to you so it is best you tell me anything that happened after I left you. What was said about the matter you were discussing?"

"What was said, Vincente, was that Peter had come to terms with the fact he had been ousted by his son into early retirement."

Vincente nodded and listened closely. "Is that all? You did not argue about who may have stolen his money?"

"No, I told you. He did not..." George had to stay calm. He did not want Vincente to badger him into a confession, "not then... not ever... accuse me. He went to bed and we dropped the matter."

Just then they heard a faint ringing sound. They both looked at each other, then around the room, listening harder. "It's coming from inside the wardrobe, George."

George opened the creaky wooden door. The sound was louder. "There!" exclaimed Vincente, "in the jacket."

George gingerly put his hand into the jacket pocket, half expecting it to be bitten off. He removed the Blackberry and looked at the flashing display screen in disbelieve.

It read 'OLIVER CALLING'

"What do we do, Vincente? We must answer it."

"No, George, not yet."

The phone stopped ringing. The display changed to 'One missed call'

"He will find out soon enough his father has died." Vincente said gravely. He then called the police, who in turn called the Coroner.

While Vincente was doing that, George checked the pockets of Peter's suit and then his briefcase. He took out a wallet and Mont Blanc pen from one inside pocket, a passport (containing his airline ticket) and a slim white sealed envelope from the other inside jacket pocket. The side pockets were empty except for the car keys. George had forgotten about the car. He turned over the envelope and looked in surprise at the name neatly hand written on it; *George Morton.*

He put everything on the dressing table, together with the contents from Peter's briefcase. He picked up the envelope and held it up to the light as if expecting to see what was written inside. He tapped it on the dresser a few times deciding if to open it or give it to the police. If it contained information about any suspicions he may have had against him, it would be best to keep it back. He put the envelope in his back pocket and picked up the Blackberry and erased all the 'missed calls', and turned it off.

"George." Vincente was standing close behind him. "What have you found?"

George turned suddenly. "Don't do that. Do you want two heart attacks on your hands?"

"Sorry, I did not want to startle you," he said with an innocent grin. "What did you find?"

"Usual things; passport, ticket, keys, pen, wallet." George picked up the leather wallet and opened it. "Three hundred Euros and two credit cards." George looked at Vincente with what his children called his '*quizzical*' look. "There *was* something else." George took the envelope from his back pocket, and handed it to Vincente.

"You have not opened it? Do you want me to?"

"I'm not sure. Why would he come here with a letter already written? Before we had discussed the robbery or any other possibilities..." George's eyes opened wide, looking at Vincente, who was trying to keep up with George's thinking.

"He had already made up his mind about me, although he gave me a hard time last night. I bet this letter confirms his suspicions."

"George," Vincente whispered.

"Yes?"

"Open the letter."

George was about to tear it open when there was a loud knocking at the front door.

He folded the envelope again and replaced it in his back pocket.

The police chief talked to Vincente for some time, then turned to George, and said, "Mr Morton, I am sorry for your loss. Mayor Caldas has explained everything. My sincere condolences."

He shook George's hand, turned to Vincente and shook his hand, and left. Vincente had given the Police chief all the personal possessions of Peter Barnes, including his suit jacket and briefcase.

The Coroner's people took Peter's body away and that was that. All over within an hour.

"What did you say to the police? Don't they want a statement from me?"

"No, George, well yes, but they will send someone back to take it later. I said you were too distressed to talk now - having just lost a dear friend." Vincente smiled his knowing smile. "I explained poor Mr Barnes was a close friend and had a heart attack, brought on by too much sun and brandy last night. And they should contact his family immediately."

George held out his hand and Vincente took it willingly. George felt the firm grasp as he had done before, but this time Vincente did not remove his hand so quickly. He shook once, slowly, and nodded to George, as people do when there is a mutual understanding - when words are not necessary.

George felt very uneasy about Peter Barnes' death. The fact that it had happen at his home, and that Barnes had paid him a visit too, was disturbing enough, but George also felt these events would only advance Oliver Barnes' agenda. George sent an encrypted email to Colin Jackson for an update on Oliver's whereabouts. If Oliver is going to play his hand, it would now be soon, and George needed to know how much time he had.

***

Four days later, George received a call at 7.00am from Maria. "George, it's me, Maria."

"Yes, Maria, I can see it is - you are on my phone, but why are you whispering?"

"Sorry, George," she said, increasing her voice to near normal level. "He has gone, Papa, he must have left about an hour ago. Is that too late George, can we still find him with the tracker?"

George dressed as quickly as possible and grabbed the laptop and iPhone, and dashed out of the front door... into... nothing. "Shit," he said aloud. The car he had hoped Martin would find him had still not arrived, and he cursed again. He stood looking all around him hoping by some miracle a car would materialize out of thin air. There was only one thing for it - the bike. He opened the barn doors and grabbed the pushbike, placing the laptop in the front basket. He pedaled furiously down the hill into town, narrowly missing a farmer pulling out of a side lane on his tractor. Another Spanish swear word to remember.

He skidded to a halt outside Martins flat at 7.23am. "Martin." He called to the window above, where he hoped was the bedroom. "Martin, por favor. It's me, George."

A few moments later the shutters opened on the second floor and Martin peered out. "George, what do you want so early... no, wait there I will be down."

Martin opened the front door and stood there in black boxer shorts and not much of a smile. "Martin, I need a big favor. I need to borrow your car for a couple of hours. I can't explain now but it's a matter of life and death - mine - on both counts."

Martin of course did not understand completely what George was going on about, but he recognized a friend in need, and gladly gave him the keys to his Seat Leon FR.

"Thank you, Martin. I will explain everything later."

"OK. Just bring it back in one piece," he called out, but George was already turning the corner and heading towards El Tango.

Maria was waiting outside the bar and in the car in seconds. "What about Jorge?" George asked hurriedly.

"It's OK, Angel is coming over in ten minutes, but he is still asleep, so let's go, quickly George, we must not lose him," she said in a mixture of panic, frustration and fear. George put a hand on her shoulder. "Maria, calm down, it's OK. We will not lose him. The tracker has a range of over one hundred miles, and he can't have gone that far yet." George opened the laptop, turned it on and placed it on Maria's lap.

"Now, let's see what we have."

A few seconds later a map appeared on the screen with Calabaza in the centre. George entered a pin code in a box on the screen and waited. Twenty seconds later a faint flashing light appeared and Maria squealed with delight, as if she had been given a wonderful gift. "He is there, on the E5 heading north east.... " She turned to George. "North, George, I told you so."

They drove out of town and picked up Vincente's trail. They drove in silence for a while - Maria transfixed by the laptop screen, following her father with the realization her relationship with him may never be the same again.

Vincente was obviously in no hurry, which allowed George to make good progress in closing the gap. By 8.30 they were only fifteen minutes behind him, and they could now see he was heading for San Sebastian or somewhere near-by.

They continued on the A8 main road passing San Sebastian town centre and drove another fifteen minutes, following the faint blip, blip on the computer screen, until it eventually stopped.

"George, we have lost him. It is not moving!" Maria shouted at George.

"Calm down, its fine. It means he has stopped. Probably at his final destination," he said matter-of-factly, trying to calm her down. "Do you recognize any of this area Maria? Have you been here before?"

Maria studied the map in front of her. "We are in Hondarribia, but I do not know it. I cannot think of any of my mother's family ever coming from here."

They drove slowly through the up market avenues lined with grand villas on each side. Large iron security gates adorned each entrance. "Wow, I bet these cost a few Euros. Maybe you have some rich relatives, Maria."

Maria was not really listening. She could not work out why Vincente would come here. She had never seen a letter post-marked Hondarribia or San Sebastian as long as she could remember. Her few surviving relatives sent New Year cards and birthday cards from Pamplona, where her mother was born, some one hundred miles further south.

"I do not know why he would come here George," she said leaning back in her seat and stretching, "but I must get out soon. Three hours is too long without a stop, and I need to go... you know where.."

George pulled over in a lay-by outside some shops. "I will go and find a toilet and buy some drinks."

Maria leaned over and kissed George on the cheek.

"Thank you George for doing this."

"Thank me when it's over - you may be disappointed with the outcome," he said, hoping he was wrong.

***

Vincente pulled into the large parking area, and the electric iron gates closed silently behind him. Rosanna Maria Mendoza stepped out to meet him as usual, accompanied by her two golden Labradors. "Hola, my love. Did you have a good journey?" She asked, caressing his face with her left hand.

"Very good. Time flies by knowing I am on my way to see you."

Vincente leant down to meet Rosanna Maria's lips, and kissed her passionately.

"Come my love. Let's go in and have breakfast, and tell me the latest news on your Englishman friend and Maria."

***

Maria returned to the car carrying soft drinks and packets of crisps. "Hardly breakfast." George complained. "You are welcome," she said, opening up the laptop. "Has he moved yet?" she asked nervously, focusing on the flashing blue dot.

"No. I think we have arrived, Maria," he said quietly, looking at her.

"That is only a few streets away from here," he said, studying the map.

"Are you sure you want to go on? We can turn around and go home if you want to."

Maria leaned back and closed her eyes. She reached out taking hold of George's right hand and squeezed it. "I want to do this George. Will you be with me, whatever happens, whatever we find?"

George leaned over and kissed her on the mouth. "I promise. I will never leave you alone. Never," and they kissed again, and she knew then her life would never be the same again after today.

They parked a few yards from where the blue dot was flashing, and walked slowly along the quiet street.

"I assume his car is parked behind that gate," George

guessed. He had transferred the software to his iPhone so it was easier to carry, and to still to be able to observe their prey.

Vincente sat at the kitchen diner and tucked into eggs, ham and tomatoes. "Are you not eating with me, Rosa?"

"No my love, I had some bread earlier. I am not eating so much these days, and besides, you are probably going to cook an enormous meal later for our guests, so I must make sure I appreciate it, as always."

Rosanna Maria Mendoza looked elegant in her black slacks and black T Shirt, embroidered across one shoulder with a pair of colorful peacocks, and didn't look anywhere near the seventy-five years old she actually was. She sat opposite Vincente, happy to watch him eat after his three-hour journey. A journey she knew he might not be taking for much longer. They were not getting any younger, and although still in good health, and able to partake in many pleasures, she felt the time was soon approaching when she would need, and appreciate, more permanent company. Her days were, for the most part, lonely. She read a lot and walked the dogs each day, but not as far as she used to. Siestas became longer, and the nights shorter. Twice a week she played bridge with some neighbors, and they took it in turns to visit each other's homes.

Senora Mendoza had been a widow for nearly twenty years. She had been married for almost thirty-five years when her husband had drowned while out swimming one day. She never remarried, although she was never short of admirers. Her not so modest inheritance may have had something to do with her offers of marriage, but she never thought badly of the gentlemen who wooed her. She sat reflecting on how the world had changed so fast around her. She preferred the days of yesteryear, when, for the most part, the world she lived in was more orderly.

"Rosa my love, are you daydreaming?" Vincente asked, finishing his second cup of coffee.

"Just remembering. That is what we do now, is it not?" she smiled back at him. And remembered how she had let

Vincente into her life those ten years ago, when she had rejected all others.

Not that he was a stranger to her, indeed no. In fact, she could well have been married to him already if fate had not intervened. Rosanna Maria and her best friend Estella hailed from Pamplona. Work was hard to find for two eighteen year olds in the 1950's, and they wanted to experience something of the world, or the rest of Spain, before they were married off by their parents. They both decided to leave home and find work in Madrid - anything, as long as it was legal and paid well. Both were trained in secretarial work, and soon found jobs in the largest newspaper publisher in Spain, ABC.

They worked hard, and within two years had secured good positions. Estella worked for the day editor and Rosa for the political editor. Their social life was good and they had many boyfriends, although Estella was always complaining about how immature they were. "Oh come on E," Rosa would say, "enjoy life. Who knows what tomorrow will bring."

"More war probably." Estella would answer thoughtfully.

"No, I promise you. Things are better now. Spain is getting prosperous and we are part of this new Spain." Rosa would say, repeating what she heard and read about in the political columns of the paper. "Let's live life to the full, and remain friends forever." Rosa would hug her friend and Estella would be reassured once again.

Spain was indeed heading for a prosperous period. Franco had relaxed many regulations and had allowed free enterprise to flourish. One day Rosanna Maria met a tall handsome young man who said he lived in the Royal Palace, and had many friends with good connections. Rosa kept this new young man to herself for several weeks, until she invited him back to her apartment for dinner. It was the 3rd June 1959. Most Spaniards remember that date because Real Madrid won 2-0 against France in the European Cup Final in Stuttgart.

The whole of Spain celebrated. Some people however had to work, and Rosa had been transferred to the sports editorial desk four weeks earlier, and was now required to work late on the coverage of the game.

She tried to get a message to Vincente that afternoon, but what with the excitement of the win and her work at the paper, and the office celebrations, she eventually forgot about her dinner date.

That was when fate intervened and tore her friendship with Estella apart. Vincente arrived as promised at the girl's apartment, and was met instead by Estella. The rest was history.

"Rosa my dear, what is it that makes you look so sad?" Vincente asked with concern, seeing her staring into her memories.

She shrugged, and forced a smile. "Nothing of concern. Come, let us sit outside for a while until our guests arrive," she said, changing the subject. They were just about to leave the kitchen when the gate buzzer rang announcing visitors. "That can't be them, it's far too early." Rosa said, picking up the intercom phone, and studying the video screen.

"Hola, who is there?" she asked, looking closer at the black and white flickering screen, but could not see clearly without her glasses.

Vincente was beside her now and gently took the phone from her. "It is OK my dear. I can see who it is. It is family," he said softly, and pressed the button to open the iron gates.

"I think we have some explaining to do my love. Are you up to it?"

Rosanna Maria Mendoza opened the front door to the unexpected guests. George and Maria stepped nervously over the threshold and met her father, Vincente, holding hands with Rosa. He greeted them with a smile and a sideways glance. "Maria my love. I did not expect to see you today," he said breaking the ice.

Maria was in shock. "Papa, who?. . .why? .. ." she tried to form a sentence but words failed her.

"What I think Maria is trying to say," George continued, "is, what the hell is going on?"

"Come my dear," Rosa said to Maria and guided her away

from George, who she nodded to in recognition, and into the large sitting room. "Let us sit here and I will explain everything from my side..." she said calmly, ".... but you may have to ask your father for his reasons."

George was about to follow when Vincente stepped in his path. "I think we should let the ladies talk a while. Lets us go outside and we can talk... if you want to," he said casually.

The two women sat on the edge of the two-seater settee, and Maria realised the splendor of her surroundings. She had never been in such a glamorous room with such beautiful furniture and fine fabrics, and soft rugs. Rosa stared at Maria while she was distracted. She had seen photos of her as a child that Vincente carried in his wallet, but now, here in the flesh, she looked so like her mother, Estella.

Rosa touched her hand. "My dear girl, it is so good to see you at last. I have wanted to meet you for a long time."

Rosa proceeded to tell the story of how she and Maria's mother had moved to Madrid to find work, and how her best friend ended up marrying Vincente.

"So Vincente," George wanted to know "how do you know this lady, and why is she such a secret?"

Vincente begin to tell the story of how, by chance, he came to meet Maria's mother in 1959.

"The two had a huge row, and Rosa threw Estella out of the apartment. She had to go somewhere, so I took her into my rooms at the Palace. I had a job there, as is the custom if your parents are in-service." He paused to make sure George understood this. "Yes, yes, go on." George demanded.

"Well," Rosa continued, "after your mother left me we never spoke again. I had no idea where she had gone, as she did not return to work. I also could not send any post to her."

Maria looked at the older woman and a tear swelled in her left eye. She went to wipe it away but Rosa reached up and dabbed it with her tissue. "Thank you," Maria said feeling embarrassed.

"After a while I met someone else, a business man in

property, and we married a year later." She paused to consider, as she often did, if she married out of spite or revenge, it was certainly not love, not then. "We had a good life but I was unable to have children, which was a strain on our marriage. Then Ralph, my husband, died whilst out swimming one day. That was twenty years ago."

"Estella moved in with me in my small two room apartment in the servant's wing. My parents were kind to her but did not really approve. She left her job, not being able to face Rosa, and I got her a job as a cleaner." Vincente smiled at his own memories. "We were in love George, really in love. Do you know that feeling?"

George certainly did - with his beloved Aimee and now with Maria. He understood why Vincente would have wanted to be with her forever.

"Everything was fine for six months until someone found out Estella was Basque. Whispers spread and tongues wagged until the chief of staff came and told me she, or we, had to leave."

"I met Vincente, again, by accident one day in Madrid. I very rarely go there now, but had to attend some dinner in honor of my husband, ten years after his death. It was all very formal, and to be honest very boring." Maria said nothing but kept looking at Rosa, her curiosity increasing all the time. "Well, I do not go to Madrid often so I made an appointment to see my solicitor the following day before travelling home. After the meeting I decided to walk a while as it was a perfect September afternoon. The leaves on the oak trees were turning autumnal orange and the air was crisp but not cold." Rosa had been staring at the window, but now turned to face Maria again. "I walked along the Calle Gran Via to take a look at the old ABC building where we worked and wished I had not. I came over dizzy and nearly fainted." Rosa closed her eyes at the memory and shook her head slowly. "The gentleman, who helped me that September day from falling over, was your father."

"So you both left?" George guessed.

"Yes, we left and returned to her home town, Pamplona. Her mother let us stay, and when she died, we inherited the house. A year later, we had Maria. I worked for a local carpenter where he taught me the trade, but there was little business to be had, and money was scarce."

Vincente looked out to the horizon and the vast expanse of the Bay of Biscay. "I should have followed everyone else at my age and become a waiter or barman. Tourists were everywhere and the hotel business was booming - all the lads in town were moving to the coast for work, even without any experience." He paused again for a moment. "As luck would have it I got an evening job as cook in a local restaurant. The owner thought the tourist trade would benefit Pamplona with the increasing popularity of the *encierro*, the running of the bulls. He was right and business was good, and I learnt a new trade."

Maria gasped. "That was... amazing.... how... why... was he there?" she asked, wanting to know the whole story now.

Rosa sighed and was still holding Maria's hand. "At first, of course, I did not know it was Vincente... it had been nearly forty years since I last saw him," she paused and smiled broadly. "He leaned over me and said, *"Rosa, are you falling for me again?"* Well I did not understand at first, and then I looked into his eyes and knew it could only be one man." Rosa paused for a moment more. "He took me to a cafe and we talked and talked for hours. He had been working at the reception I had attended the previous evening and saw me on the top table. He had been asked to help in the kitchen by the owner of the catering company, someone from Pamplona, where he learnt to cook."

Maria remembered something too. "Yes, I do remember him going to Madrid to help a friend but it was a long time ago..." she said, realizing that was around the time he started to make unannounced trips away from home.

Rosa looked away, feeling guilty for the deception that had been born out of their deceit. "He had followed me back to my hotel, and then again in the morning when I went to my solicitor, and afterwards for a nostalgic walk, where I fell into his arms." Rosa leaned back on the settee, exhausted with storytelling.

"I am sorry if this is difficult for you..." Maria started to say.

"No not at all." Rosanna Maria interrupted, "It is us who must apologize and put things right. I am glad you are here. It is appropriate as well," she said in a matter of fact way, as she rose from the sofa.

"I worked then in his restaurant in Pamplona for five years until Estella died. I could not stay in our house without her, so I sold up and found a small bar and restaurant in Calabaza. Maria was not happy. She was just sixteen and had to leave her friends behind and start a new life in a small town." Vincente closed his eyes reflecting on his words. "You think it was a mistake, don't you George?"

"I am not in a position to judge you, Vincente. God knows I struggled with leaving family and friends behind to do much the same as you did." George said, offering some cold comfort.

The two men looked at each other with solemn faces. "I like you George. You understand what needs to be done when something needs to be done!"

George blinked, as if it would refocus the statement Vincente had just delivered, but it did not. Was he trying to be philosophical, or was it another cryptic message which he was supposed to pick up on?

Just then, luckily for George, the two women joined them on the patio, arm in arm. "I think we are in need of refreshment my dear. Will do your magic for us all?" Rosa asked Vincente with a smile he could not refuse. Maria sat next to George taking his hand and squeezing it. "That was an amazing story," she said in English to George, "both sad and romantic at the same time."

"How much did you know about Vincente meeting your mother?"

"Nothing. He always said they met in a restaurant. I knew nothing of Madrid or her life then." Maria looked drained and tired, still coming to terms with the day's events.

"I think I should get you home. We can talk more when Vincente gets back." George suggested.

Rosanna Maria was not fluent in English but picked up on 'get you home'.

"Maria, you must stay and eat, and we need to talk some more," she said almost desperately.

"Yes, I need some food, but we must return. I have left Jorge with a friend and I did not know we would be so long."

Rosa smiled at hearing Jorge's name. "How is he? Vincente tells me he is growing fast."

"Yes, very, but he will be missing me. Perhaps you can visit." Maria suggested.

Rosanna Maria smiled at the thought. "That would be nice. One day soon, if you think it. . appropriate," she added, still not sure how Maria would view her father's relationship with her mother's rival.

Vincente arrived carrying a large tray of cold meats, salad, tortilla and chorizo. "It's not much but we are cooking for friends' tonight," he said opening some wine.

"I was saying, papa, we must really go. Jorge is with Angel and it is not fair to leave him so long. I must just call her to say what time we will be back," and she went into the lounge for some privacy.

"George?" Vincente said, pouring the wine. "Just how did you find me here, miles from home?" George knew he would ask the question eventually, and he still had not thought of a suitable answer. "To be honest Vincente." he paused and looked at Rosa, "... which is what we seem to be doing today, I bugged your car. I tracked it here."

Vincente was translating to Rosa, who laughed loudly. "It is not that funny," he complained. "It violated my... space."

"Oh, be quiet you dear man." Rosa said, playfully slapping his arm. "I think ten years is long enough, don't you? And I do not want to hear you have been cross with them. We brought this on ourselves, remember? She finished on a more serious note.

Vincente shrugged, but did not translate for George. "We will talk about this again," he said to George, smiling, so as not to displease Rosa.

Maria returned saying they must go. "Angel has plans for later so we must get back. Papa, I am sorry if we have upset you, but we... I... needed to know, I am not sorry for that."

Vincente took hold of Maria's hands and kissed each one. "I would not do anything to hurt you, but I really thought you would not approve of Rosa if you knew the truth. I am sorry my dear, but I thought it was best at the time. I see now perhaps I was wrong." Vincente was not used to apologizing, and Maria could see he was humbled.

Her emotions were still mixed, and although she had heard the reasons for the charade, she was going to need time to digest this new information, and whether it would have any long lasting effect on her relationship with her father.

Rosa said her goodbyes on the patio and Vincente walked with George and Maria to the gates.

"Vincente, this apart, I do want to talk to you about El Tango sometime." He said offering his hand, adding, "I hope there are no hard feelings."

Vincente shrugged and raised his arms as if the past couple of hours had been nothing more than a social visit. "Feelings are a peculiar thing are they not?" he replied, leaving George even more perplexed.

"Papa." Maria intervened. "We must go." She turned and walked out without saying anymore, and not even attempting to kiss her father.

This time it was George's turn to shrug.

George caught up with Maria at the car. "You did not say goodbye to Vincente . .or kiss him."

"George, I am not in kissing mood just now. Can we please leave?"

They drove back mainly in silence, although Maria did sleep for a while. They arrived back at El Tango at 4.00pm, and George returned the car to Martin.

"That's a long two hours," Martin said, looking at his watch.

"I am so sorry. I will explain one day, but I must get back now and get some sleep."

George put the laptop in the basket of the push-bike, and cycled slowly back up to the farmhouse. He slumped on the settee exhausted, not only from the drive but the sheer realization of what they had discovered today. His last thoughts were of Maria and how she would cope in the coming days and weeks, and it was the first time, he later realized, he had fallen asleep without thinking of Aimee.

Chapter 7. September

After Aimee died, George was devastated by the loss of his true love. It may be a cliché, but she had been his soul mate, friend, lover and wife.

They had shared so much in common, which can be unusual in a marriage, especially after thirty years. They listened to music, watched films and swopped books. Went to the theatre and liked the same food. Aimee had also built up a good small PR company which Bonnie now runs.

George would lie in bed and curl up with the spare pillow and cry, just thinking of her. *Bed can be the loneliest place in the world when there's no one to share it with.*

Now he was doing the guilt trip. How could he be falling for Maria? Well, that was easy he thought. She had many attributes that Aimee has.... had. She is attractive, intelligent, self aware... George hesitated... she also has a child, a business, and a routine that she may not easily want to break. She also has a father who has a lot to say in the running of her life, although that may have changed owing to recent events.

George smiled at the thought. 'Who knows what Columbus Day will bring?' If I learnt the Tango will it really make a difference? 'No' George said, out loud, 'that only happens in books and films. Am I ready for marriage? Marriage would be complicated just now.'

At least twice a year Aimee and George would have a 'weep-in'. They would open a bottle of wine. Fill a bowl with peanuts. Curl up in the middle of the large sofa and watch Les Miserables - the 10th Anniversary DVD edition.

They had seen the show in London in 1991 and fell in love with it instantly. It had all the emotional triggers that a good weepy should have; atmospheric music, haunting voices, a villain, a hero, a death, a marriage, and a good rousing ending.

George had tried to get hold of tickets for the 10th Anniversary show at the Albert Hall in 1995, but failed. So they bought the video and vowed to watch it at least once a year (the other weepy they watched alternately with Les Mis was Moulin Rouge, the musical, which has the same emotional attributes).

Even by the end of *I Dreamed a Dream*, both of them would be crying, and by the very end, sobbing uncontrollably. They would lie in bed afterwards just holding each other. Afraid to let go. Fearing what it would mean to lose someone they loved.

Now George knew how it felt. 'Like shit, that's how it feels', he repeatedly told himself.

It was the second Sunday in the month and Vincente and Maria were due to come over to hear George's ideas on an investment plan to open El Tango a few evenings a week for dinner. George was convinced the potential was there to expand. They were only fifteen minutes from Aranda de Dueru, the nearest large town, and with some good advertising and marketing, it could stand a chance.

George was not sure how Vincente would react, but since their 'discovery' a few weeks ago, he had been very agreeable to Maria, and almost everyone else. The plan was simple. George would offer to invest two thousand Euros to cover decor, (it badly need a coat of paint) and fixtures and fittings (some tables needed repair or replacing), plus the advertising. The menus would be simple, but adventurous, and where possible using local farm produce. At least the olives would be free.

George liked Sundays. Although most days seemed to merge into each other, Sunday always seemed like Sunday. Maybe it was the sound of church bells, or the smell of roasting meat, or the stillness that came over the town like no other day. Sunday was also a good day to catch-up on the family. George had got into a routine - the only one he allowed himself, to Skype the kids. After a quick shower and shave, and a careful choice of attire, (he still had the memory of being caught nearly naked by Alex a couple of weeks ago), he was ready to call.

He would call Alex first. Mainly because Christopher would not be up before noon, and he would get all the relevant news and gossip from Alex before he spoke to the twins.

The Skype dialing tone rang for two minutes but no one answered. The screen showed Alex was on line, which the other two were not, so why did she not answer? Alex is always there, she is always reliable. George sighed, and caught his reflection in one of the two monitors. "OK, so they've gone shopping. No problem." He looked at the connection status of everyone in his Skype address book. No one else was on line. He checked his watch. 11.20 here. 10.20 in UK. Someone must be up by now he thought. He sighed again and put on some music. He opened up Spotify and selected the Quantic CD, Apricot Morning.

Finding himself with nothing particular to do George was feeling frustrated. The weather was, for once, cloudy. Standing on the patio he could see dark storm clouds forming over the western hills and threatening the day with rain.

Looking down over the town, no one was in sight. Not even a cat or dog. He felt so alone. The cheerful sound of the Quantic CD was not helping. He was melancholy, and changed the music to reflect his mood. He chose Jan Garbarek.

He checked his watch. 12.10pm. He dialed Alex's Skype number again. Still no answer.

He called Maria. Vincente answered. "Ha, at last. Someone is awake." George sounded relieved.

"What are you talking about George?... Of course we are. Maria has had to visit a sick friend in Aranda. I drove her there this morning at 8 o'clock, and Jorge is staying with some friends today. What did you want George?"

"I was wondering if you wanted to come to lunch instead of dinner, but if you are alone it can keep until Maria returns."

"I can still come over, George. We can still talk. I will be over at two."

"Damn," thought George. An afternoon alone with Vincente was not what he really wanted, but at least it was company on this dull and unexciting Sunday.

George had just enough time to make the Tagine for lunch, although it was to have been the evening meal. He set to work in the kitchen preparing all the ingredients. He and Aimee had made this dozens of times so he knew the recipe of by heart. They had first brought a Tagine many years ago in Almeria, in southern Spain.

George prepared the lamb and seasoned it with ground ginger, cinnamon and pepper. Once the meat had been seared, he stirred in apricots, prunes, onions and tomato paste, along with some stock. George looked at his watch again, twelve-thirty. Excellent he thought. Should be ready by two. He tried Skyping his children again but still no one picked up.

Vincente arrived dead on two. "Lunch smells good," he said entering the lounge via the patio.

"I hope so. We need something warming on a day like this. Must be the coldest September in history," George responded, putting the couscous on to cook, which would take only five minutes.

They sat at the table in the lounge and ate in silence for while. George liked to think it was because Vincente was absorbed with the food, but he seemed to have something on his mind. George broke the silence.

"I wanted to talk to you both about an idea I have for El Tango." Vincente said nothing, so George continued.

"I want to invest..." He decided not to name the amount of money just then. . "some money, to open it up, initially a few evenings a week, for dinner." Still Vincente said nothing, but continued to eat. George had the feeling he was being played with.

Without any response from Vincente, he was not sure if he wanted to expand further.

He tried a different approach. "So, what do you think of the idea?" He said with some optimism.

Vincente had finished eating. "Very good lamb, George," he said, pouring himself another glass of Rioja. "Where will all these customers come from? This is a small town."

At last, thought George, some response. "I realize that, and there will be some local business, there always is, but we will advertise in Aranda, it's not too far to drive for an evening out, especially if it's worth the journey." George was sounding enthusiastic, hoping it would rub off on to Vincente.

But instead of questioning George further, he suddenly changed the subject.

"Has Maria said anymore about Rosa?" He asked casually, strumming the table with his fingers.

George sighed, and realised he was going to have to spell it out for Vincente.

"No... well... yes..."

"Which is it, yes or no George?"

"Ok, yes, we... she... talks, I listen..." George said, wishing she was here right now. "She is still coming to terms with the situation... that is all I can say."

Vincente finished his wine and poured another. "I thought as much. She will not open up to me any more George. . I don't know what to do," he said with heartfelt sincerity.

George however was not convinced. "What the hell do you expect Vincente, after all those years of keeping Rosa a secret? You expect your daughter to accept you have a lover - the best friend of her mother..." His voice was raised and his words lingered in the still of the darkening afternoon, "and another thing... did Maria's husband know of Rosa before he died?"

Vincente looked down at his empty plate, and George knew the answer.

"Yes, Juan knew, but not from the start. He caught me leaving early one morning. Back then I left around 4.00am to get the bus to Aranda, then a train to San Sebastian. It was a long journey before I used a car. I swore him to secrecy, and it seems he kept his word."

George wondered if Maria had asked the same question yet.

"After Juan died I used his car and the visits became more regular. His old car finally gave up the ghost last year, so Rosa gave me some money, and I bought the Dodge. I told Maria it was from money I had saved over the years - she seemed to believe me."

George leaned back in his chair and shook his head slowly.

"I am not judging you Vincente," he said quietly. "I just wish you had been more... open with Maria."

George looked at the 'gentle giant' sitting opposite him and thought how different he looked from their first encounter nearly seven months ago, although now it seemed a lifetime away.

"Vincente," George suddenly asked, bringing Vincente back from his thoughts. "Why did Rosa not give you money earlier.... as a friend. She seems well-off."

Vincente smiled. "She wanted to. She was insistent I took it and spend it on Maria and Jorge, but I could not. It would have meant weaving even more lies. Besides, we were not poor... not rich... but we managed... do you understand, George?"

George nodded, and smiled at the enigma.

"What is there to smile for George?" Vincente asked, looking a little hurt.

They talked a while longer about where Maria had gone, and where Jorge was today. There was more silence. George offered Vincente a brandy, which he accepted, and asked about Rosanna Maria.

"She is fine. In fact I am going to see her next weekend," he said in a matter of fact way, "and yes, before you ask, I have told Maria."

"Is she coming to the Columbus Day fiesta?"

Vincente shrugged and sighed. "No, she has other plans unfortunately. That is why I am going next weekend."

No matter how big and bear like someone looks, there is always one thing that will make them sad-eyed and vulnerable as the rest of us - love. Vincente was in love.

It was now 3.15pm and both men were feeling a little

jaded. George wanted to talk more about the restaurant, but the mood was too somber now. It would have to wait.

Suddenly the light outside, what there was of it, virtually vanished. Both men went out on to the patio and saw the darkest sky either of them had ever seen. At that moment deep thunder roared above them, and a few seconds later lighting bounced off the distant hilltops. It was like a scene from a disaster movie, thought George. Then the rains came, hard and fast - sheet rain, and both men dashed inside, and George closed the patio doors tight. "Wow that was amazing. No rain for five months then the Apocalypse."

Vincente smiled, shaking off the rain. "You are almost right. I hope it is not our deadly *Gota Fria,* which strikes without warning, and has no mercy on people or property."

George poured two more brandies and proposed a toast. "To Spain, where the rain can stay on the plain."

"Salud." Vincente echoed, with a somewhat forced smile.

It was a bold move, but George had a wicked thought. Let's watch Les Miserables. It seemed Vincente needed cheering up. Watching a 'weepy' to cheer yourself up does seem like a contradiction, but the 'feel-good' factor at the end overtakes any other emotion by a mile.

"Vincente, have you ever seen the musical Les Miserables?"

"No. I have heard of it, but opera is not my thing."

"Well it's not what I would call an opera proper... "

"It is all singing, no?"

"Yes, but....

"Then it is an opera." Vincente shrugged.

"Look, come and take your drink and let's sit on the sofa and watch it. It is a wonderful story of love, war, politics and freedom. And the music is... exquisite."

"I will sit and have a siesta. You watch, I sleep."

OK, George thought, at least he is on the sofa. He put the DVD in the player and the forty-two inch wall mounted TV echoed with the sounds of the Les Mis overture.

George settled down to what he knew was coming, but

always enjoyed watching someone who had never seen the show before. Either there would be an emotional reaction, usually by *I Dreamed a Dream*, and they were hooked, or, as in Vincente's case, they would go to sleep.

Strangely, and George does not know how or why to this day, Vincente stayed awake. Out of the corner of his left eye he could see the big man's lower lip quivering by the end of Act One, and by the finale, he was physically shaking.

Still looking at the screen, Vincente spoke softly. "If you ever tell anyone about this I will kill you."

George handed him a tissue. "Agreed."

***

It was not until the following evening that George managed to contact Alex. She and Tom had been visiting his parents, but she had no idea where Chris and B were that day.

They caught up on all the gossip and George filled her in on the Peter Barne's death.

"Poor man," she kept saying. Alex, as ever, always tried to show concern for her fellow man, whoever they were.

"He died in his sleep, Alex. Peacefully." George said, trying to sound as reassuring as possible.

There was silence for a few seconds.

"Are you still OK for us coming over for Columbus Day?" Alex broke their thoughts.

George smiled. "Of course. Looking forward to it. Apparently, it is a great weekend. Dancing, fireworks and eating of course. Have you booked the flights?"

"Yes, Chris has taken care of everything. B was not sure but she has said yes. Hope she does not change her mind at the last minute."

"I'll get Chris to email me the flight details."

"How are things with you and Maria, dad?" Alex asked, genuinely interested.

George smiled broadly. "Been too busy to think of anything else."

"Liar," she shouted back at the screen, but laughing.

"Ok. We see each other of course, but nothing has happened, if that's what you are after – well nothing I am prepared to discuss with my daughter."

Alex blew him a kiss and touched the screen. "We all want you to be happy dad." She said, trying to stop her eyes welling with tears. "She is a lovely lady."

"Hey, that's enough of that." George said gently. "Don't start me off, and wiped an eye.

"Sorry dad. Glad you are happy - we all are - that's all."

George blew her a kiss and they finished promising to email each other.

***

Yes, Columbus Day, George thought. I really need to do something about that.

The following Sunday afternoon George cycled down to Martin's workshop but stopped about twenty yards away. Should he or shouldn't he? What if it was just a joke, and she didn't really mean it? On the other hand he did not know if *she* was learning to jive. If she was, and he did not learn the tango, he would feel really foolish. He was just about to decide when Martin's front door opened and Maria came out. George ducked behind the garbage cart. *"Hasta la proxima semana, Martin adios."* George could not hear what she said in detail, and even if he had, he would not be any the wiser. She walked briskly past the garbage cart and around the corner out of sight.

George noticed she was wearing a most unusual outfit for a Sunday. Fitted black t-shirt with spaghetti straps and a short flowing skirt. He walked slowly to Martins door and rang the bell.

Before Martin could say anything, George walked in and started accusing him. "What has been going on here Martin? I just saw Maria leave here wearing the most ridiculous outfit."

Martin smiled. "Sit down, George, and have a beer."

"I don't want a beer... yet. I want some answers."

Martin moved over to the CD player and pressed play. Out boomed Bill Haley playing Rock around the Clock.

George looked dumbstruck. He also felt a complete fool. "You've been giving Maria a dance lesson?" He shouted over the music.

Martin turned the CD off.

"Si, for ten times now. She is very good." Martin smiled, enjoying the moment.

"How's your Tango?" George asked, looking very depressed.

'Why have I left it so late?' George asked himself, looking in the bedroom mirror. He struck a tango dancers' pose. *'Maria secretly having lessons from Martin.'* He could not get the image of Maria out of his head, walking out of Martin's place wearing a T Shirt and a mini skirt.

'If she is taking it that seriously then I am in real trouble.'

Martin had told George he could teach him the basic moves of the Tango which would get him through a three minute routine. After that it was all over. Just three minutes - what could possibly go wrong?

***

George opened the front door and stood staring at the young woman standing in front of him.

"Hi, Uncle George."

"Evie... what on earth..."

"Surprise...?" she said as she walked passed George into the lounge.

"Wow... great place, Uncle George... must have cost a packet."

George was still looking out of the front door trying to put his brain in gear and assess what had just happened.

He turned into the lounge without closing the door. "Evie... it's great to see you... but what are you doing here?"

Evie was around five foot five, long blonde hair, blue eyes and a pear shaped freckled face. She looked sixteen, but George knew she was at least twenty four, and Colin Jackson's daughter. Her hair was caught back with a scrunchie with designer sunglasses perched on her head. She was wearing a Ted Baker pattern T-Shirt and shorts – very short shorts, and the only sign of luggage was a large leather shoulder holdall which she dropped by the front door.

"I wanted a break so decided to do Europe. I looked in Mum and Dad's address book and noted where all their friends live. Did you know they have friends in almost every

European country - isn't that cool - I could travel for ages for free."

At last she stopped to draw breath and slumped onto the soft leather sofa and hung her legs over the arm, giving George a nervous smile.

"Does anyone know where you are Evie, especially Colin and Judy?" George thought of sitting next to her but remembered it was an advantage to stand over someone when questioning them, to gain control, and respect.

"They properly don't give a shit where I am," she replied in a half thoughtful, half angry way. "Got any food in Uncle George? - I'm starving." She suddenly changed tone, got up, and walked over to the kitchen.

So much for control and respect, thought George. He shook his head trying to refocus. "Evie, yes... I can make you something - how about an omelet?" he suggested.

"Great, thanks, and a long cold drink. I'm parched."

"Help yourself. Plenty in the fridge."

George sat on the kitchen stool watching her. She hasn't a care in the world, he mused. Comes in like a whirlwind, and will probably leave the same way in the middle of the night.

What on earth were Colin and Judy thinking... did they even know where she was?

"Hang on." George, he told himself. She is a grown woman, although she does not look it, and has the same rights as anyone to go globetrotting. George thought how frail and vulnerable she looked. Not exactly anorexic, more Kate Moss than Calista Flockhart.

"Evie, how are your parents. It was good of them to come and see me off last March, but not heard much since," he said casually, wondering how much she knew of his working relationship with her father.

She sipped on a cool glass of blueberry and ginger. "They're fine, I guess," she replied without any real thought, but added, "I don't see them a great deal since I left home."

Evie and Bonnie had seen a lot of each other growing up. Parties, BBQ's, holidays, etc., but with Bonnie looking three years older and Evie looking six years younger, they grew apart for a while. George did remember Bonnie said something about bumping into her in Harvey Nics in London, and she had told B something about moving in with a boyfriend.

"Yes, of course," George replied, sounding positive. "How's the boyfriend? Hope it's going well."

She gave him a sideways stare. Then she let it all out. "He left me, the shit," she cried aloud. "Just went one day and hasn't come back, Oh Uncle George I'm so in a mess."... she almost fell of the chair and slumped in George's arms, sobbing and shaking so much the glass of blueberry and ginger slopped alternately onto the floor and then onto George's left arm. George rescued the glass and set it down before his cream cotton shirt was stained beyond repair.

He put his arms around this frail and vulnerable girl and hugged her as he would one of his own, which he had done on many occasions - that's what Dads are for, aren't they?

George, however, was not Evie's dad. "Hey, come on, things are never as bad as they seem, especially when you talk them through," he suggested, trying to install some composure into the girl. He was also wishing Alex or B were here right now. He was comfortable sorting out his own children's problems, arguments and even tantrums, but someone else's kid? George was feeling decidedly uncomfortable right now.

What if Maria suddenly came in? Oh heavens, what if Vincente came in. George shivered at the thought.

"Why are you shaking as well?" she said half sobbing, and half with a curious expression.

"Ahh, it's... err... energy transference... I'm absorbing your... err...."

Evie suddenly stopped shaking and pulled away from him, but still holding his hands. "Uncle George... you're full of shit," she burst out laughing.

George sighed with relief. "You saw though me," and they both laughed - George more nervously than her.

"Make yourself at home while I go and change my shirt. Senora Torres will kill me if this juice doesn't come out."

"Wow, you have a lady that does for you... hope she's not the jealous type Uncle..." but George stopped her this time.

"Evie, listen." She could see he was serious again.

"No she is not. She's over sixty five and happily married, and secondly, while you are here you must stop calling me Uncle. It makes me sound a lot older than I care to be."

"OK... I promise," she said, offering a Girl Guide salute.

George sprinted up the stairs to his bedroom to change his shirt. He sat on the bed seriously considering calling Colin to tell him his daughter had come to stay. How would that go down? Young woman shacks up with old. . err man. He could hear the tongues wagging here and back home. He was many things, but he was not Harrison Ford. He had to make her see sense and call home. He washed the sticky juice off his arm, chose a clean shirt, and went back downstairs.

To his surprise, Evie was whisking eggs and had butter melting in the frying pan.

"Not sure how many eggs you use, but I use four and some milk, got any herbs Unc. . sorry George."

"Yes, I'll get some. They're on the patio." He returned with a handful of Basil.

"Great, my favorite," she exclaimed, and poured the egg mix into the pan. She then expertly took a fork and started to tease the omelet from the edge of the pan, the French way. "Make yourself useful and chop the Basil would you."

George was glued to the spot and transfixed at what he was watching. "Sorry. Yes chef, right away chef," he replied sarcastically, and chopped the herbs coarsely just as she plated the finished dish.

"That looks fantastic - I didn't know you could cook." They took the plates on to the patio. "Why should you. There are probably a lot of things you don't know about me George, same as I don't know a lot about you." She looked him straight in the eyes with a look that made George feel a little uncomfortable again. Was she probing, or just making conversation?

Evie finished her omelet and leaned back in the chair.

"I hear you had some trouble before you left England?" she asked cautiously.

George looked at her but was not shocked or worried about the question. Many people - friends and relatives no less, were probably still talking about the 'problems' George had before he left England. *"Did he or didn't he?"* was the most obvious question. Some were even saying *"Did he kill his wife?"* But not the people who matter. No, the most obvious question was, *"did he rob that bank?"* and if yes, *"where's all that money gone"* or *"He's living the high life in Spain - isn't that where all the villains go?"*

George smiled politely. "Yes, I had many problems as you say before I came here. My wife died for one, and I was arrested for robbery." He wanted to pick his glass up but knew his hand would be shaking at the thought of these memories.

"I'm sorry Unc. . sorry George." Evie put a hand on his and squeezed gently. George pulled away on instinct. "It's OK, Evie. I came here to start a new life. I will never forget, or be out of love with Aimee, but I felt England had nothing else to offer me after the other business, so I came here."

Evie sighed as if she understood everything. "So what did you do, stick a pin in a map?" She laughed.

George relaxed and smiled too. "Well almost. We knew southern Spain quite well, but I had never seen much of the north. So I took into account ferry routes, coastal routes, and time to travel from Madrid or Barcelona airport, *"and I surmised young lady"* putting on his Sherlock Holmes persona, "that this location is ideal for all eventualities," he paused briefly, *"especially for a quick getaway."*

Evie looked serious as hell and she knew she was blushing, and was not sure how to respond, but George burst out laughing, and they laughed aloud together.

George cleared the plates away and Evie offered to wash up, but George said the dishwasher would do it. "Well young lady, you have the choice of three bedrooms. One is in the basement without any windows, or one of the others on the first floor."

"Where is yours?" she asked sheepishly.

"I have a room on the second floor," he replied causally.

"OK, the basement sounds good. Never did like daylight waking me in the morning."

George showed her to the bedroom, and then gave her a tour of the house and outside grounds.

Back in the lounge, George's thoughts turned to what the hell he was going to do with her. She wasn't related to him, but was the daughter of good friends, so he felt obliged in some way to take her in.

"Evie, I really think you should call home and let your parents know where you are. Do they even know you are in Europe?"

She was sitting on the sofa looking forlorn. "OK, I promise. But can I take shower first and change. I have been travelling all day."

George thought this was a delaying tactic, but she did look as if she could do with a change of clothes.

"OK, but as soon as you come back down we call home."

She jumped up from the sofa and threw her arms around George. "Thanks George. I promise"

"It's OK, I just want you to do the right thing by them," and released himself from her somewhat embarrassing embrace.

She retrieved her holdall from where she had dropped it and ran upstairs to have a shower.

George walked back to the patio and took in the still of the late evening. September was a good month in any country he thought. It didn't have the blistering heat of previous months when you spend almost every minute searching for shade. September was a neutral month. On the horizon, he could see forests of deciduous trees change colour every day. He also enjoyed seeing the sun set every evening, but now looked forward even more to seeing it set in the coming months, against the backdrop of this ever-changing colorful scenery.

He wandered back inside and sat at the computer. He checked his email, half expecting mail from Colin asking if he had seen his daughter. Nothing of importance was in the 'in-box' so he shut Outlook down. He was just considering seeing if Colin was on Skype when he saw a reflection in the PC monitor. He turned the swivel chair quickly, to surprise Evie saying, "That was a quick..." but stopped in mid sentence, and froze with an expression that was going to be hard to explain.

Maria stepped back at George's sudden turn, and nearly lost her footing, but grabbed the edge of the sofa to balance herself.

"Oh, I wanted to surprise you..." she said, smiling and regaining her posture. She walked up to George and gave him a kiss.

"What did you say about being quick... who or what is quick?"

Maria sat on George's lap facing him. "Do you think it will hold us both," she asked with a smile, putting her arms around his neck and kissing him, but George was not listening. Instead, he was looking behind Maria at Evie who was standing there with just a bath towel wrapped around her thin, naked body.

"George, what is it you are look.... ing." Maria hit the floor before the last syllable had left her mouth - a mouth that was now open as wide as her eyes. She had slid off George's lap having turned to see Evie standing there, almost naked.

George sprang to try to catch Maria, but missed her hand and instead tripped over her, propelling himself in Evie's direction. He automatically reached out with his left arm to grab something tangible, but the only nearest tangible object was Evie's shoulder, which, being wet, caused George's hand to slip off the shoulder and down to the towel, which came away in his hand, and ended up covering his face as he lay sprawled out two yards away, on the other side of the room.

Maria was now sitting upright, against the back of the sofa, trying to focus on what just happened. George moaned, and turned over just as Evie retrieved the towel and covered herself with it. She offered a hand to George, which under any other circumstances would have been hilarious, but George helped himself up from the floor. He knelt down next to Maria. "Are you OK?" He asked, but Maria pushed him away and stood up. "I guess that's a yes then." George offered, stepping back. "Maria, this is Evie, the daughter of an old friend who arrived unexpectedly a few hours ago, and she is staying a few days..." George's sentence trailed off as he realised Maria was not looking at him, or listening to him. "Maria, I'm trying to explain."

Maria then turned to George, and George suddenly knew what Vincente felt like when she let rip at him for being AWOL. But, much to his relief, Maria was calm.

"I hear you George. Now I suggest we get this young lady some clothes before she gets cold, si?"

Before George could say anything Maria had taken Evie's hand and led her off to the bedroom. "And some coffee would be good George," she called out as she left the room.

George smiled to himself, scratching his head. "That could have been worse... " he thought, "unless it's still to come".

He made coffee and poured himself a brandy - he felt he deserved it. He kept playing the scene over and over in his mind, but could not at any point remember seeing Evie, well. . naked. Maria must have, but he was pleased how she had kept her cool, especially after sliding on to the floor and nearly being trodden on.

A long ten minutes later Maria and Evie came back into the lounge and sat opposite George on the other sofa. Evie had dressed in jeans and a black T Shirt which had 'FCUK' printed in large pink letters across the chest.

George forced himself to focus on Maria, who was not yet smiling.

"So, where are our brandies?" she asked.

"Yes, of course, I'm sorry." George spurted out as he went to the sideboard. He poured two generous shots of brandies.

"Trying to get us drunk I think," Evie said with a straight face.

"And have his way with us both." Maria nodded in agreement.

George sat dazed, for more than once that day, looking at Maria, then Evie, and back to Maria.

After several agonizing seconds when no one had spoken, Maria smiled and then laughed, as did Evie.

"You... we have a word for that." George waved a finger at the two women, who were enjoying his torture, "but I'm too much of a gentleman to say what it is."

This made the girls laugh even more. "Oh, come on Uncle George, we were only playing with you."

"Si, *uncle* Jorge... *only playing with you*." Maria mimicked.

Maria got up and sat next to George. She linked arms, and gave him a kiss on the cheek. "All better," she said and kissed him again.

"That was not fair. I was very worried about you and what you may have thought."

"I have a confession, George." Maria paused to ensure she had his attention.

"I knew Evie was here. She came in to the bar asking directions, and we got talking. But I did not know she was walking around half naked. That was a real surprise," she admitted, giving Evie a mocking glare.

George shook his head. "Well that's the last time I trust a woman in need." But eventually smiled and put his arm around Maria before adding. "Any more surprises for me?"

"Yes, actually, but you will have to wait until Columbus Day to find out."

***

George was fully aware of the time of year and the approaching 'Festival', when he was going to either make a fool of himself, or, ...or what? Leave, run away... *'out of the question'* he told himself. *'Then what?'* Feign illness? Twist an ankle? The problem was, he actually wanted to be there and dance with Maria. So what was troubling him?

He had a foreboding about the 12th October that was not planned, and he felt sure Evie had something to do with it. She had spent the last week since her arrival being very helpful around the house, much to Senora Torres' displeasure, and had helped in the restaurant kitchen as Angel had been off ill for a few days.

Evie said she had called home, and George had heard her talking on the mobile, but did not speak to Colin or Judy himself. Evie said they were fine with it and thanked him for 'taking her in'. When he said he would like to talk to them she always had some excuse about them not being there much, or they were just going out.

George had expected to spend the last eighteen months being paranoid after the 'robbery', and the subsequent enquiry, but the move had been good for him and apart from the Peter Barnes episode, things had gone well. Until now. Now that paranoid feeling was back again.

Chapter 8. October

The Skype call came at seven p.m local time. It was Alex.
"Hi love, nice surprise. How are things?"
Alex looked tired. "Hi, dad. Fine thanks, just wanted to see how you are coping with the lodger."
George grinned at the screen. "She's fine. I suppose B told you all about her. She said she wanted to stay a couple of weeks and then move on. What could I do?" George asked sincerely.
"Have you spoken to Colin or Judy yet?"
"No, not been able to get in touch with them. Ex directory," he lied.
Alex grinned. "Thought you could do anything with that computer, Dad."
George looked thoughtful for a moment. "Yes, I could, but I will never admit it to anyone but you," he said, finally, smiling.
"Listen, Dad, we are all coming out next weekend for the Festival. It's all arranged."
"That's great news!" George said excitedly.
"We've taken the Friday off and I've booked a flight to Madrid arriving eleven-thirty, and we fly back Sunday evening at nine o'clock. I know it's a rush but we wanted to be there for you... and... "
"And what love?"
"Nothing... just looking forward to it."
"That's wonderful - thank you Alex," and he blew a kiss to the screen. "I just hope it's not a disappointment."
"It sounds fun. I've been looking it up on the web. Most towns and villages have dancing and fireworks, and of course lots of Sangria. By the way Tom's coming as well, so we'll all be there for you."
"That's great, haven't seen him in a while, except on the screen. Where is he by the way?"
"Football of course. Should be back soon."

"Do email me the flights won't you? Are you hiring a car?"

"Yes, Chris has done that."

Alex paused a moment as if collecting her thoughts. "Dad, you will be careful won't you?"

"Of course love, always. Have a good weekend. See you soon and thanks again, and don't forget your party frock." They both blew each other a kiss, and George closed the connection.

He sat looking at the screen wondering what Alex had meant when she said, "You will be careful." Careful of what? Dancing? Getting run over? Getting caught? Take your pick, George.

The following day George made breakfast as usual and called Evie to come down... no, up, from the basement for breakfast. She had elected to sleep in the downstairs bedroom without any natural light, and George was happy to let her.

A bleary-eyed Evie appeared in T Shirt and shorts. "You look terrible, Ms Jackson."

"Gee, thanks, George. Not what a girl wants to hear," replied Evie, looking around for her sunglasses. "Martin asked me back for a coffee. He wanted to talk about vintage cars. And he *did* want to talk about cars. You could have told me he's gay," she said with some bitterness.

George smiled back. "I can't go around telling you everyone's preferences," he whispered, as if the whole town could hear him.

"Well, he looks straight to me, and bloody good looking - it's not fair," she sulked, and took her revenge out on a slice of buttered toast.

George let her cool off a while before approaching the subject of her arrival.

They talked casually about home back in England, and what she had been doing for the past few years. George almost changed his mind, but he had to find the truth, but before he could say anything more, Evie's mobile rang. She looked at the screen and then turned it off, looking somewhat embarrassed, George thought.

"Who was that, Mum or Dad?" George enquired.

"No, no one I recognized. Probably a wrong number." She tried to sound convincing but was not.

George finished his coffee and decided to get it over with.

"Evie." He cleared his throat. "Do you have anything you want to tell me?" He tried to sound sympathetic and not too heavy handed.

"What do you mean, George?" she replied, with a genuinely puzzled expression.

"How did you come to be here really?"

"I told you. I decided to travel some to clear my head, and found your address in mum and dads' address book."

George was not convinced.

"I've known your Dad a long time Evie. We have done work together. Did he send you here to spy on me?" He sounded more threatening than he intended to, and the girl winced.

Evie just sat there for what seemed ages biting her lip. George could see she was trying to decide what to say. "I'm sorry Evie. I didn't mean to get all heavy with you, but I need to know what's going on."

She took a deep breath. "Oh shit, shit, shit. I told Dad this was not a good idea." George said nothing. He sat waiting for the rest of it.

"I *am* on holiday - that is the truth. I was thinking of where to go and dad suggested Spain. OK, I said, Ibiza, Majorca, Tenerife, all sound good to me, but he said how about a quiet village in the middle of Spain, miles from nowhere."

George was smiling.

"It's not funny, George. I could be having a ball right now... sorry, no offence, but I am not a country girl."

George tried to look serious. "No offence taken Evie, but why did Colin want you here?"

"It's something to do with the job he's doing for a bank in London. Something about the one you worked for once. ." George had stopped listening. His mind was racing. What was Colin doing, sending his daughter to spy on him?

George looked at Evie and she recoiled slightly. "I'm not

going to hurt you, never think that, but what did he tell you to do here, I need to know."

Evie sighed. "Well, that's the strange part. He just said, have a good time and stay as long as you can. What's this all about George?"

The pair of them sat there thinking. George stirred his coffee and Evie just stared at George, waiting for some response.

"Do you want me to call Dad and you can speak to him?" she suggested, thinking that was a good idea and all would be resolved. She found her iPhone and was about to press the speed dial number.

"No love. Don't call. I don't think he wants me to call. I can't explain it, but I see what he has done now." George smiled as if he had found the meaning of life.

"Your old man is right. Have a good time, and you can stay as long as you like."

Evie almost ran over to George and hugged him. "Thanks Uncle George. I thought you were going to throw me out."

"I would never do that. . and your dad knows that too."

They finished breakfast, and George told her of the *en masse* arrival on Friday of his children. "You may have to share with Bonnie for a few nights."

"Great, we get on OK. She's also my size in everything, and I may need to scrounge something for the party."

When he was alone later that day, George reflected on the morning's conversation with Evie. He knew Jackson Securities had been hired by Oliver Barnes to investigate him, as Peter Barnes had said back in August. Colin would have agreed to send an 'operative' to keep an eye on him, but who that was would be left entirely to Colin Jackson's discretion.

Oliver seemed obsessed with nailing George, and would seem to have had the backing of the board to fund such an arrangement. George hoped he had not come cheap.

12th October - Columbus Day

George suggested they walk into town. Driving was out of the question if they were to be drinking most of the night.

"No way! Not in these heels!" Bonnie announced.

"I agree, dad. Not an option for us girls," Alex confirmed. Her sister gave her a condescending smile. "See," Bonnie exclaimed rather too excitedly," even Alex agrees, so no walking."

George looked at each of his offspring in turn, and was heartened by how they had each made an effort to look presentable for the party. Not that it was a formal affair, but he had always instilled a sense of occasion into them, and thankfully, they seemed to have remembered it.

Chris was wearing Calvin Klein jeans with a white Paul Simon shirt.

Alex wore a navy summer dress with a small paisley print. Not designer, but very nice.

Bonnie wore a very pretty yellow strapless Stella McCartney dress, with a white belt and Louboutin shoes.

The other two members of the group were equally smart. Evie had borrowed one of Bonnie's second choice outfits, and George could not help noticing how similar they looked standing together.

He also looked down at the girl's choice of footwear and sighed. "No. Not only will you not walk into town in those, you probably won't even be able to dance in them!"

"Let us girls worry about that, Dad." Alex said, and put her arm through her dads' arm.

"Well, I'm ready to party, so let's go," making the decision to drive an easier option for George. "OK, he conceded, "but we'll have to get a taxi home. I'm not going on fruit juice all night."

The Columbus Day festival in Spain is held every year on the 12th October to celebrate the discovery of the new world by Columbus, for the Spanish Crown, back in the fifteenth century, and it is traditional for the Mayor to have the first dance to formally start the evening off, and Vincente was not going to break a long tradition.

The 'Morton' party arrived *en masse* at eight fifteen, and George saw Maria and Vincente sitting at one of the large round tables they had reserved. George and Maria kissed and he introduced everyone again, including Tom, who was very impressed with Maria.

"Tom, come and sit next to me," Alex called over to her husband. Tom blushed and obediently sat down. "You ladies look beautiful. George, should I be jealous?" Maria asked.

"Only if they were not my daughters, or a close friend." He added, looking at Evie.

George sat between Maria and Vincente. Alex was also next to Vincente, then Tom, then Bonnie and Evie and finally Chris, leaving one empty seat between him and Maria.

"Are we expecting anyone else?" asked Chris.

"You never know," George offered. "It's always good to have a spare place for an unexpected guest," he said, giving Evie a warm smile. She smiled back and blew her uncle a kiss, and mouthed, 'thank you.'

"So, Vincente, who is the lucky lady tonight - I mean for the first dance of course." George asked, turning to face him. He then realised it may not have been a good move to have sat next to this giant of a man. Elbow room was going to be a problem, and *what on earth* was that cologne he had on?

"Ah yes, I have not chosen yet, but any of you can offer." He grinned, looking at the three ladies around the table."

"I was thinking of your daughter actually," George suggested.

Vincente looked surprised and a little hurt. "George, please. This is my choice. Not a family matter," and winked at him.

George understood all right. "I hope he is going to behave himself tonight," he whispered to Maria.

"I can always disown him, again," she suggested and smiled, putting a hand on George's knee, which made him swallow hard.

Just then little Jorge came over to say hello. "He is on a table with many friends. It would not be so much fun with all the grown-ups," Maria explained. She then introduced Jorge to everyone around the table, and he nodded to each seated guest. His mother gave him a kiss and brushed his hair with her hand, making the boy wince with embarrassment. He escaped as quickly as possible to return to his own world without grown-ups.

George checked his iPhone was on. "Hey, Dad. No work tonight." Alex gave him a stern look.

George pocketed the phone quickly as if to hide his actions. "Sorry, force of habit."

The background music which had been playing from a CD player suddenly stopped and spontaneous applause resonated around the large hall.

Everyone turned to see the band take their places, with Angel centre stage, microphone in hand.

"Buenas tardes" she shouted in to the microphone. Everyone replied in unison - *buenas tardes.*

She looked stunning, thought George. No wonder Vincente was always flirting with her. At least he hoped it was just flirting, especially as they now knew of the existence of Rosanna Maria.

Angel explained what was to happen this evening; when the buffet would be ready, what time they have to finish etc, etc, and oh, yes, of course, the tradition of the first dance by the Mayor. Angel seemed to be padding these announcements out, and she kept glancing at the main door, and back and forth to Maria.

Vincente, on hearing his name, stood and was about to walk over to Angel when Maria caught his shirtsleeve. "Si, what is it my dear?" leaning down to hear her reply.

Maria however gently kissed his cheek and turned him to face the door. Standing there was Rosanna Maria, looking a little nervous, but also very glamorous. Maria went over and kissed her and took her hand and led her back to the table. She stood in front of Vincente, who was for once, speechless.

"Hola, Vincente, may I have this dance?" she whispered.

Vincente looked around the hall. Everyone was looking at

him and this stranger who had appeared from nowhere. *"How, why, where"* raced though his mind. He knew he did not have time to get all these answers now, so he did the only thing he could.

"My dear Rosa, I would be honored."

The room exploded with applause, and everyone stood and clapped the couple to the floor.

George leaned towards Maria. "I assume this was your doing?"

She half turned to face him. "Si." She smiled with some self-satisfaction. "I could not say anything George in case she decided not to come. I hope you can forgive me," and kissed him on the cheek, (which was kiss number two, according to Bonnie).

"It is Vincente you may have to ask for forgiveness." He said, nodding in the couple's direction.

"He is potty in my hands." George smiled and was about to correct her when the music started. Vincente and Rosanna took hold of each other, and to everyone's surprise waltzed effortlessly around the hall to continued applause.

"I had no idea your father could dance, I mean, looking at him it's not something that comes to mind." George winced, hoping he did not sound too patronizing.

But Maria was equally surprised, and stunned, at what she was witnessing.

"I had no idea he danced this well. It looks like he is talking to her though."

George caught Vincente's expression as they passed close to their table.

"He's not talking Maria, he's counting. He is counting in time to the music." Maria looked at George and finished the sentence, *'as if he had been taught it.'* She said, and they laughed so loudly they had to sit down.

"Dad, Maria," Alex called over, "what's so funny? I think they look good together. Who is she?" By now, Alex had sat next to George who was still trying to control himself.

"I'm sorry, Alex." But Maria started to explain who Rosanna Maria is in Spanish. "Ok, I understand, but why are you laughing?" Alex insisted.

"It seems Vincente has been taking dancing lessons for tonight from..." George looked around the hall. "Where is he Maria? I thought he would want to see this."

"Who, Dad, who?" Alex was now tugging his shirtsleeve.

"Our very talented car mechanic, Martin. It seems he is good at many forms of dance instruction." He said, looking Maria in the eye.

She smiled that wonderful smile and her green eyes glistened. "Si, OK he taught me too. You will see later if he did any good."

George did not want to think about that. If she was willing to Jive tonight, it meant he was going to have to Tango. Could he slip and break his ankle? No, that really would hurt and would mess up his plans for later.

"George, look, I see him, over there." Maria pointed to the side of the stage.

Martin was standing behind the upright piano taking a video of the dancing couple. George shook his head. "He is a dead man Maria."

"I hope not. You may need him again one day," she laughed. Alex wasn't sure what that meant but suggested it was about time to go and dance as well.

"Yes, come on, lets join them," and as soon as Maria and George stepped onto the floor, many others followed, and George saw out of the corner of his eye, Vincente stop and hug Rosa, and kiss her on the cheek.

Back at the table, Vincente was as gracious as ever. He introduced Rosanna around the table, and poured a glass of wine for her. He raised his glass and everyone followed suit. "To family and friends. "Salud." "Salud." everyone echoed.

"So," George started to say to Vincente, but Vincente leaned over, and in a low voice said, "Was this your idea or my daughter's?"

George straightened up and looked past the big man to Rosa. "Good to meet you again, Rosa. I hope you enjoy the evening." Maria translated and Rosa said she was pleased to be there, if only a little nervous meeting all these people.

If Vincente had more questions, he did not have time to

ask them. Fellow guests, friends and colleagues came and shook his hand, and insisted on an introduction to the attractive stranger by his side.

The evening continued as expected. Everyone danced. Angel's band was in fact very good, and played styles of music to suit all ages.

At nine-thirty, the buffet opened, and an orderly queue shuffled past the extensive choice of hot and cold food.

Others stepped outside to get some air, or for a smoke. George slipped out the door while Maria was getting her food. He nodded to various familiar faces, but realised he did not actually know many people that well, apart from Maria, Vincente and Martin, and of course Mrs Torres. He considered lighting up but decided against it. Just as well. Alex crept up and slid her arm in his. "Not thinking of..."

"No, not at all," he said, smiling unconvincingly.

"Good, because I do not want you breathing smoke over your grandchild."

It took a few seconds for the penny to drop. "Alex, that's fantastic, *when, how?*" George blurted out, his mind racing. "Sorry, not how of course."

Alex laughed, and tried to suppress a choking feeling, but a tear rolled down her cheek as she burst into tears and she hugged her dad.

"Oh darling, I'm so happy for you. Why didn't you say anything earlier?"

Alex sobbed some more. "I wanted you to be the first to know, and we haven't been alone since we arrived."

More sobbing.

"I just wish mum... ," but she couldn't get the words out.

"I know my love, I know." George hugged her again and people nearby looked on wondering what was going on between this young woman and this older man.

Tom appeared at the door and saw his wife and father-in-law, and knew what had been said. He came closer and put his arms around Alex and she turned and kissed him.

"Congratulations son. I'm so very proud of you both."

"Thanks, George," Tom said, and the two men hugged.

More looks from the onlookers, and many then knew something was either very wrong or very good, but could not make out which it was.

Then Martin appeared with his video camera strung around his neck on a lanyard.

"Hey, there you are. What's happening here?"

George explained the good news and Martin smiled and congratulated George, Alex, and Tom with kisses and hugs. He turned to the nearby audience and explained in Spanish, which resulted in a cheer and sounds of 'congratulations' and 'good luck.'

Alex was suddenly speaking Spanish too, and acknowledging the compliments.

They worked their way back inside and stood at their table.

"What's going on? What was all that commotion?" Chris asked.

Tom and Alex looked at each other then at her brother and sister.

"Well," deep breathe, "you're going to be an uncle and auntie."

Gasps of delight and squeals of pleasure filled the hall, and people turned to see what was going on.

Chris and Bonnie rushed around the table and kissed and hugged their sister, and Tom.

"Why didn't you tell us before? That's not fair," Bonnie said, trying to sound annoyed.

"We wanted to tell dad first - I thought it only fair," and wiped away another persistent tear.

More hugs and kisses. This time Vincente, Maria and Evie joined in and food was forgotten for a while.

George sat in silence, looking the proud 'granddad-to-be', and watching his daughter accept the accolades. Maria slid next to him and took his hand, and squeezed it gently.

He squeezed back but kept focusing on Alex.

Finally Maria asked, with gentle concern, "Are you OK?"

"I'm fine," and turned to Maria and kissed her on the cheek. "I'm more than fine. It's a perfect evening," *and it's not over*, he reminded himself.

Maria smiled, but knew he was thinking of someone else. It would be hard for him over the next few hours, and days, not being able to share this news with his wife.

In the last six months she had discovered it was possible to fall in love again, at her age, and she knew it was right. Why not have a new life, a new man - if he was ready to renounce his beloved wife.

Martin came to the table with a plate of food, which seem to remind the others that they had not yet eaten. "There's plenty left," he announced.

"Do you want me to get you some food, George?" Maria asked.

"No, I'm fine thank you. I can always share," and picked up a white asparagus stalk from Martins plate.

"Hey, get your own." Martin joked.

"So, Martin, you taught Vincente to dance. How long has that been going on?" George enquired.

Martin finished a mouthful of battered fish. "He came to me a couple of weeks ago. Said he had just remembered the tradition of the first dance. He was hoping to have it with Angel," and shrugged. "Where did this lady come from, and who is she?"

Maria had returned with her food and explained in Spanish - it was quicker. Martin let out a long whistle.

"Then you expected to film Vincente and Angel, didn't?" George asked.

Martin smiled. "It was something I planned to do. Not just the first dance. I have taken film of everyone for..."

"Posterity?" George offered.

"Si, George, for that, and I have more to film, yes." He winked at Maria, who may have blushed, but George was looking at Martin, and considering snatching the camera from around his neck.

Vincente and Rosa had found a quiet spot in the back of the kitchen. Not romantic, but at least private. "My love, why did you come tonight. I thought you wanted our relationship to be... discreet."

She touched Vincente's face. He took her hand and kissed

it. "Oh, my dear, lovely man. Don't you think this has been going on for too long? Now Maria knows, what is the point of keeping it a secret, that is, unless you have someone else here you do not want me to know about," she asked, raising one eyebrow.

Vincente feigned hurt. "Rosa, how could you think that? I enjoyed our discreet meetings, sneaking away in the night; it made me feel young again."

"You are a romantic - I know that. I love you Vincente, as much as my dear departed friend did. We are not doing anything wrong, but now we should be open about it.

Vincente was listening but his emotions were mixed. Rosa continued. "I want to sell my house and move to somewhere else, maybe in the south, or even Ibiza, and I want you to decide if you want to come with me."

Now his mind was racing. This was not what he was expecting. She is giving me a choice. *Continue openly and leave here, or say goodbye - maybe forever.*

Angel and the band took to the stage again. "Ladies and Gentlemen, we have two dances for you tonight by a couple who bet each other to learn how to dance."

"Wow, that sounds exciting, I wonder who they are." Alex said looking around the hall.

"What, what did she say, Alex?" George asked.

"A couple are going to dance for us."

George turned red. "Oh shit," and turned to Maria. "What is she saying? Tell her she is fired if she keeps it up."

"Too late, lover, I think it's our cue to dance," and Maria grabbed his hand and pulled George onto the dance floor, to a burst applause.

"Ahh, and here they are, our very own Maria Julia Caldas, the best boss in the world, and her partner, George Morton." More applause.

Maria was translating as fast as she could. "She said I was a good boss," smiling and waving at her friends.

"She won't have a boss after tonight." George promised, through clenched teeth.

"She is telling everyone how you have been here six

months and are enjoying your new home in Calabaza." More applause.

"She is saying you are a lovely man and hope you will settle down here and make the owner of a certain restaurant very happy..."

Maria turned to face Angel with hands on hips. "Sorry Maria. He told me to say it."

"Who?"

"George." She whispered out loud. Everyone laughed.

"What did she say Maria, my Spanish is not good yet?" He said smiling broadly.

"You planned all this. You two," she said, glaring at Angel. "You, you...."

George held onto her arms to keep her from hitting him, and calm her down.

"Can we talk about this later? I think they want us to dance." He gestured to the waiting audience.

Maria faced George and blew him a kiss. She turned to Angel, "OK, ready," she confirmed.

"One, two, three," Angel called out, and the band struck up a familiar rock n' roll number.

Everyone was on their feet again, clapping and shouting *"Well done Maria"* and *"Show him how it's done, Maria"* and *"Best jive I've seen Maria"* but she was concentrating on the routine Martin had taught her, and found it exhilarating. She could jive! She had won.

They sat down to the sound of applause all around them. George was breathing heavily. "Want some water, Dad?" Bonnie offered.

"More like mouth-to-mouth," Chris suggested.

"Thanks for the concern but I am fine. It was just a little faster than we agreed."

"We? Who is *we*?" Maria asked, turning to George.

"Well... I had agreed the tempo with Angel... but she must have changed her mind."

"No, that is strange. Martin told her what he had taught me so she could play that tempo."

"Really?" George looked around for Martin who was not in sight. "I will have words with him," and then a terrible thought occurred to him. "What tempo is the Tango?"

"Do not worry my dear, the Tango is all the same."

"Did we miss something?" Vincente and Rosa arrived at the table carrying a tray of glasses and champagne.

"Only your daughter dancing the jive." George replied with some pride.

"Ahh, good, I hope Martin has it on video. Sorry I missed it, Maria, but we were... getting the champagne."

Maria looked at her father with suspicion. "Yes I see, but what for?"

"For the happy couple." Maria and George looked at each other.

"To Tom and Alex of course, on the news of the baby."

Everyone raised a glass and toasted, *"Tom and Alex's baby"*

"Thank you very much Vincente that was a very kind thought." Alex said, noticing Vincente looking at her. He raised his glass again in her direction and nodded.

Dessert was announced. "Good," said George, "I missed most of the main course," and rose to join the queue. Maria and Martin followed him, as did nearly everyone, except Vincente and Alex. They were sitting opposite each other across the table.

"Not hungry?" she asked in Spanish.

Vincente shrugged. "I do not eat so much these days, more bits and pieces. What is it they say now in English?"

"Grazing." Alex confirmed.

"Ahh, si, grazing. Like a bull, gracefully, not a pig greedily."

Alex smiled at the definition. "You should smile more. Not cry. You are very pretty when you smile," he said with sincerity.

Alex looked at him with a puzzled expression and frowned.

"I will be smiling more now I am to have a baby soon."

"Soon, not for what... six months," he guessed. She was silent. She wanted to leave but also wanted to stay.

"I am very happy. I love my husband," she said suddenly, fiddling with a napkin, not sure why she said that, but feeling compelled to do so.

Vincente smiled and leaned forward to whisper. "Is that me you are telling?...or yourself?"

She was deep in thought when Bonnie and Chris came back chattering to each other. "Alex, help us. I have no idea what we are eating here. It looks like a sponge doughnut"

For a short moment, Alex had been mesmerized by Vincente and was still in another world. She came round as soon as she heard her sister's voice, and shook her head to clear her mind of its doubtful thoughts.

Alex looked at the plate of pudding. "That's rum-baba," she confirmed.

"See, I was right" Chris said triumphantly. "OK, you have it brother, I'm going back for the fruit jelly, at least I know I like that.'

People were drifting backwards and forwards from the buffet, deciding what to have. George and Maria took a crème caramel each and headed back to their table.

"I'm glad Papa is getting on with your daughter. I think it helps that she can speak some Spanish."

"What have you two been talking about then?" George enquired sitting back next to Alex.

"Oh, nothing really, just solving the world problems as usual, dad," Alex quipped, and rose from the chair. "I think that looks good. I'll see if Tom got me one, back soon." and she was gone.

"Everything all right Vincente? You look... concerned," George asked.

"It is all OK, George. I am having a wonderful time, maybe too many sangrias."

Just then, Rosa came up behind Vincente and put her hands on his wide shoulders.

"Come my dear, come and dance with me again, or would George like to?" raising her glance in his direction.

George looked at Maria and she translated. "Would you dance with Rosa?"

"It would be a pleasure, Rosa." And they both took to the

floor, halfway through a slow number being played on the CD player.

Maria saw that her dad too was looking a little thoughtful. "Are you cross with me, Papa?"

"No, no, of course not my angel." He gestured for her to sit next to him. "There was something I enjoyed in the secrecy. I know it's childish, but we revert back to childish things when we get old."

"Papa! You are not old," Maria contradicted. "Childish maybe... sometimes." She smiled, and kissed him on the cheek. "But how does Rosa feel now she is no longer the 'secret'?"

Vincente sighed and took a sip of wine. "She wants me to make a choice, Maria. To stay here or... go to live with her.... maybe even further away."

Maria was not shocked, but was taken aback a little. "I had no idea she would want you to leave here Papa. I am so sorry." She took her Dad's hand and squeezed it. "What are you going to do? Have you decided?"

Vincente was about to answer, when everyone seemed to rejoin the table at once, including Martin. Vincente nodded to him. "I hope you have a good video this year, Martin." he said, just to make conversation.

"It will be a masterpiece of course, by the time I have edited it, and put it on YouTube," Martin replied with pride.

George and Rosa returned. "That was delightful, gracias Rosa" he said and offered a seat to Rosa next to Vincente.

George stood behind Maria with his hands on her shoulders. "I cannot believe it was six months ago I moved here." He looked around the table. "It's been a personal journey for me," he said quietly, "but I have to say it was made a lot easier for me with good friends around me." He looked in turn at Vincente, Martin and then Maria. He took her hand, and was about to say something else when Angel announced that everyone should be dancing.

George's face changed to a broad smile. "Yes, come on you lot, let's dance the night away."

Everyone, except Vincente and Rosa took to the dance floor.

George with Maria
Chris with Bonnie
Tom with Alex
Martin with Evie

"Shouldn't you be dancing with Martin?. ." Bonnie shouted in her brother's ear.

Chris looked in Martin's direction. "He hasn't asked me yet, and my Spanish is rubbish."

"Liar," Bonnie shouted back and blew him a kiss.

11.30pm. George looked at his watch and fingered the iPod in his trouser pocket.

"Stop doing that or people will start talking." George frowned on hearing the voice, but it took a second to realize it was Tom.

"Stop what?" George asked abruptly.

"Playing with your phone? I assume it is your phone."

George took his hand out of his pocket, like an embarrassed child being caught stealing sweets. "Err, yes, old habit Tom. Did the same with my lighter when I smoked."

Tom grinned back and nodded. "Are you enjoying the party Tom?" George thought small talk was best with his son-in-law.

"Yes, very...err Spanish."

They both surveyed the hall. People were dancing, talking, taking photos and drinking. Some were still eating, and children skipped around the tables, or pretended to dance.

"It's what I more or less expected," he added in his broad Welsh monotone accent.

George turned to look at Tom, and was about to ask more about the baby, when Tom added. "Is everything OK, George? Does Alex need to be worried?"

George's face changed instantly from inquisitive to fearful. He stared at Tom for several seconds. "What do you mean?" he said, moving nearer, but leaving an empty chair between them.

Tom coughed and dipped his head for moment, collecting his thoughts. "Alex has been worried about you for a while."

"In what way?" George asked, defensively.

Tom looked around to ensure Alex was not nearby. He saw her dancing with Martin and smiled.

Turning back to face George he said, "She has not said in so many words George... but she had doubts about you and the..." Tom fidgeted, and looked around him again, then lowered his voice even more, and leaned towards George "...bank." He sat upright abruptly, mainly because he wasn't sure if George would hit him.

But George just sat there taking in those words. In all the time since he had been arrested, not one of his children, or friends, had asked him outright. *'Did you do it, George?'* Now, here of all places, his son-in-law, of all people, had the nerve to ask.

"George, are you OK? We... Alex, was concerned, that's all. She... we... want our baby to have a grandfather... George?"

11.50pm. George smiled to himself. Then, looking at Tom said calmly, "Tell Alex all is fine. My grandchild will have me around for a long time." Then he got up and walked slowly out of the hall.

George breathed in the cool night air. It had been a good day. It had also been a good eight months. He was at peace here, in this small Spanish town, making a new life for himself. A life he deserved after having the previous one destroyed for him. His beloved wife, murdered by a drunk driver. The pathetic seventeen year old was given a twelve month suspended sentence, and a year's driving ban. What justice was that?

George had thought long and hard about revenge. *Kill the bastard*. That would not bring Aimee back, but it would be satisfying. *Kill someone he loves*. Ruin *his* life.

In reality, very few, if anybody, actually carry out revenge like that. They do it in their mind, repeatedly, avenging their loved ones, but not in reality. George, like most people, is a decent law-abiding citizen. He has three children to consider, and Aimee's parents. If he ended up in prison what would become of them? After three months of agonizing, George came to the only conclusion he could - direct revenge was out of the question on the bastard driver, so he needed to do something that was totally unrelated to him, but would give George the satisfaction of having done something to revenge his wife's murder.

He turned to the one and only thing he was good at. His job.

He knew he would have to sweat it out. Keep calm and let them investigate. And maybe in a couple of months they would let go.

Wrong. It was twelve months before he got the call;

"Hello Mr Morton, George, its Chief Inspector Cox here. Are you OK, you sound distant?"

Do I? Thought George. You try having your life ruined and see how that affects you.

"I'm fine, Chief Inspector," he replied, trying to sound not too distant.

"George, I wanted to call myself to tell you officially we are not investigating you any further. The CPS has decided not to pursue the case against you, and the bank agrees... are you there George?... Mr Morton, can you hear me?"

George had heard all right. He had replaced the receiver and started to cry. *'For you my love, for you,'* He whispered into the dark, and started on plans to move to Spain.

"Here you are. Sneaked out for a cigarette? Who are you calling? - everyone is here." Vincente asked, seeing the iPhone in George's hand. Vincente's voice brought George back to the present day.

"Ah, no, just getting some air, or I should I say clearing the air."

Vincente gave George a quizzical glance. "I do not understand you George."

George smiled. "No matter," he said, but added casually, "I was calling my wife's parents in Scotland to tell them about Tom and Alex's news."

Vincente was still looking vague. The mix of alcohol and

the night air had made him a little slow, and he was having trouble hearing.

"I did however want to ask you something", George said. "Let's walk over to the bar."

Vincente nodded and shrugged, and followed without question.

As they walked to El Tango the town clock struck midnight, and fireworks lit up the night sky. Vincente looked up in wonder and smiled, and threw his hands up to sky. "Magnificent, magnificent."

George still had his iPhone in his hand. He gently rubbed the screen, as if deciding what to do. He too looked up to the night sky and thought what a fitting finale.

The iPhone screen lit up with an IP address, and he pressed SEND.

***

Tom McPherson opened the small electronic notebook George had left him nearly nine months ago on his last visit, asking him to keep it safe, and well hidden. He put on his reading glasses and opened the letter George had sent him three weeks ago. It read *'Open 12th October 10.55pm'.*

Tom checked his watch, it said 10.56pm and he continued to read.

Plug in the notebook and press the ON button
Wait until 11.05pm then switch off immediately

***

Oliver Barnes looked at the incoming call on his Blackberry. It was the office. He checked the time on the screen, 11.14pm.

"Sorry to trouble you, sir, but there is something you need to see here."

"Harris, what could possibly be important," he snapped back. "I'm having a party and I'm not interested in work."

Oliver was on the balcony of his Penthouse in Canary Wharf, wearing only his KC boxer shorts.

"Ollie baby, you promised me something stronger than pot. Where do you keep the Tutti Frutti..." the slurring of a woman's voice echoed out of the living room for half of London to hear.

"Shut up, you stupid cow... and keep your voice down," Oliver shouted into the room. His other guests looked over with a dazed expression.

"OK, Harris, tell me again." Oliver took in a deep breath of the chilled October air, and looked out over the City and East London skyline, with its mix of modern and traditional architecture dominating the horizon.

"Well sir, you asked me to let you know of any unusual activity."

"Yes, I remember. So what is it?" Barnes said irritably.

"We have had a large deposit made tonight."

"Well that's good isn't it? We are still a bank after all," he snarled.

Harris gulped. "Yes sir, but it has been paid into an internal private account."

Oliver was now a little more interested. "Internal? You mean directly into one of our clearing accounts?" He asked, taking a slug of Tequila.

"It *is* an internal account, yes sir." Harris replied with trepidation, and was a little relieved his boss was on the phone and not in the same room - for now anyway.

"What account number?" Oliver asked, almost respectfully.

Harris hesitated a second. "Yours, sir."

Oliver went pale. He dropped the shot glass and grabbed the balcony handrail.

"What was the amount deposited?" Oliver asked nervously.

Harris looked at the screen displaying the account.

"Well, the *first* deposit was one million pounds at 11.02pm, then another one million pounds at 11.07, and another at 11.12..." Harris's voice trailed off. "Every five minutes it seems sir."

Harris and Barnes looked at their watches. 11.16... 11.17..." Sir, another deposit. At 11.17pm. One million pounds again."

Oliver Barnes walked back into his living room and sat on the white leather sofa. "Get me a brandy." He barked at the woman lying half-naked on the opposite sofa, "and get dressed. The party's over. Everyone get out, now!" He shouted to the other six bodies lying around the room in various degrees of undress.

"Harris, you there?"

"Yes, sir."

"I won't get there in five minutes, so we will wait until 11.22."

"Do you think there will be another deposit sir?" Harris asked with a little more confidence.

"I bet my life on it." Oliver replied in a calm voice, and downed the brandy in one.

11.19

11.20

11.21

The suspense was getting to Harris in the small transaction room. He loosened his tie and wiped his clammy right hand on his trousers leg.

11.22... the flat screen monitor bleeped once and displayed a new deposit.

Oliver got up and walked back onto the balcony.

"Well, Harris?" Oliver asked with new concern in his voice. "Is there another payment?"

"Yes sir, there is...but... "

"But what, Harris. . tell me man," Oliver spat down the phone.

"The amount sir... its one million pounds and... one penny. That's really odd isn't it sir?" he added, with genuine innocence.

Oliver collapsed onto the cold balcony stone floor, and sat there with his mouth wide open staring into space.

After several moments he uttered, "The bastard. The cheeky bastard."

He tried to focus. "Trace the payments. You must be able to find the source," he demanded, shouting into the mobile phone.

"I have tried sir, but each one came in via at least eight other countries. I cannot trace where the server is. The trail is bouncing all over the place. Whoever they are they do not want to be traced."

"Oh he's good all right, and I know exactly who HE is." Oliver stood up and collected his thoughts.

"Harris, I'm coming in. Do nothing. Tell nobody. Do you understand Harris?"

"Yes sir, but the security sweep will have detected the transactions by now and they will be coming...."

"Forget security. I'm running this one. I know exactly what's happening."

***

Tom McPherson closed the electronic notebook and placed it in the small padded neoprene pouch it had come in. He crept upstairs to check on his wife. He opened their bedroom door gently and saw she was asleep, book in hand.

He crept back downstairs, put on an overcoat, and picked up the dog lead.

"Come boy. Fancy a late walk?"

Josh, the Border collie, looked up from his bed in the kitchen and wondered why Tom was going out at this time of night, but a walk was a walk and he was never one to shy away from such an offer.

Anyone seeing him observed a man out for a late stroll with his dog, and carrying a folded newspaper under his arm.

The October wind was biting more than Tom would have liked across the Forth, but he pressed on to his appointment. Josh was confused when they crossed the park and headed up the slope towards the Forth Bridge. This was not their normal evening route. "Don't worry old boy," Tom assured Josh, "we won't be too long. Just going to run an errand."

Tom walked up to the Forth Bridge Hotel and took the path through the car park. It's not an obvious route unless you know it, but a convenient short cut, which brings you out directly onto the bridge.

The giant bridge is just over one mile long, and Tom was not too sure how far he would have to walk out to find an appropriate spot for his clandestine arrangement. He looked over to the more magnificent sight of the Firth of Forth rail bridge, which always gave him a feeling of pride, knowing his grandfather worked on it for eight years. The giant red bridge, and the distant lights of South Queensferry sparkled in the clear October night sky and Tom heard the last train of the day cross over, heading for Edinburgh.

Traffic was flowing well on both sides of the carriageway, but there were no other pedestrians. If he was picked up by the CCTV cameras he was just someone out for a walk with the dog, probably going to take a photo of the famed Edinburgh lights. After walking for ten minutes he reached the first giant pylon and could see he was over deep water. The tide was in thank goodness, so he did not have to walk any further in the now bitterly cold wind. He casually opened the folded newspaper and let the concealed object fall, like a pebble, silently, into the vast blackness below. "Well, George. I hope you know what you are doing," he whispered, and turned and walked briskly back towards the hotel, and home to a well deserved dram.

***

Oliver Barnes reached his office at exactly midnight, and was greeted by Harris and head of security, Sam Cohen.

"Mr Barnes, I understand you are aware of the recent deposits into your personal account this evening. Five million pounds."

"Five million and one penny actually, Sam, and that is the crux of all of this... the one penny. He said he didn't owe me a penny, and now has the audacity to send it back with one penny interest."

Sam Cohen looked puzzled. "Sir, what are you talking about?"

"Morton of course... that bastard George Morton!"

"I did hear about that episode sir, but he was cleared..."

"Cleared!" Oliver shouted back. "Cleared? He was clever, very clever, but now he has made a mistake, and we have him." Oliver was smiling, perhaps a little too much.

"Two years ago my father was prepared to let the police handle it, but they couldn't find anything. Three months ago I rehired the private security firm to reopen the case and monitor Morton, and all his activities. They have an operative out there now - watching his every move," he explained with a dash of satisfaction.

Sam Cohen looked uneasy. "Sir, did you clear that with the board. I don't remember seeing approved expenditure on that..."

Oliver looked at Cohen and Harris across his wide modern desk. "I'm sure there is some paperwork on it somewhere," he said more calmly. "The point is we have him. Can you see that Sam, we have him! I can get Jackson Security to pick him up and have him brought back to the UK." His tone was now triumphant.

Harris felt he should be elsewhere now. He had done his part as his boss had asked, and if anyone else asked... well, he had nothing to hide. Except the fact he should have informed security of the deposits first.

He stood and went to take his leave.

"Stay where you are, Mr Harris," Sam Cohen insisted, "I need you as a witness."

"Witness!" exclaimed Oliver. "What are you talking about? We need to get Morton back, now." He slammed his fist on the desk, causing a very expensive piece of *objet de art*, to fall over.

Before Cohen could reply, Oliver had dialed a number.

Jackson Security was a private 'specialist' in surveillance equipment, especially Asset Trackers, and the retrieval of 'property.' Colin Jackson, being ex-SAS, would do better than the police and M15 put together. Oliver really did not care what he was as long as he brought Morton to justice.

"Yes, Mr Barnes, how can I help you?" a soft clear voice asked.

"We've got him. Bloody got him. He has deposited the money, all five million, back into the bank."

There was a muted silence the other end.

"I assume you have tried to trace the route without success?"

"Yes, my people have tried, but I am sure your people can do better. Don't you have a computer forensics team," Oliver suggested, sounding now rather agitated.

More silence.

"It seems that as the money has been returned, in full, our services are no longer needed."

"No longer needed!" Oliver raised his voice even more. "I want that bastard brought to face trial. I know it was him. That's what I'm paying you for." He was shouting into the mouthpiece.

"This was an unofficial enquiry from the beginning, Mr Barnes. Your father asked us to investigate the matter quietly, and the bank hid the disappearance of the money under the cloak of the Icelandic bank collapse last year."

Oliver's mouth was dry. He loosened his tie and sat down.

"Furthermore, DCI Cox, in conjunction with the fraud squad and various forensic agencies, were unable to prove satisfactorily who was responsible. We therefore respectfully suggest you lick your wounds and be grateful for the return of the money. The case is closed. Our invoice will be emailed. Goodbye Mr Barnes."

Oliver Barnes stared at the Blackberry. "Bloody armatures," he muttered to himself.

The Outlook icon on Oliver's computer screen came to life letting him know he had new mail. He clicked open the mail and printed an invoice for £100,000 from Jackson Security Ltd, payable in 7 days.

"Holy shit!" he exclaimed out loud, and sank into his chair, totally deflated.

***

George poured two brandies, and he and Vincente sat on bar stools.

"Cheers, my friend," said George. "The past eight months have been... interesting, and wonderful. Thank you for being a friend, Vincente," George said with sincerity, and raised his glass. "To friends, Salud." Vincente touched glasses with George.

"Salud, George." Vincente smiled a warm smile, but behind those narrow blue eyes lurked suspicion.

"What was the real reason you wanted to drink my brandy, George?"

George smiled back. "You are not as drunk as you look."

And sipped at his drink. "But to answer your question my friend... I would like to buy 50% of the restaurant."

Vincente was usually sure of himself, and prided himself on being a good judge of character. With George, however, he had changed his mind several times since they had first met back in March, when he caught him taking his jukebox off the wall. He had however warmed to him, and his family, but there was still one question he did not have an answer to.

"Fifty percent! But I already have a partner, my daughter, we have fifty percent each."

"Yes, and I want to buy Maria's half. There is a good future here as a restaurant and we can make it work, all three of us."

Vincente blinked twice and leaned forward. "Why would she want to sell to you, George?" he asked quietly, and to George's mind, somewhat menacingly.

"Because it will be a wedding present to her."

Vincente looked puzzled. "But who is she marrying?"

"Me. of course. If you will agree," George asked most humbly, and a little nervously.

"Ahh." Vincente cried out, "You think you can buy my daughter." He pointed a finger at George, who instinctively leaned back as far as it was possible on a barstool.

Vincente however had not finished. He got off the chair and came closer to George, finger still pointing. Now it was prodding. "You, a stranger. Been here five minutes and think you can buy your way into our lives." George recoiled even more.

"No, no I'm not asking that at all, and you know it Vincente. I love Maria, and Jorge, and... I like you a lot as well." George closed his eyes waiting for the next verbal onslaught.

He heard Vincente laughing, a deep belly laugh.... "OK, I accept on her behalf." His face lit up with a wide smile. "You had better go and propose, no."

George looked at his watch. It was almost 12.30.

"Go, George, I will lock up." Vincente insisted.

"Thank you, Vincente, thank you." He grabbed his hand

and shook it hard. He thought about hugging him, but decided against it. Vincente said nothing, but he felt a warm feeling inside, and perhaps also a little nostalgia. George turned to leave.

"One thing George. I must know. Do you have that bank's money or not? I need to know what my daughter is getting into, you understand." His voice was calm and sincere.

George looked Vincente square in the eyes. *Does he know something or is guessing?*

"No, Vincente, I can honestly say I do not have the bank's money."

The two men stood staring at each other, still holding hands, firmly.

"Vincente, one thing I need to ask you as well. Is Juan's killer still on the run?"

Vincente squinted and half turned, as if he had not heard the question, but he had, and knew George was also holding an 'ace'.

"No, George, I can honestly say he is not."

George knew then Maria had seen blood on the car. Vincente must have caught up with the man, and either hit him accidently, or... or what, either way, Vincente and his friends knew the forest well, and if a man was to disappear, then the wildlife, especially the boars, would leave no trace of a body.

They shook once more, and George nodded, as did Vincente. Nothing would be said about either subject, ever again.

George left the bar and headed back to the assembly rooms. Before he got there he took out his iPhone and checked his messages. Just one: *'Thanks for the business. Keep the 'tracker.' CJ.*

He smiled at the message and then removed the Sim card and broke it in half. *'Thank you Thomas. I hope it was not too cold on the bridge tonight.'*

He had estimated there would be enough money to open several restaurants from the interest that had accumulated over nearly three years. No money in the world would bring back his Aimee, but he now felt a sense of accomplishment, and of closure. He knew he could now do what he was going to do with a clear conscience.

Vincente finished his brandy, and George's, and turned to leave when the door opened.

"I thought I saw you come here." Angel was standing there in her stunning red silk dress with strapless top and wearing black stockings and red high heels.

Vincente looked her up and down. *"My Angeles,"* he sighed heavily. "You look wonderful and you sounded great, but as much as I hate to say this, we must leave. You have one more number to perform." He took her hand and before she had time to protest, or even understand where they were going, Vincente had turned off the lights and locked the door.

The music had finished but everyone was still there, standing around, talking about the evening. George joined his table. "Hi Dad, where have you been, you missed the fireworks," exclaimed Alex.

"Yes, George, where were you?" asked Maria taking his hand as he sat down next to her.

"You are cold, George, and shivering," What has happened?" she asked.

He held her hand tightly, on top of the table for all to see, and looked at his family and friends. "I have come a long way in the last two years, but even further over the last eight months."

Alex felt a swelling in her eyes, and both she and B went to grab the same paper napkin on the table. Bonnie won it but tore it in half and gave half back to her sister.

"I could not have done it without you, all of you. I know you all had concerns, and to be honest so did I, but here we are eight months on, and I have family and friends around me."

He paused to look around the table. "Chris, thank you for everything." Chris smiled back and raised his glass to his Dad. "Cheers Pop."

"Alex and Tom. Great news about the baby. I'm very happy for you both."

He turned to Bonnie and Evie.

"Bonnie, you have done wonders with the business, Mum would be proud," which started both Alex and Bonnie sobbing. "I'm sorry," Bonnie managed to say between blowing her nose.

"It's true though," George continued. "You are great." He then looked at Evie sitting next to him, "and Evie... as we say in England, *all's well that ends well.*

Just then, Vincente came in and whispered in George's right ear. At the same time they heard Angel make an announcement on stage.

"Senores y senoras, tenemos tiempo para una ultima baile, con permiso del alcalde."

George turned to Maria. "What is she saying?" but before Maria could answer, Alex was standing up. "They are having one more dance Dad, come on everyone."

"Shall we?" George asked, turning to Maria. "Si senor," Maria said "but not if it is a Jive." They walked to the dance floor as the band struck up a Tango.

George froze. "I thought she had forgotten that."

"Come... it will be fine," Maria whispered and pulled him gently towards the floor.

George started counting the steps to himself and was surprised that he was moving so well. They moved back and forth completing two lengths of the floor when George stopped and knelt down on one knee. "That's not one of the dance moves," Maria said, looking down at George.

"I know, but it is one of my moves," and held her hand in front of him. Others around gradually stopped dancing and the band slowed down, and Angel eventually stopped singing.

"María, haces que mi vida valga la pena de Nuevo. Te casaras conmigo?"

He asked her to marry him in near perfect Spanish. He had practiced it for many weeks.

Maria, looking down at him, pulled him up from the floor and put her arms around his neck. "Si," she smiled, and they kissed long and lovingly.

A rousing chorus erupted, and cheering and clapping

could be heard the other end of town. Jorge came running up to his mother and hugged her, but was not sure what had just happened. Alex, Bonnie, Chris and Evie joined in the hugging and kissing, and Angel and her band upped the tempo, and everyone danced the night away, on what would be the first of many *Columbus Days* for George Morton.

Two months later, on the 5th December, El Tango opened its doors for evening meals. Three days a week, at first, but gradually increasing to six days by the following March as it grew in popularity.

Six months later on 18th April, Alex gave birth to a baby girl, they named her Amanda. George and Maria were there with them.

Nine months later on 4th July, George and Maria were married in the tiny register office in Calabaza, by the new Mayor Rodrigo Sanchez. Angel was bridesmaid, Martin was best man and Jorge was a reluctant pageboy. Christopher, Alex and Bonnie were witnesses.

Oh yes, Vincente sold his share of El Tango to George for a very large figure, and he and Rosanna Maria moved to Biarritz... to live a long and happy life together.

The End.

Acknowledgements:

Sincere thanks to my many friends who have encouraged me to finish this book, especially Ros McCaul who was unyielding in her spotting the sublime to the ridiculous (which 'Word' had not noticed) and for her editing skills.

Also from the same family, Kate McCaul for her invaluable knowledge of the Spanish language.

Thanks also for help, encouragement and advice, in no particular order, to Robin King, David Freeman, Annie Stevens, Alonso Herraro, Carol, Nicole and Lindsay Balaam, Stewart Ferris, Kim Whitecross, Simon Robinson, Jamie Oliver, John Cordara, Rick Stein, Kate Percy, Michael Cowell.

Gratefully acknowledge permission from Eland Publishing to reproduce excerpts from Peter Mayne's book A Year In Marrakesh.

The WOMAD Music Festival in Cáceres is held in May each year, not July. Visit http://womad.org/ for more information and dates.

Visit David's website and read all about the author: http://www.davidbalaam-books.co.uk/